WHERE THE RAIN FALLS

Where the Rain Falls

Subhakar Das

ROMAN *Books*
www.roman-books.co.uk

Copyright © 2012 Subhakar Das

ISBN 978-93-80905-31-0

Typeset in Adobe Garamond Pro

First published in 2012

1 3 5 7 9 8 6 4 2

British Library Cataloguing in Publication Data.
A catalogue record for this book is available from the British Library.

ROMAN *Books*
26 York Street, London W1U 6PZ, United Kingdom
2nd Floor, 38/3, Andul Road, Howrah 711109, WB, India
www.roman-books.co.uk | www.roman-books.co.in

Printed and bound in India by
Roman Printers Private Limited
www.romanprinters.com

for Kalia, of course

1

Every day at dawn, when the wind shrieked past the bamboo thickets and hurried for the company of the waters of the Dikhow nearby, households stirred and weary souls, startled out of sleep, stared at the darkness. In obedience to the summons of routine bred by birth, tired bodies hurried out of homes like machines destined for a lifetime of labour. Their bare feet walked through the dimness to the fields basking in the promise of the rising sun. In the afternoon, when the sun was a reflection of its morning pledge, the villagers trod the long road home. The soil smacked beneath their tired feet, and the gravel crunched with each step. Their bodies smelled of sweat and their faces wore a drained look. As they neared the village, they walked faster for work was over for another day and food and rest awaited them at home. The day, like all other days in their lives, was past. For the time being, they were happy and contented for they could rest in the warm bonding of family and friends.

The men knew no respite from their daily slog. They worked every day except during Bihu and Puja or when they fell sick or died. Burdened by a weariness accumulated over years of hard work, they lightened their shoulders with drink. When the liquor had taken its toll, they huddled together bonded by their miserable life. They talked of the things they wanted out of life like little taboos. Their voices were full of optimism, their hopes meagre and needs simple. When evening turned to night, and the storm clouds gathered, they hurried home. In the flicker of kerosene lamps, they quarreled with their wives and swore at their friends and, when the children cried, they often beat them.

They ate their one good meal of the day - beaten rice with curd and molasses, wild fowl from the nearby jungle or magur or goroi from the swamp - and feeling tired and pleased, they slept till another day dawned and work beckoned.

The villagers lived bounded by a fanatical sense of obligation towards their god-given existence. They treated each other with faint disregard, their feelings dominated by a lurking sense of animosity brought about by the constant worry and the exhaustion of mind and body from the endless tasks. They never learned to love or hate, and their emotions never found expression or a friendly shoulder. Birth meant an invitation to a life of suffering and never ending work, and of the inevitable sickness and death from which there was no escape. This feeling haunted every person like a malady. Most went through life in mute acceptance of their poverty as punishment for sins committed in an earlier life. Some struggled with their situation for a while believing it to be nothing more than a coincidence of fate, but they soon gave up and sought solace in prayers and penitence.

The young fought their circumstances with brave new dreams. They bore no malice towards life. They studied hard for a while, but battered minds are reluctant sponges and they struggled to soak in the might of a pen, and the promise of an education never held sway. Then, like condemned men, they gave up, picked up spades and axes, and became unruly. They came home late at night, drunk and dirty, torn clothes tattered and bruises on their bodies. There would be much shouting and a question or two about the existence of god and why they had been so damned. The elders, roused from sleep or rest, cursed them, but having suffered a similar fate, they soothed them to sleep, only to wake them up in the morning as the hush and hustle of dawn heralded another day of work.

Few went out to visit other places and fewer passed through. The villagers were always wary of strangers, avoiding them as if they bore some dreadful disease. They were afraid of anything that might upset the balance of their mundane, but difficult life. They resisted any attempt at change, afraid it would only bring them more hardship. Distant events never touched them, but sometimes hordes of people visited the village in cars and jeeps and clamoured for their attention. They spoke of great things, but came so far apart that few remembered what they talked about or what they wanted. The villagers did as told and when elections were over, they were forgotten anyhow.

Nothing changed in the village. All that ever did were the seasons. After Puja, when the trees shed their leaves and the days grew short and nights long, a mist crawled in from the hills and hung about like an evil shroud. When winter departed with its share of souls and spring rolled in, the rains came and the river flooded, and people sought the safety of the earthen bund. In their hurry, some were swept away and some fell sick, and so a few more died. When the waters receded and the river went back to its trough, they found their homes gone and the crops ruined, but they carried on nonetheless, and so built new homes and sowed fresh seeds and shouldered the chores of the living. And hoped and prayed for their share of the simple things in life.

It was a difficult life. Nobody lived to be fifty or more, and most that survived the scavenging of the flood waters died young. They all suffered from some sickness or the other, and each, young and old alike, carried their disease like desperate secrets to their deaths.

One summer night, after many years of such a life, Bibhuti Barua died.

He came back from his usual ramble through the village and, like always, settled down on the bench by the pond. He fed the fishes and soon lost himself in the pond's reflections. When the moon gleamed on its surface, he went for a walk. It soon grew dark. There was not a soul on the narrow path. A haze was everywhere. It clouded his sight as he peered into the distance through cataract-eyes. He stumbled on a rock and lost his balance. He rolled down the embankment leading to the edge of the swamp and his head struck a boulder.

Around midnight, a tired heart gave way and a relieved soul left with a gentle sigh.

A solitary fox foraging for food came sniffing, drawn by the smell of blood. It bit into the flesh, but when it saw torches and heard loud shouts, it slunk away.

In the morning, they found the body in the dense undergrowth of bushes, as heavy as a lumbered log, and as silent as the lull before dawn.

Few came to pay their respects for Bibhuti Barua became a stranger long before death came to claim its dues. A crowd collected on the road outside his house, but it was more out of curiosity than any desire for homage. They dispersed long before the crying stopped and the tears dried. There was someone from the government, and a few teachers from the school he founded, but their condolences came more from a sense of duty than any feeling of loss. Those his age shed a few tears and shook their heads. Those younger knew nothing of the life he led. They stole a few glances, shrugged their shoulders, and went their way. They all knew him as Bibhuti Barua, the farmer, who was teacher for a while.

It was the life he resented the most. When younger he had run away to school ten miles away across the Dikhow. On clear days, they gathered cross-legged in the shade of an ancient Krishnasura and let their imagination soar across faraway lands full of magical discoveries and brave conquerors. Each day was a wakening, every lesson filled with possibilities. Bibhuti learnt of a completely different world existing beyond the boundaries of the village, which was inventing itself and marching across new frontiers. What fascinated him was the teacher's claim that they lived in the same age and time, yet lived so differently, and he spent hours thinking why life was meant to be like that. Then the classes ran out in the school, and his father told him he had been patient enough, it was time he worked the fields.

Bibhuti ran away from home and hid in the forest, and in the swamp amongst snakes and leeches. He couldn't bring himself to turn back, run away from the promise of a better future, if not an education. He confided in his mother, who despite all her ignorance, believed in him and told him to do what he thought was right. One dark night, he felt her calloused hands on his face for the last time. In Dibrugarh, he washed dishes and cleaned houses.

He went to school again.

Times were changing. There was talk of a free country and a bright future for all who cared. When Gandhi made a visit, Bibhuti stayed up all night at the maidan for a glimpse of the great man. When his words wove their magic, he fought his way to touch Gandhi's feet, and the blessings evoked their charm. Bibhuti plunged into the freedom struggle with a fierce determination, all the while thinking of a world where everyone lived equally and without prejudice. He went everywhere his heart led him, in front of processions, battling the police, even suffering his share of blows and bruises. He never flinched for a moment, never thought of turning back, never spoke a harsh word or returned a single blow.

When the British left, Bibhuti returned home to a sick father and an adoring village. It was still a place where no one lived to be old, but under his careful tutelage, it became a place where at least no one died young. He was knowledgeable beyond his education and spoke of things that could only be learnt with experience. The villagers held him in awe and their reverence increased with every small improvement in their lives. He set up a school in the village and, some years later, married. He taught in the school for a while, but when teaching and tuitions hardly made ends meet, he turned his attention to his father's fields.

Bibhuti Barua returned to the life of his forefathers. When his son was old enough, he sent him to school.

Independence never fulfilled its promises and life remained as hard as before. Nothing changed. Not the rain, nor the land. Those that lived died before their time, those born mellowed in the vicissitude of circumstances. As he aged, Bibhuti retreated into a shell from which he never ventured out. He rarely spoke, and the large watery eyes in his sullen farmer-face watched the world with scorn from under thick eyebrows. He refused to meet the people who sought his blessings at election time nor attended the function where the government announced a pension for services to the country. Like everyone before him, he gave up on life long before life had given up on him.

"Sons of bitches! What do they want from an old starving man? More taxes?" he said from his seat under a portrait of Gandhi when the postman bore him a large brown envelope with 'On Government of India Service' printed on it. He tore open the envelope with a vehemence reserved for his son, read the dull parchment and threw it away. "What do they think me to be?" he swore at the postman, who hastened to pick up the paper. "Do they think I did it for money? Is that what they think of all the time now? Money? Have they forgotten Gandhi?" He rose to his feet and adjusted the askew portrait, studying the fading face.

When Manav, his son, returned home, his mother told him what had happened. She showed him the envelope with the letter inside.

"Why don't you take it?" he said to his father, waving the

paper in front of his face. "People don't get a job nowadays and they are offering you a pension."

"How dare you talk to me like that?" said his father, hands raised as if to strike. "Do you fight for freedom for the sake of money? What has gotten into you?"

"What freedom?" Manav said in his loud, adolescent voice. "What has it given you? What has it given Ai?" he said of his mother. "She remains cooped up in her kitchen all day long and listens to your taunts. What has it given me? I can't get a college education and so never hope to get a job, never hope to have a decent life."

"At least you live an honest life," said his father. "I washed dishes and swept houses to give myself an education. I ran away from home so that I could give myself hope. What have you done for yourself?"

Manav looked away. Tears welled in the corners of his eyes. When he spoke again, his voice was a whisper. "All I ask for is a chance to complete my education, maybe get a job. What is wrong with trying to break the shackles of poverty on our lives? Is that too much to ask of a father?"

"I have given you life," said his father. "You can make heaven or hell out of it. I lived by my beliefs all my life. I'm not going to sell them for your sake." He struggled to his feet, lips trembling, eyes breathing fire. "You stand in the shelter of this roof and scream at the injustice, but you can never understand the purity of fighting for your country's freedom. It can't be bought with money," he said, before marching away.

It was the first of many fights between father and son. It was like the rain, which never went away. The house lost its peace, and Ai, her quiet. Sometimes they fought over trifles, sometimes they quarreled over their fate, but mostly they argued without reason. They stopped speaking to one another and ate separately when they could. But their house was only a small dwelling not much bigger then a pair of arms at full stretch, and the more they tried to avoid each another, they more they ran into one other.

One day, when Manav was changing his clothes, several coins fell on the floor along with a wad of change.

"How come you have money in your pockets and I buy your food," said Bibhuti.

"It is not your money," said Manav.

"It is not your money, bah. Listen to him," said Bibhuti. "Where do you think the money in this house comes from? Every paisa in your pockets is mine, every paisa comes from working in my fields." Turning to Ai, he said, "He has money in his pockets and I sleep underneath a leaking roof."

Manav turned to his mother. "Tell him it is the money I earned by selling my shoulders. Tell him it is not his to count."

Ai kept her silence. She wanted to tell both father and son what was right and how they were both wrong, but they never listened to her or asked her advice. Her voice was always kept in abeyance, heard in its silence.

"Listen to your son," Bibhuti said to Ai. "See how he talks to his father because I refused that pension from the government. Listen to him, listen to his complaints for because of this old man he suffers."

"Ai," Manav said to his mother. "How can he gloat over a past that sold our future, how can he rejoice over honour when his family suffers, how dare he boast about freedom when all it gave us was poverty."

Bibhuti to Ai: "Why has god given him two hands if not to work?"

Manav to Ai: "God has given him a mouth, but is it to speak nonsense?"

Father and son went their separate ways. Bibhuti walked out of the house by the back and Manav stumbled out of the front door. Both went out in the rain. Though they slept under the same roof, such was their fetters of poverty, it was around this time they decided they had enough of each other to last this lifetime. They parted in the soul, each blaming the other: one for his future, the other for his past. From then on, Bibhuti ignored his son. He worked when possible, but when the pain in his body rose above the pills from the dispensary and the prayers of the pujari, he stayed in bed or sat by the pond in their backyard. Most times, he fed the fish and watched the ducks frolic in the water. Sometimes he went for long walks, but he went without speaking. He never acknowledged another's presence, never paid heed to any call. Finally, the people in the village stopped paying him any attention.

His unsteady steps took him everywhere in the village.

Bibhuti watched the changing face of the village with contempt: bare electricity poles gasping under climbing pepper vines; the piers of the abandoned bridge on the Dikhow, where boys from the nearby villages rested between swims; what the Dikhow left of a new road to Dibrugarh, chunks of asphalt sticking out of the water like boat wreck. He noted the arrival of alien faces that worked for a pittance and spoke a strange language, the shops that opened in the fringes, even the police outpost set up after the first outbreak of trouble. And every day, he came home to rest for a while in the only chair in the house under Gandhi's gaze and think of all the things that had gone terribly astray.

In the house, Ai sat in a corner and cried alone, but she had cried in that corner all her married life. She watched her dead husband through the haze of incense smoke and thought about a life laid waste. She soon stopped and went to see what she could do. Manav watched his father's body for a while without remorse or tears. He thought of a future that can never be his.

15

Like his mother, he went to make arrangements for the funeral, cut bamboo for the cremation, call a brahmin.

At noon, on the banks of the Dikhow, when shadows hugged tired feet, an emaciated body went up in flames. Then the rains came and the river flooded, and washed away all traces of a life that never found its way.

2

For a month thereafter the rain stayed away. The river receded as quickly as it had risen, so that from the earthen bund it was no more than a slick serpent sneaking away. The fields dried and opened cracks. The villagers, rarely used to such a long period without rain, fretted about their crops. Lamps were lit in the namghar in penitence for sins committed. Women took to fasting and the priest approached his daily rituals with more rigour.

One day, the heat became unbearable. Leaves on trees drooped and the bamboo in the thickets burst at their joints. At noon, the sky darkened in a swathe of angry clouds. Thunder spat fire. The heavens opened as if in spite. The rain poured. It found water in wells and filled the fields sick with the stricken kothiya. Those at work sought the shelter of trees. Those on the road fled for their homes. In the mist of approaching darkness and falling rain, the village appeared bereft of a single occupant.

The rain fell without break, its rancour broken by the ringing of the namghar bell. Trees bent in the wind and swished at stragglers - those who had expected the storm to pass, only to have witnessed it gather strength with every minute. A figure appeared out of the sleet. Mumbling incoherently, his speech slurred by the unaccustomed taste of liquor, the young man paused at the namghar door. His eyes fell on the priest. Lips moving in prayer, the priest hurried through the closing-down rituals; he shut the door and turned the key on a rusty lock. The young man sniggered with satisfaction when a gust of wind blew out the lamp, throwing the namghar into darkness. He staggered forward on the muddy path. Once or twice he slipped. With a drunkard's instinct, he climbed over a familiar gate and stumbled up a garden path. He fumbled with the front door and, when it opened for him, he rushed inside and fell into bed.

Ai, who was waiting for her son, followed. With fortitude bred by endless vigil of an ill-tempered husband and, now, an ill-mannered son, she pulled off his rain-soaked clothes. She wiped him dry and put a blanket over him, and a wet towel on his brow, which glistened with feverish perspiration.

Manav's guts wrenched with pain as spasm after spasm racked his body. The food he ate some hours back with his friends churned in his stomach. He suddenly bent forward gasping for air. Before he could stop himself, he vomited all over his mother. When he woke it was dawn and slivers of light shone through gaps in the bamboo wall. In the dim morning light, he made out the glint of cobwebs, which littered the underside of the roof, while his ears filled with the chirp of birds on the trees. He turned his head and his eyes fell on Ai. Her body, battered by years of hard work, lay exhausted on the chair. Her chest heaved with every gasp of air, while dark circles surrounded grieving eyes lulled into sleep by the promise of a few hours of rest. His father ignored her most of his life because of his shattered dreams, but has he been any different? She must have longed for the love and respect, which was her due. Instead, she suffered in their neglect in the depths of her kitchen, hunched in front of the stove, cooking them their food or prostrated in prayers for their well-being. His eyes brimmed over. When he turned his head, Ai was watching him, a strange look on her face.

Manav wiped away his tears. "The rain, it's gone," he said in a choked voice, blurting out the first words that came to mind.

"It's all we've got," said Ai, looking out of the window. "It gives us food, renews our lives, takes away those that are weak. It's our enchantment, our giver, our guide. It is our fate, our destiny. It's all we have." She was silent for a while. "Sometimes I think it's god's law meant to wreck vengeance on those that are evil, and reward those that are good. What else could we do, but accept the choices god makes for us?" She rose to her feet with a sigh, grasping the chair for support. At the door, she said: "This is your life and it is best to accept things the way they are. Nothing is going to change it. Don't make it hard for yourself."

The storm and the deluge renewed the crops that looked to fail. It also washed away Manav's sloth. As the days passed, he assumed a serious demeanour - gone was the languor of his age, the anger at the futility of his fate. But discontentment brewed in his eyes. He questioned in sullen resentment the few opportunities that came his way. He grew pale and thin, and his eyes grave and questioning as if searching for answers he could never hope to find. His lips were always drawn together in a stern line, and when he grew a moustache, it gave him the severe look of a forty year old mourning the demise of a life he never had. He became busier by the day and more mysterious. Sometimes he stayed away for a day and night, sometimes more, but when Ai went to look for him in the morning, he was always at work in the fields.

Ai noticed the faint traces of a budding maturity, but she grew afraid lest their circumstances took a toll. She was glad her son was not like the other young people in the village, who had to be pushed and prodded to do their share of work or mind the money they had, but dark fears beat at her heart. With each passing day, Ai's foreboding grew till it became a mountain which threatened to crush her. She often sat up at night thinking what could be troubling him. Her thoughts never remained in one place. If she came from a wedding, she thought: "Maybe he is thinking of getting married. Yes, that's why he repaired the house and bought new clothes." If she met someone returning from the college in the next village, she thought: "Maybe he wants to go to college. That's why he brought all those old books." When whispers about the Sangathon, a mysterious brotherhood fighting for freedom, reached her ears, her worries rose above her head: "What if he is mixed up with these people? How can that be possible? He has made no new friends and his old friends never visit him nowadays." Each thought brought about by a recent event and modified by a circumstance of her creation.

Manav never explained, and to Ai, he seemed to talk less and less. She spent hours thinking and finding no tangible explanation her heart grew heavy with a sense of something out of the ordinary. Ai kept her worries to herself. Unable to calm her qualms, she sought solace in prayers. Once or twice, she asked him:

"Is something wrong?"

"Why didn't you come home last night?"

"Where were you in the rain the last few days?"

"Have you heard about Molu ka?"

That was the only time he responded. The police and a contingent of soldiers had swooped down on the village one night and took away two men for no reason. One of them was Molu ka. The other, Jogen kai, limped home three days later. He appeared all right, even talked with a smile, but everyone was unanimous there was something different about him, something sad. Some of the villagers spoke of bruises over his body and a bleeding nose, but Jogen kai denied anything was wrong with him. He was at work in the fields the very next day, though he never lifted a spade again. Molu ka never came home.

And another week was already past.

Manav stopped in his stride. His voice was a thin rasp: "Everyone thinks he is dead."

"So I heard," said Ai in surprise. "But how could anyone know for sure?"

"When have you heard of people walking out alive out of an Army camp?"

Ai was silent for a while. "He was mixed up with these Sangathon people. Why would the Army take him otherwise?"

"He was a good man, Ai. Better than most. That's all we need to remember," said Manav, stepping outside.

In the village, there was silent acceptance of Molu ka's fate. The men followed Jogen kai's example and returned to the fields in groups of threes and fours. They all pretended nothing occurred in the few days they stayed away from work and talked of a week past like it was yesterday. They were careful not to utter Molu ka's name or veered their conversation towards him. But there was a sadness in the air, and to dispense with the gloominess, stories about the Sangathon were passed around in a spate of promises, which were never kept. Within a few days, Molu ka became a valiant soldier of the struggle, and a martyr. He was a farmer all his life, but gradually his life became one to be idolized. He became an example of the brave and the selfless. He was the patriot. Suddenly, there were stories galore about his adventures and every villager tried to outdo the other in narrating their proximity to the missing man. There were indignant words against the police, all spoken in private, about how the law had turned against its own people; even whispers of a protest, a hunger strike, of sending someone to town to meet reporters. Everyone talked, initially, quite reluctantly, then, more freely, but still within the confines of homes or sanctity of close friendships. They asked questions, discussed answers, even grew a little afraid lest somebody else found out. A glimmer of hope shone in every heart. It was this faint hope that drove the villagers to gather for a discussion at the namghar. Everyone was in attendance: children, women, even the old and infirm, and of course, all the men. Everyone agreed they cannot accept Molu ka's disappearance without a reasonable explanation now that so many days are past. After the meeting, the men walked in a procession to the police outpost and demanded the police handover Molu ka. They raised slogans, sat in dharna and even got someone knowledgeable, who knew English, to write a letter to the District Commissioner. The daruga, the officer in charge at the outpost, refused to meet anyone, even the gaonbura, the village headman, and the men returned home in the darkness, unheard and ignored. That night, everyone sat together to decide their next move. Nobody had been taken away from the village before, so no one knew what to do. They all agreed they must return and plead with the policemen. They talked of Molu ka and reminisced about him to pass the night. By dawn, when memories ran out and their stories became far-fetched, their discussion veered to how he must have died. Nobody in the village had been killed before except once by an elephant, that too by accident, and before memory years, so nobody knew what to say. In the village there were only as many people as gooseberries in a child's pocket, and when the men returned to the police outpost in the morning, emboldened by prayers and the belief their cause was just, they were caned. Even the missing man's wife, who had tagged along was not spared, nor were the women watching from afar. That afternoon, every house in the village nursed a bruised body or a painful limb. Some of the men sat in hurt silence, and a few, who had escaped the policemen's barrage by running into the forests, talked of a fresh protest. But too many have been injured and concern about Molu ka's fate was diminishing with the fading light and the increasing pain. They all agreed in their hearts that his was a soul that will remain restless till a body was found or a life returned. As for his wife, she must begin her eternal wait.

Some distance away, at the edge of the village, Manav removed his arm from a sling around his neck, and repeated: "Ai, I'm leaving in the morning."

"Leaving? Where?" Ai looked up from grinding a bunch of harbhanga leaves in a mortar for the swelling in Manav's arm.

"I've some work," said Manav, but in a small voice so as not to annoy his mother.

Ai squinted at him in the dimness. "Does this have something to do with what happened to Molu ka?" When Manav didn't answer her for some time, she peered at his face: "Yes?"

"Don't drag Molu ka into this - his was such a gentle soul," said Manav. "Ai, trust me and listen to what I have to say," he added, stammering a bit. He didn't know where to start, but there was very little time and he must leave at dawn. He told his mother of the day not far back when a stranger stopped to address the young people in the village. The stranger, Barman, was a man making his way through towns and villages with a message for anyone who cared to listen. They had gathered in the darkness of a classroom in the village school, the one his father founded, and with the chowkidar keeping watch, he whispered the Sangathon's vision of a free Assam. He was succinct and polished and didn't waste his words, and there were facts to back up what he said. He liked the fervour of Barman's appeal to join the struggle, and his honesty about the hardship they would face. It didn't make much sense the first night, but after a few days of thought, he found Barman's rhetoric reasonable.

For a long moment, Ai sat like a statue, a petrified expression on her face. Only when the first tear rolled down her cheek, did she burst into a fit of sobbing. For a moment, she thought she was dreaming. "But a country of our own," she said between tears, her words coming out in a rush as if they must be told quickly lest they lose their meaning. "It is too much to ask. I've heard that before, seen what it meant. For us poor people, it means nothing. I've seen one freedom struggle in my life. I don't have the strength to suffer another."

"Don't judge me by what happened to father," said Manav. "It is because of people like him that we have to do this all over again."

Ai has never been angry in her life, but when she spoke, it was with a measure of admonishment. "Don't blame your father for what's in your fate. If you really hate your father, why follow in his footsteps? How miserable he was all the time, a burden he brought on himself. I pitied him all the time, the poor thing. Is that a way for a man to live?"

Manav made an impatient sound. "Don't harp about father now. He expected the government to come rolling with riches and schools and hospitals, when what we have for rulers are thieves with about as much vision as snakes."

"Your father used to talk just like that when he was young," said Ai, wiping away her tears. "He too dreamt of a better life and his dreams came from a belief in one man. When Gandhi was shot, he was heart-broken. He told me this country would go down the drain." She paused to catch her breath. "He was right."

"His faith in that man was blind," said Manav. "Do you know he called our land a paradise on earth and yet was prepared to give it away? Him and Nehru later on - they were no different from all the other Indians - selfish and uncaring, and blind to the problems of its people." He pointed at the portrait of Gandhi on the wall. "I don't know why you still have him here - should have thrown it out a long time back."

Ai shook her head. "It's all I've to remind me what a brave man your father was, how he gave so much for so little."

"The Indians are an ungrateful lot. They've always been like that - use, use, use, take, take, take - that's all they know." He told her what Barman had told him about the exploitation of the land, all the oil and wood that had been ferried away, all the people that had been killed trying to stop it, the trouble that had been ignited just to keep a few people in power, how they planned to change all the injustice, build themselves a better world.

Ai listened fascinated, grinding on the mortar all the while. Her eyes caressed the diminutive figure before her, talking of things that made her wonder. She pinched herself to see if it was a dream from which she would wake up to find her world in the same miserable state she left it. Her son was still of an age when people were finding their own feet, leave alone think about taking care of others. She was happy the words came from someone she always took to be so simple and ordinary to be quite incapable like everyone else in the village. When Manav told her about the men martyred, how they had been tortured, and how so few returned home, Ai was horrified. Being a mother, with only a son to look forward to in old age, she grew angry with the people who had led her son on a path of constant danger.

"Did Barman tell you all this?" said Ai, peering into the mortar to see if the grinding was done. "How can you be sure he is not lying? He could be another one of those crafty politicians!"

"He made me see the light," said Manav, "and what he said made sense." He took the mortar from Ai and applied a thick smear of the paste on his arm. "You know how it is here, Ai. The life we lead, how we die. Because we belong here, the police or soldiers are always going to come after us. One day, they will

25

take me away and torture me to death even if I am innocent like they did with Jogen kai and Molu ka. So why not join the struggle, make something of my life while I can. Barman offered me a way out, a job, if you like, one you do for your country."

"It's a job that makes you take life," said Ai. "When life is not yours to give, how can there be any sense in killing people? How can killing serve anyone's purpose?"

"But we just can't sit still and wait our turn to be killed or beaten. Yesterday, it was Molu ka. Tomorrow, it could be me, anyone in the village."

"Perhaps this is what fate left us."

"Fate doesn't teach us to accept, Ai. Fate is what our past is. Destiny is what we make of our lives," said Manav. "I'm afraid too. I don't want to be shot for no fault of mine or hacked to pieces like an animal. We work so hard, strive so much for so little. Sometimes I think this is hell and we are all sinners together." He was silent for a while. "I don't want to end up fighting you when our enemy is someone else. Let me go, Ai."

Shortly before dawn, in the hush of the night, Manav left on his journey. He went to Ai's room before he went, touched her feet and said a prayer for her well being. He hurried to his room to pick up his clothes and a couple of letters for the post.

He glanced behind one last time at the hut that had been his home before scampering through the fields towards the road.

3

In the forests north of the village, not far from where the Dikhow meandered into the Brahmaputra, two men sweated in the slight chill of a new day. Their heads bent over a railway track, clammy fingers connected a mass of wires to a device crammed underneath a wooden sleeper. A few metres away, another man stood on watch. Hands in pockets, keen eyes scanned the jungle as it blended into a veil of thin mist. He lit a cigarette and sauntered round a bend in the track. He knelt on the gravel and placed his ears on the rails.

"Don't worry, we have enough time," called out one man, glancing up from his work taping two pieces of wire.

The man by his side passed a clipper. "They are always on schedule for being late. Now we know why this country is always lagging behind."

The man keeping watch returned for a look. "How much longer? We are running late," he said in an anxious voice. He kept glancing at his watch. "You can never trust these fellows with time. What if the train is on time?"

"Don't make a fuss," said the second man. "Bloody Indian railways are always late. 10.30 for Dibrugarh actually means the 11.45. Good for us, makes our job easier."

"Can't be too careful…"

"You worry too much. We'll have them shitting in their pants."

"They are not that lazy these days what with the security detail and everything." He flicked the cigarette into the woods and wandered off down the track mumbling to himself.

The first man stood up from his work.

"About done," he sighed with relief, wiping his brow on the sleeve of his shirt. "Five more minutes and we can say goodbye to our friends in fatigues." He checked the contraption under the track, running through a checklist of chores in his mind. Satisfied, he picked up his tools and trailed off a roll of wire down the embankment into the dense shrubbery of the forest below.

A thin rain fell drawing a curse from the second man. "Can't keep away this infernal rain, can you? And where is that idiot Jogen off to now?" he said. "Why does he have to walk so far down the track? Why did we put the explosives here, why not at the bridge?"

"Calm down, my friend. You are as bad as Jogen," said the first man. "We want the train to slow down enough for us to see where the soldiers are. Anyway, he'll be along when he hears the train." He glanced upwards, noting the sudden increase in intensity of the rainfall. "Not sure he can now," he added.

"At this rate we are going to miss the train. We should've been done and ready yesterday."

"Couldn't have, not with the track inspections and a policeman every mile. Too bloody careful the railways these days, can't blame them too."

"Yes, not after what happened at Gossaigaon."

"The Tigers doesn't have any qualms about targeting civilians," said the first man, breathing heavily from the exertion of clambering up and down the embankment. "They were ordered to blow up the train and that's what they did - wouldn't have cared if their mothers were inside it. We can't be like them."

"Don't know why we have to bother with whom to kill. There will always be innocents dead."

"You won't be talking like that if you were one of the innocents."

Their conversation was interrupted by Jogen running down the track. He was waving his arms and shouting, but his voice was drowned in the roar of a train.

"Why isn't it late? Why isn't it late?" said the second man in an urgent voice. "How far are you done?"

"Almost there," said the first man without looking up.

"The defense compartments should be the last three bogies."

"Won't miss the buggers for anything."

"We'll teach them a lesson for coming here to fight."

"Damn right we will."

The massive engine rounded the bend in the track.

"Get out of the way, you fool," the two men shouted at Jogen. "Jump!"

Jogen leaped off the track and rolled down the embankment. The train rushed past in a muddle of metal and smoke. He struggled to his feet and watched the blur of faces and blue-beige bogies. The two men crouched in the shadows. The first man tightened his grip on the plunger in his hand. The last of the bogies rounded the corner. He paused, waiting, watching. Then, gunshots.

Between Dikhowpar and the only railway track connecting Lower with Upper Assam stood subtropical forests, which wandered into a narrow expanse of fertile land several miles wide as it reached the Brahmaputra. Those in the fields were hard at work at work despite the heavy rain. Some of the men were settling down to a breakfast of beaten rice and molasses when they heard the bomb going off. They stopped and stared at each other trying to make some meaning out of the explosion in the jungle. They whispered among themselves, deciding it had to be a bomb, but not very sure whether it involved the oil pipeline or the railway. It was only around noon that a passing villager brought news about the blast on the railway track leading to town, and how so many soldiers escaped certain death. All told with wary glances and fast promises not to pass the story to another soul lest someone finds out now that the Sangathon had dared the military. By nightfall, everyone in the village had a different version to tell of the attack. Some said the attackers had been shot. Others spoke of charred bodies of dead soldiers scattered across the track. There was even the odd curious look at the Barua's house, and a few whispered suspicions about Manav's disappearance.

Ai remained closeted in her hut and heard little of the rumours. Nobody told her about the bomb nor did anyone spoke about the attack on the soldiers. She led the life of a mother suffering from the sudden departure of an only son. Her days had passed in a reluctance of routine, interspersed with expectation for some news of her son. Every morning, she sat by the window, full of the common motherly ills of worry and fret. Sometimes she sat in Manav's bed and cried. When her tears dried, she wiped her face and, with the enormous endurance of long suffering village women, resumed her daily cycle of life. Even when busy, her mind drifted to her son, every scrap of his memory, their last conversation. All her thoughts ended with a prayer for his safety. Sometimes she thought about the mysterious people Manav told her would come to visit, and whom she must shelter, and she was nervous about those unknown people who were to come and stay in her house. They had shown Manav this foolish path, and because she was lonely, she hated them.

Of course, nobody came. No one brought Ai any news of her son. Not a stranger showed up at her door. No one climbed the fence or pushed back the gate; nobody knocked at the door or whispered Manav's name.

The rain gathered strength with every passing hour, covering the land in a pall of gloom. The river found its life renewed and flowed with terrifying energy. In the bleakness, day turned into night, and the wind howled and shook the doors and windows of the hut. Ai sat through the fury of the storm. She sat on the wicker bench in the verandah, hands clasped together, eyes fixed on the gate just beyond the marigold bushes. She hardly noticed the hostile darkness or smelled the fury of the approaching floods. The steady rhythm of the rain and the whisper of the wind soothed her, and she found her eyes closing. As the water surged and flowed with gay abandon, she sat oblivious in the verandah, her head resting against the wall, waiting for those unknown people and news of her son...

She dreamt of strangers creeping about in the rain around the house. The sinister figures ran for cover behind the bamboo thickets when she turned her head. Someone from amongst them was stealing round the house, body pressed to the walls, hands feeling forward, hiding from the rain, hiding from her. She heard the clatter of the gate opening, but the sound drowned in the din of the rain. Then, damp shuffling of muddy feet, a squishy-squashy sound, which drew nearer. Ai started out of her drowsy state, her brows raised, eyes squinting into the distance.

A tall figure emerged out of the rain. The man stooped through the doorway and straightened. He wiped his face on his sleeve and smiled at Ai. A deep voice said: "My name is Neal. Manav must have told you about me." He settled down on the murrah by Ai's side with a sigh as if from relief at the end of a long and arduous journey. "You shouldn't worry too much about him. He will be all right," he added, looking up at Ai.

Ai sat like a statue, her hands clasped, now more tightly. She peered at him in the gloom. His face was young, but not very young, and a neatly-trimmed moustache stood out on a fair face. Large eyes flickered in the dim light and danced with eagerness. There was a calmness about him, a reassuring

31

demeanour as if nothing fazed him. It dawned on Ai he was just the sort of person her son would want for a friend. She called him inside and gave him a towel. Her thoughts were on the one question tormenting her mind. "Manav...do you know where he is? When he will come back?"

Neal shrugged his shoulders. "I doubt Manav himself knew where he was going till the last moment."

"So you don't know," said Ai, disappointed.

"Nobody does," said Neal. "That's how the Sangathon operates. It's their way of protecting him, everyone. Ours is such a hard life, Ai, but we do as told."

Ai was shaken by the answer and her face clouded. "So will I ever see him again?"

Neal grinned. "You will see him sooner than you think, Ai, but he will be a different man."

"Do you know why they have taken Manav? I heard they teach how to kill."

"They teach us to fight, defend ourselves."

"So they teach you to kill," said Ai in a voice that told Neal her mind was made up. "What about you? Have you...killed?"

The young man squirmed in his shoes. Before he could answer, there was the hurried patter of steps. The door flung open. A young girl, not more than eighteen or nineteen, entered the room. She was not very tall, but she was pretty. Her long hair was tied in a bun and her clothes were wet in patches form the rain. Her eyes searched out Neal.

"Haven't you heard?" she said, quite out of breath. "The soldiers - they have found out about Arun and you!"

Ai stared at the young girl in front of her, and the young girl at her.

Neal paced the room. "Where is Arun now? Does he know? Why hasn't he come?"

The girl shook her head. "Be patient. He is on his way here.

32

He should be here any minute now." She turned to Ai. "They must stay here for a few days." When Ai hesitated, she said, "It's very important."

"If they must," Ai said in reply, finding the situation beyond her understanding. She sensed something was wrong and all kinds of terrible thoughts ran amok in her mind: "Why are Arun and Neal in trouble? Why are the soldiers looking for them? Who is Arun?"

As if in answer, the door burst open and a massively built man staggered in. His body was hunched with the weight of much physical labour, and his eyes were tired and bloodshot. A thick, bloodied bandage clung to his arm. Pudgy fingers wiped water from his face and fierce eyes darted around the room till they rested on Ai.

Ai's heart beat in alarm. Yes, yes, he was the drunken man from the brawl in the weekly market some years back. Sarmani, her friend, told her how he almost bludgeoned a man to death in front of everyone. From then on everyone in the village treated him with awe and fear. His father, shamed by his son's rowdiness, promptly disowned him. "No, not him too?" she thought, shaking her head.

Arun read her mind. "I know what you are thinking, Ai. But I've paid my debts and thanks to these nice people, I've changed and become a better person."

Ai pointed to the bandage on his arm. "What happened to you? Are you hurt?"

"The bastards," said Arun. "They were shooting at us, remember," he said to Neal. "I think one of the bullets nicked my arm."

The injured man sat on the floor and groaned in pain. The others sat surrounding him. Neal pulled away his shirt. Ai hurried to get her bottle of tincture and hot water to clean the

33

wound. Nina held up a lamp and examined the wound.

"Lucky you," she said, cutting away the rough bandage. "It's just a superficial wound. The bullet scratched your shoulder."

"Your first honest wound, Arun," said Neal. "A few inches to your right and you would've been a martyr."

"Better that than this," said Arun with a grimace, raising his head to take a look and falling back from the pain.

"Can't see why you have to hang around to watch your handiwork," said Nina, scrapping off the caked blood from around the wound.

"We were told not to use a remote device," said Neal. "Much easier, but a lot more casualties including civilians. We were only after these army buggers."

"The train was on time. Why was it on time?" said Arun. "That's when it all started to go wrong. And the rain, it could have waited ten more minutes - can't trust anyone with time these days."

"Jogen didn't see the train until it was almost upon him," said Neal. "And then the soldiers spotted him."

"Foolish boy," said Arun. "Something must be wrong with his eyes not to be able to see a train. And then he stood up to watch - made a mess of things. I had a bad feeling about the whole thing, knew something would go wrong."

"You'd think he never seen a train in his life the way he was watching," said Neal.

Ai returned with the medicine and a bowl of hot water. She settled down beside the injured man and placed his arm on her lap. She cleaned the wound. The others crowded around her full of advice. The injured man glared at them and bit his lips. He let out a cry when the tincture stung.

"Put this in the wound," said Nina, holding up two halves of a capsule she fished out from her bag.

Ai bandaged the wound with clean linen and placed the

arm in a sling made from a gamocha tied around Arun's neck. "You need to change the dressing every day," she said, stooping to pick up the dirty bandages from the floor. She stopped and turned to Arun. "I suppose the soldiers must have a very good reason for shooting at you."

The three looked at each other, then at Ai. Arun looked away. Nina watched a train of ants scampering for the safety of dry ground. Neal sat by her side, elbows on knees, a smile on his face. He straightened and faced Ai.

"There was a bomb blast on the railway track north of the village yesterday," he said, but in such a small voice as if talking to himself. "There were three of us including Arun. We planned to blow up a train carrying a large number of soldiers. The bomb went off, but it didn't do much damage. We were hiding by the side of the tracks in the bushes, but the soldiers spotted us. They started firing. One of our friends was killed on the spot and Arun took a hit while running away. We separated and each went our own way. But they kept coming after us. Manav told us we could use your house as a hideaway and we decided to come here."

Ai stared at each in turn. Thoughts weaved through her mind. How could these nice, young people in front of her be capable of so much violence and yet be so casual about it? She was shocked by Neal's admission, but she was more scared of the implications of two men fleeing the law hiding in her house. What if the police came looking for them? What a slur it would be on the name of her late husband, who once fought to free his country from the British, and whose house now sheltered extremists and seditionists. Yes, that was what these Sangathon people were called in the papers. And her son had become one. They had always been poor, but never disgraced, never had to lower their heads. Her heart felt heavy with a deep sadness.

"We don't mean to cause any trouble," said Nina, coming

closer and holding her hands. "Arun needs to rest for a few days and we will leave as soon as he is better."

"What if they come here?" said Ai.

"They might if they do a house-to-house search," said Neal. "But they have a big area to cover and there are too many houses and very little time."

"It's only for a few days," said Arun in a weak voice. "I'll leave as soon as I get better."

"But the bomb - why did you do something so bad? They will kill you when they find you, just like you tried to kill them," said Ai.

"They won't find us," said Arun.

Neal nodded in agreement. "Ai, we are not afraid. We haven't done anything wrong. We are in the middle of a fight and when people fight, people get killed - sometimes for all the wrong reasons, even without reason. Wars are always unreasonable. The tragedy is that we are the ones who belong here, yet we are the ones who are being hunted and killed."

"Still," said Ai, "all this violence - bombs, guns, deaths..." Her voice trailed off and she shook her head.

"If we don't fight them, they will wipe us from the face of this earth, take away what is rightfully ours," said Nina.

"We may be poor and ignorant, but we want to live a life worthy of human beings, and with the dignity and respect we deserve," said Neal. "We must show our enemies that this life of drudgery hasn't made us weak or kept us from being their equals."

Ai gazed out of the window. The hum of their voices receded to the background. Tears welled in her eyes. She had always led a troubled life, but somehow all her problems involved overcoming the next obstacle in her battle against poverty. She had never led a complicated life, never faced the fury of outraged law, never seen the harsh reality of daily deaths. Now, she was suddenly scared for Manav, his life and everything he stood for.

Nina rose to leave. "I'll come back in the morning. Have to get Arun some medicines. And I've an errand to run."

"In this rain? No, go in the morning," said Ai, not wanting to have another worry on her hands.

"I'll be all right, Ai," she sang from the door, but her words were lost in the wind. She covered her head with a shawl, opened her umbrella and stepped into the rain.

Ai felt uneasy, even guilty, at letting her leave. Her heart missed a beat as she watched from the window. The wind whirled about Nina and tugged at her umbrella trying to snatch it away. The rain beat down harder. She staggered forward with great difficulty, her feet sinking in the mud. When she reached the bamboo thickets, they bowed and screeched like wicked witches on a full moon day.

Ai watched the narrow path leading out her house for some time, long after the figure of Nina had disappeared into the gloom of evening. "God, what has the world come to when little girls have to fight such lonely battles," she thought with a shudder.

For some reason, she thought she had seen Nina for the last time and it made her sad. Later, when she prayed in front of the idol tucked away in a corner of her kitchen, she cried. The tears were for her son, and for the young people, whose lives would be lost to death and injury. It was also for the end of days when people marched armed with the ideals of Gandhi in their hearts. Those days were long past and Gandhi meant nothing more than a fading memory of a giant, whose portrait hung in dark corners of offices and houses. She was still weeping when she lit the stove to prepare supper, but as always, her poverty and her hard life stood her in good stead.

By the time she served her guests, she had regained her composure.

By the time she went to bed, she was her normal self. But

women have their sixth sense, and for some reason, a vague fear clutched at her heart warning her of an ominous event. And Ai had learnt to trust her premonitions all her life.

That very minute, in a nearby village, an olive green truck screeched to a halt in a slurry of mud and filth. The tailgate tumbled down with a crash and a number of soldiers jumped on the ground. They fanned out through the village. They hounded the surprised villagers out of their houses into the rain and herded them into the open field in the middle of the village. They separated the men from the women and children.

An officer approached the men. He spat on the ground in disgust as thin bodies shivered in the cold and prayed for divine intervention. He watched their faces for a faint trace, a sliver of a clue, anything. All he saw was fear. He sighed in disappointment and pointed randomly.

"Take him…and him and him."

4

Manav closed his eyes and counted to three. Slowly. Like he had been told to. One. Two. Three. When he opened his eyes, all he saw was the soldier watching him, a cold look in his eyes, the dark bore of his gun pointed at him. He held his breath and took careful aim. There was a tightness in his arm, then a taut release as if the gun belonged to him, an extension of his body. His finger tightened on the trigger. At a sharp command, he fired, noting the patch of torn paper between the soldier's eyes. He kept on firing until all that remained of the cutout was a mangled piece of cardboard.

"Not bad," said the instructor stopping by Manav's side, his eyes on what remained of the cutout. To all the men hunched over their guns, he said: "Never waste your bullets, make every single one count. Think you are shedding your own blood with every shot. Think of the soldiers as leeches, leeches who suck your land dry. They will kill you if they had half a chance, so kill them without mercy." He glanced at his watch. "Fifteen minutes," he said, before turning on his heels and walking off.

Manav heaved a sigh of relief. He hustled to his feet, unlocking the magazine and depositing the gun in the armoury. He joined the queue at the food hut, and when the thick ghoulish mass thudded into his plate, he hurried for the shade of a nearby tree. He wasn't hungry. Not for food. The mass on his plate made him sick, but he managed to spoon a mouthful, reveling in its warm stickiness when he swallowed. If only he could rest, get a good night's sleep. He closed his eyes.

They were nine men on the road from Ledo, nine men,

who pledged their lives in the fight for freedom. They were met by their guide at the monastery, who confiscated their watches and money, and forbade them from talking to one another, even stare or steal glances. They were driven forty kilometers down the Stillwell Road in the back of a lorry to the frontier with Myanmar. It was an ordeal from the moment they crossed the border. Everything was suddenly different, everything felt worse than it was. It was like stepping into another world, full of mistakes and regrets, and vile serpents and deadly insects. The people on the road treated them with an empathy reserved for animals taken away to be slaughtered. They were taken to Myitkyina in Kachin Burma and put on a bus, which let them off in the middle of nowhere after a three hour drive. They were handed over to another man, a Burmese from the few coarse words of Assamese he spoke, who told them they'd have to walk the remainder of the way to the camp somewhere in the jungles close to the border with China. He led them through jungles so thick it was dark during the day. Several times, they narrowly missed running into Burmese soldiers. And all along they kept a careful watch for the dim-dim, a tiny pest, whose bite is known to itch, paralyze and kill, and claimed more lives than skirmishes with government soldiers. Three days later, they arrived in the camp run by Kachin insurgents, an encampment of huts surrounding a clearing in the jungle not far from the border, and the Chinese town of Mengmao in Yunnan Province.

Manav went to bed the first night with all the excitement at the beginning of a new journey, but sleep eluded him. He tossed and turned on the hard bamboo matting, which felt like a bed of sharp nails. He drifted in and out of sleep, lost in a myriad of dreams, which were strange and vague, and warned him of coming trouble.

It was still dark when they were startled out of sleep by the blast of a whistle. The whistle blew again. It was louder and imperious, and there was a tremor of impatience in its shrillness. The door of the hut burst open, heavy boots smacked off the mud floor and angry oaths broke the morning air.

Someone's bare feet slapped on the floor. One of the sleeping men gave a yawn; another turned on his side and went back to sleep. More men rushed inside. They kicked out at those in bed and they sat up with startled looks on their faces. Within minutes they scuttled out of the hut like frightened chickens and gathered in the clearing. They shivered in the cold and stared at each other with half-open eyes, and then at a short, squat man, almost invisible in green fatigues. He climbed the mud lectern and barked out instructions in a staccato of broken Assamese.

The group set off on a barefoot run in the dark jungle. All Manav remembered in his sleepy stupor was the constant slapping of his cheeks by the thick foliage on which an occasional leech fed itself before falling off. They must have run for an hour or so, but by the time they returned to camp, thirsty and bruised, it was bright and sunny. They were given five minutes to eat, and another ten for their toilet. Still panting from their exertions, they gathered in a smattering of silent individuals in the clearing.

It soon grew hot, but there was no respite for the men. Hour after hour, one lesson followed the other. They learnt how lethal their hands could be, how to fabricate guns out of plumbing, put together explosives, even shoot with all manners of weapons. In the afternoons, there were lectures to attend to, and Lenin to learn about and Mao to memorize. Their heads stuffed with visions of an egalitarian society, sleep engulfed the group the moment heads hit the floor. A breeze blew through the open windows and brought with it swarms of mosquitoes. They bit the sleeping men with carefree frenzy.

It was the beginning of the sickness and the shootings.

On the seventh day of their training, one of the men

stumbled and fell on their morning run. He was left on the trail, burning with fever and vomiting his previous night's meal. When they returned to camp, they saw him on the ground in the shadow of a hut, eyes closed, muttering to himself. They kept an eye on him during the day, but his condition deteriorated with every passing hour. By late afternoon, he was unconscious and didn't even stir when two of the guards poked him with their guns. Manav heard his shallow breathing and feverish incoherence all through the night. He sat up wondering whether he should help, then remembering the strict instructions from the guards not to. The next afternoon, while they ate and swatted at flies, they saw two guards carry the sick man into the jungle. They came back wiping sweat from their brows and a large hunting knife; it glinted in the sun and still had traces of blood. It was the moment they realized the camp was without a doctor or medicines. Too fall sick meant death. Their life, they were told that night, was in their hands.

A week later, another man fell during rifle training. Manav knew him well for they had taken the same bus from Margherita to Ledo, each lying to the other the reason for the visit, and laughing about it as they fed the dogs at the monastery waiting for their guide. He was sick for several days, puking after meals and holding his stomach between drills, but having seen what happened to his comrade, carried on nonetheless. The short, squat man took one look at him before deciding his fate, but Manav was glad to notice he was at least angry about it, shouting at the guards for losing another man. Like the one before him, he was dragged to the jungle. All they heard sometime later was a single shot and the startled cries of birds settling down for the night.

That night, they were provided with mosquito coils. There were strict instruction against lighting a fire at night, and after a discussion on the matter, it was decided in favour of the coils.

Manav spent the night tossing and turning in bed, and staring at the darkness. If only they were allowed to talk for the silence between the men was beginning to stifle and choke. They exchanged the odd fleeting glance at meal times, and there was even the momentary meeting of scared eyes, but they never broke their enforced silence.

The days passed in a blur of time.

Manav soon lost count. They were devoured by their routine, which gradually intensified. For the flicker of a moment, there was the muted longing for Ai and the village, but the feeling passed. Two more men in the group fell sick and were shot in the courtyard. It didn't matter much to the remaining men nor did they flinch or close their eyes when the guards shot them as they lay sick and shivering on the ground. It only made them more resolute to see their training through, become what they had set out to do.

After ninety days of such an ordeal, it was over. The whistle didn't blare out the morning after, but the men woke all the same. The short man nodded with a pleased expression on his face when they gathered in the clearing. For the first time in many months, he spoke in a voice that was not harsh and even sounded polite. It was as if they deserved the respect and the accolade for seeing their training through. The men were allowed to break their silence and speak, mingle amongst themselves, ask questions. They stared at each other, squinting in the tender light of dawn as if seeing each other for the first time. They stared at their hard, tanned faces, the blank expressionless eyes and their gaunt bodies, the pain and the agony they had borne in silence, all the suffering of a survivor. They were ready for their moment of reckoning. In the rising sun of a new day in foreign soil, they found their lives renewed.

In Dikhowpar, it was still dark. It was around the time the men prepared to leave for work in the fields. The women were beginning another day of coping with an endless stream of chores while the children held their grandparents and slept without a care. They stopped and listened as the distant rumble of engines grew louder. They doused their lamps and peered out from the windows. Two trucks came to a halt in the village square. The tail gates opened and a number of soldiers jumped out in a rush, their boots crunching the muddy gravel. They divided themselves into two groups and spread out through the village.

Ai was still in bed when she heard the distant crash of the gate. The noise startled her out of sleep. She sat up in bed and stared in the dim light trying to catch the sound again. Like all village people used to gentler sounds of animals calling or a man toiling with his tools, it left her anxious. She heard the rustle of leaves and twigs snapping, harried shouts and the heavy thuds of boots on the verandah outside.

The door burst open.

A tall soldier, an officer, appeared by her bed, followed by another shorter man, a policeman. A couple of soldiers ran past, kicking open the back door and rushing into the kitchen.

Ai drew back in bed. "What are the soldiers doing here? Neal and Arun - where are they? What have they done to them?" she thought.

"So where have you hidden them, woman?" said the officer.

The policeman glared at Ai. "We have information you are hiding two ultras. Where are they?"

"I live alone. I don't know of anyone hiding here," said Ai. She pulled the chador over her shoulders and leaned against the wall, her eyes following the men inside the house.

"Have you looked there?" the officer pointed to the door by an almirah.

A soldier kicked the door open and rushed inside. Ai held her breath. "Nobody inside, sahib," he reported in a crisp voice.

44

The two soldiers returned from the back. They looked at their leader and shook their heads.

"I'll find the two motherchods. They can't be far," said the officer. To Ai, he said: "If you see them, let us know, and we'll remember not to kill you." He pointed the gun at her and nodded as if to convey he meant what he said.

Ai looked away. Her eyes filled with tears. Nobody in all her years had spoken so harshly to her as this evil man.

"Spare your tears, woman," said the officer, "or you won't have any left for future use. Rain and tears, that's all you have." He spat on the floor.

The policeman glanced at the officer before turning to Ai. "I know what's going on here, you see. You can't lie to me. I'll catch you one of these days and then they will come and drag you away. If you are lucky, they will spare you the pain and kill you."

Ai shuddered in fright and lowered her eyes, sensing a merciless soul who had little respect for life. The officer barked out orders to his men. They left the house, breaking down the front door and sending the wicker bench in the verandah crashing into the courtyard. They jumped into their trucks, the engines started with roars, and within minutes all that was left in their wake was the slush of tires and the silence of a village shaken by fear. As soon as the sound of the engines died in the distance, Ai wiped away her tears and hurried outside. The gate lay in tatters and the garden was a mess of broken flower pots and wrecked flower beds. She hardly gave it a glance, darting everywhere, peering into the blurred greenery of the bamboo thickets behind the house, and the trees behind the cowshed, and even in the heavy undergrowth further ahead. She looked everywhere, but Neal and Arun were gone. Her heart pounding, she entered the house when the two men jumped out from behind the sacks of grain. "Where were you? Why are you wet?"

she said, an incredulous expression on her face.

Neal showed her the papaya stem in his hands. "The fools, they looked everywhere, but they missed the pond. We kept the fish company." He noticed the scared look on Ai's face and stopped. "Did they hurt you, Ai? You were very brave."

"They were very rude," said Ai. "They tried to scare me, but I told them I don't know anything." She paused. "They know you were here."

Arun shook his head. He didn't appear pleased with his early morning bath. His bandage had come off and he was shivering. "No, they don't. That's the way they treat people. For them everyone is a cheat and crook, but they are the bigger criminals."

"They will talk in the same accusing tone to everyone in the village," said Neal. "Sometimes a villager might stammer out something in his nervousness. Then all you can do is pray for him to die quickly because these soldiers can be brutal and they know how to kill."

Ai shivered at the thought. She saw something she hadn't seen in any of the three young people: fear. But they told her they were ready to die. Perhaps more than death, they feared the agony of capture and the torment of torture.

"They will come back?" she said.

"I know they will," said Arun. "They are a persistent lot. They can't lose sleep over two people roaming free with bombs for them."

"If they fail, they will think of something else," said Neal. "They won't think twice about stooping low, do what they like."

Ai was silent for a while. "Nina. I'm worried about her."

"She will be fine, Ai," said Neal. "She is braver than all of us put together, and she knows how to stay out of sight."

Ai nodded, but somehow she didn't feel reassured. The day had an ominous beginning and she was a believer in portents all her life, so much so she'd scare and hide every time she had a premonition, shudder in fright at her sense of unease. And every single time, it had come true, harmed or killed, changed things beyond repair. She felt the same way now.

"Do they really torture people?" she said, quivering at the thought. "Break bones or pass electricity? It's awful. How could one human being do that to another?"

Neal sighed. "They do that and much worse. They wring out your soul and they torture that too. Even if you are not dead, you wish you were. You welcome death."

Nina returned with the medicines the following day and news that the soldiers had picked up five men from the neighbouring village.

"See, I told you," said Neal. "Cowards! Why can't they fight like men instead of picking on innocent people?"

"That's their way of getting back at us," said Arun. "They think it will make us turn ourselves in, but you can't blame them for being stupid."

Ai gave a sigh and lowered her eyes. "Who can blame them when they can't see who they are fighting? Maybe they are more afraid of you than you are of them."

"So they pick on innocent people, people who struggle to put together two meals, wear decent clothes, try to be happy with what they have." Neal paused for a moment and shook his head. "Now they will take away whatever little they have, even their nothings."

Ai turned to Nina. "Did you see them?"

Nina nodded. "Two truckloads armed to their teeth to pick on a village of twenty families who hadn't had a decent meal for such a long time even they must think hunger is an insatiable natural feeling. Such courage." She lowered her voice and her face darkened. "I was lucky. They'd have taken me in too, but I hid in the bushes by the road."

Ai drew her breath. "You poor dear, but they don't harm women and children, do they?" She noticed the three exchanged glances. Their faces dropped and cheerful faces clouded.

Nina smiled and placed her hands on Ai's shoulders. "Oh no, they don't, except that in the middle of so many thin and taut bodies, I'd have stood out like a well-fed chicken."

Something that was almost envy - no, admiration, touched Ai's heart. "I wish I was like you, so casual and yet so brave, but I'm too old for all this now. I was never brought up to be brave. All I was told was the work I'd to do as if it's the most important thing in my life, like a ritual, every day of my life till the moment I die."

The news of the arrest of the five men set off a fierce discussion between the three. Neal, Ai observed, talked more often and with more intensity. He was always gesturing with his arms, trying to make his point. Arun spoke once or twice. Nina listened with a severe expression in her eyes. She occasionally interrupted Neal, and though he never listened to what Arun said, he always stopped when Nina spoke to make a point. Their discussion turned into a furious debate, and then into a heated argument. Nina went away in a huff to sit by the pond. Neal paced the width of the room, forehead furrowed in thought. A couple of times, he stopped to stare at the portrait of Gandhi on the wall. Arun slept. Feeling tired herself and finding her eyes closing, Ai went to rest for a while. When she returned in the fading light of dusk, Neal and Arun were gone and Nina sat in a corner, a worried look on her face.

"What happened?" said Ai, rushing to her side. "Where are the boys?"

Nina didn't answer for some time. Then with a sigh, as if of defeat, she told her. "The fools. What if they get shot? What if they are killed?"

Ai stared into the gloom, sensing her premonition coming

true. "Why does life for the poor always had to be about redemption?" she thought. "Why must the meek always suffer? Why has the military stooped so low as to pick up five innocent villagers? What can she do to stop such foolhardiness from Neal and Arun?" She stared at the portrait of Gandhi, fading with the light. Manav's words rang true in her ears. What he said made sense. Gandhi's vision belonged to a world that was long gone. It was a world that died with him. Ai always believed in her prayers and with all the fervour of her belief, she knelt in front of her idol in the kitchen and prayed. She prayed for the men corralled in the Army's custody and for their families, but most of all she prayed for Neil and Arun for despite their careless ways they had the good of other men in their hearts. There she remained, palms joined together in solemn entreaty as dusk turned to night and a pale moon picked out Neal and Arun many miles away at the end of their trek deep into the forest north of the village. They were soaked to the skin in sweat, but they had the anxiety of the task ahead in their hearts to keep up their frantic pace.

In the confines of a small shack in the forest, the two men busied themselves with the job in hand. They worked in the sullen silence of discord realizing they faced a more formidable foe in a circumstance of their creation. Eyes peered in the light of a kerosene lamp and sweat glistened on their brows as the two men assembled an improvised explosive device. An hour later, the bomb inside the pack on Neal's shoulders, they hit the trail again. Like before, they walked in silence, their thoughts on the five villagers in the Army camp. They kept up a relentless pace, eyes focused on the dimness ahead, ears alert for the slightest sound. Arun stopped every now and then when his arm pained, and Neal not at all.

Two hours of fast-paced walking brought them within sight of the only bridge worth its name on the Dikhow. They slid down the grassy bank to the water's edge to have a look. From below, the iron spans were as solid as the day they were cast by the British a hundred years back. But time and the raging waters of the Dikhow had taken their toll. Only the interlocking spans and the clever design ensured the bridge's survival as it endured the battering from buses and trucks, carts and cars. Neal estimated they had enough explosives to give one of the pylons a knocking, make a large enough hole to stop traffic for a week, kill a few soldiers in the bargain. They didn't want to damage the bridge too badly and disrupt all communication with Dibrugarh.

Neal crawled up the support wall, a torch between his teeth, fingers digging into gaps between boulders where the cement had fallen off till he was underneath the footboards. He grabbed one of the many loose planks above his head, changing his hold to the one in front to move forward. Ten minutes later, he was directly above the river. From somewhere below came the smell of a carcass in the water. He twitched his nose and ignored the smell. When he found a suitable place for the explosives, he hauled his feet into a gap between the planks. With a knife he scraped away at the wood. Fifteen minutes later, when he had enough space, Arun passed him the explosives from above. They trailed off a roll of wire to the river bank below and settled down to wait. Neal was sweating profusely, and every now and then, Arun cast a worried look at his wound. He broke the silence.

"Do you believe they will really let the five men go if we blow up one of their trucks?" he said all of a sudden.

Neal didn't reply for some time. "What else could we do? We can't rescue them from their camp, can we? We'd be shot down like dogs before we make the gate. We are responsible in the first place for what is happening to those villagers right now. We can't just hide and look away and hope everything works out fine. What if they are killed?"

Arun nodded in the darkness. They had this conversation all through the day, debated and argued, and he was still not convinced.

"What if they see us? What if we get killed?"

Neal gestured impatiently. "That's the idea, my friend. We want them to see us, we want them to know that the two bomb-makers are still out there. We want to tease them, tell them we are waiting for them to come after us. And does it matter if we die? Anyway, it's a lot better than carrying the death of five men on our conscience all our life. But we are not going to die. We will be back with Ai by this time tomorrow and things will be like before. The soldiers will look in the jungle, but they are such fools, they won't find a trace of us there and they will give up taking other people to kill instead of us."

"What if they don't?"

Neal glared at Arun. "Then we make another bomb and shove it down their throats!"

The patrol came as dawn was breaking over the horizon and the sun was rolling down its light across the hills. In the hamlet nearby, people were rising to another day of work. Arun was the first to hear the distant sound of the engines. He shook awake Neal, who had fallen asleep on the grass, and was snoring. They ducked behind the bushes.

The roar of a truck grew louder. In the still morning air, it drew sharp cries from the birds out on their first flight of the day. A blur of green grew larger. It took the shape of an enormous truck with a gun mounted at the top, and a soldier behind it.

"Careful," said Arun, raising his head. "Not much time now. Don't miss the bastards."

The truck roared past them in a cloud of dust and onto the bridge, which shuddered under its weight. One of the soldiers at the back of the truck was dozing after a night of wary vigil. He blinked and raised his hands as a gust of dust flew into his eyes. He had a momentary glimpse of a head springing out from behind the bushes below him. He let out a yell of terror.

"Kuch garbar hai," he shouted. Something's wrong.

The truck screeched to a halt. The soldier at the top of the truck turned the gun around searching the ground for intruders. The others clambered down from the truck and took up positions on the road, scanning the ground below for any movement.

Neal heard the shouts above him and realized they had been spotted. There wasn't any time to lose. He pulled the detonator as the soldiers were about to fire. The explosion ripped a hole in the bridge a few feet in front of the truck. The whole structure shook violently and pieces of mortar and wood fell on the water with loud splashes. Startled cries of birds rented the morning air. The soldiers shouted and ran for cover. In the nearby village, people held their breath and prepared themselves for more horrors.

For Neal and Arun there wasn't another moment to waste. They jumped out of the bushes and started running for the safety of the trees. The soldier behind the machine-gun had fallen back when the bomb set off, his head hitting the side rails of the truck. Still groggy, he shook his head and steadied himself. From his perch, he caught fleeting glimpses of two men as they fled towards the trees, brief streaks of blue and white mud-soaked shirts through the tall kohua. He turned the gun around and caught the blue-shirted man in his sights. He watched the figure disappear into another patch of kohua. Ahead, he made out a gap in the grass. He adjusted his sight and waited. When the man appeared, he took careful aim and fired. The body faltered in mid-stride as if held back by a powerful hand, tottered, and fell, the momentum of the run carrying it a further few feet ahead.

The following day, the soldiers returned to the village with Arun's body inside a jute sack. They made straight for his house, dumping the body on the courtyard. A couple of soldiers went inside and dragged out the parents.

The officer leading the men, a tall man with a loud voice, ran a knife through the sack. He uncovered the dead man's face with an expression of disgust. "He tried to ambush my men by blowing up the bridge over the Dikhow," he said in a shrill complaining voice. "Been after him for some time now, him and his friend. He escaped, but we will get him. We always do."

Arun's father, a short, thin man with ribs that glared out of his chest, stumbled forward. Tears streaked down his cheeks at the sight of his son's face. The mother ran forward with a cry of anguish. She stared at the body at her feet and fell on the ground, wailing and beating her chest.

The officer tapped the woman on her shoulders. "Cut out that sound, you stupid woman. I'm not here to listen to your screams. I'm here to let you know that we will soon put an end to all this nonsense. Thanks to your dead son, we can now release the five innocent men in custody." He took a few steps around the courtyard watched by the silent crowd on the road. He motioned to his men to push the crowd back with a contemptuous wave of his hand. He came over to the sobbing father and patted him on the shoulders. "That other man we are looking for, we will find him. If he comes around, you send that behenchod to me. If I'm in a good mood, I might kill him quickly." With a crisp turn of his heels, he climbed into his Jeep and drove away with a burst of speed.

Ai was feeding the fish in the pond when the soldiers arrived with the body. She had heard bits and pieces about somebody

53

shot in the forests, but didn't give the matter much consideration. Rumors have a way of copying the truth, and as she often found out, they were never far from it. She turned her mind to what Nina told her about Neal and Arun and dismissed the thought, deciding it had nothing to do with the two. A passing neighbour broke the news.

She hurried to Arun's house, her heart heavy with sorrow, a faint hope in her heart that there had been some mistake. But the silent throng in front of the house and the taunts of the officer left her in little doubt. As soon as the soldiers climbed into the Jeep, she rushed forward, tears falling from her eyes.

When she returned home several hours later, she found Nina in a corner of the house, wiping tears from her eyes.

"The fools," she said. "I knew this would happen."

Ai said: "Have you any news of Neal? I heard the soldiers are looking for him."

"They won't find him," said Nina. "He knows his way better in these parts than they know the back of their hands."

Ai nodded, but she wasn't very convinced. "Do you think they will come here again?"

"No, they won't," said Nina. "They have nothing more to find or kill here."

But the soldiers returned to the village that very night. It was a moonless night and they came at the darkest hour. They surrounded the dead man's house and tore it apart. They did the same to the house next to it, which belonged to the village grocer's.

In the morning, Ai had a visitor in the village grocer. As soon as it was light, he hurried to each of his neighbours - anyone he knew, reliving a slightly exaggerated experience.

"What did they do your house, Bora? They broke my door, made a mess of my garden," said Ai, offering him a betel nut and paan, tinged with a sliver of lime.

He declined, pointing to his mouth. "My mouth's full, Ai. I had too many," he said. "Anyway, let me tell you what happened." He paused for a moment to spit out some crumbs. "They were very rough. Nasty fellows. I was afraid the officer would shoot me because I refused to cooperate. Why should I when none of this is my fault? What were they doing when these kids were hatching their conspiracies? He shouted and stamped his foot. He kicked at the furniture and shot my radio to pieces. 'I'll put you in jail for this,' he shouted. He asked all sorts of questions. 'Have you seen anyone else in their house? How could you not know staying only a few feet apart?' As if I have no other work." He shut his eyes for a moment and pursed his lips, pushing back his hair with a quick movement of his hands. He pointed at the portrait of Gandhi on the wall. "His soul must be a tormented one seeing his dreams come apart like this. The young - they can't take care of themselves and they want a country of their own." Then, staring at Ai with large, febrile eyes, he added, "The other boy, the one with Arun, he's in for a tough time. They will find him for sure, and when they find him, they will kill him without any mercy."

"Do you think they will be able to catch him?" said Ai, looking him in the eye.

"I hope they do," he said, rising to leave. "It will give us back our peace. This is bad for business. Now all people do is talk about the Sangathon."

"I don't like him one bit," said Nina after he left. "He is a cruel, heartless fellow."

Ai cried out in pain. "Who isn't, dear, who isn't?"

There was no sign of the soldiers in the village that day, but a patrol kept a keen eye. As evening approached, news filtered in about searches in the neighbouring village. There were several beatings and a broken house or two, but nobody was picked up. Ai hung on to every word for news of Neal. When nothing gave her succor, she went to bed on an empty stomach and a prayer on her lips.

She slept pitifully that night, meandering between bizarre dreams, wandering far away from home in a strange land, looking for Manav and finding Arun instead. She woke with a start, reflecting on her dream, searching for some significance, deciding it must be from watching Arun's pale dead face and the sudden longing for her son. She thought she heard the faint rustle of leaves outside the window, but dismissed it for the wind, which picked up and blew a fierce gust. She was awakened by the sound of steady knocking at the back door. Whoever it was kept pounding with remarkable persistence. She saw Nina stir beside her, then get down from the bed and crawl into the space behind the almirah.

The knocking grew louder. There was something alarming in its stubborn insistence. Ai threw a shawl over her shoulders and went to the door, pausing before opening it.

"Who's there?"

"Me," said a hoarse voice.

"Who?"

"Please open the door," the voice implored.

Ai recognized the deep, guttural tone. She lowered the latch and pushed the door open.

Neal staggered in. He was covered with mud and his clothes were torn and tattered. There were bruises and cuts all over his arms and face. He stood unsteadily on his legs.

"They saw us, the devils," he said. "They got Arun."

"I know."

Neal looked at Ai. "How could you know?"

"The soldiers handed over his body to the parents," she said. "But they freed the five men."

"Just like I expected," said Neal. He heaved a sigh of relief and sat down on the floor. He removed his shirt and with a gamocha cleaned his face. "I was lucky. I fell into a ditch. I heard them looking for me. There were crawling all over the place, the devils. I held my breath and hid in the ditch and they passed me by. I saw two of them - they were three feet away, but blind as bats in broad daylight. I stayed there the whole day. When it was night, I crawled out. They were gone by then. I got up and started legging it and here I am."

Nina appeared in the doorway. "Didn't I warn you something like this would happen?"

Neal paused for a moment before answering. "It was Arun's mistake. We were hiding in the bushes by the bridge waiting for the morning patrol. I don't know what came over him, but he got up and a soldier spotted him. I couldn't wait and set the bomb off. We both started running towards the forest, but they had a machine gun mounted on top of the truck. They got him. He must have died instantly."

"Did you go back to find out?" said Nina, a tinge of sarcasm in her voice.

Neal pretended not to notice. "I wish I could, but then the soldier turned his gun on me. A minute more and he would have found his range. Thank god, I fell down that hole."

Nina could see he was pleased with himself, pleased with his adventure, pleased for the fact that he got away.

"Yes, thank god," she said, glaring at him.

5

Manav died the day he completed his training around the time Arun was cut down by a hail of bullets and Neal escaped by falling into a ditch. He was dismissed from life like he was never there, never had a mother, never toiled the fields of his forefathers. In his place, by a single intonation and the flourish of a ball-point pen, Hirok Hazarika was born. He was now of a different faith, one that claimed what remained of his life by an oath to his mother land.

"Hirok Hazarika!" He repeated his name like a mantra when the instructor introduced him to scattered applause from the camp inmates. Gone were the burden of a past and the prejudice of fate. In a flash of enlightenment, he found his life explained and his destiny decided. "Better than a job pushing files," thought Hirok. His mind darted back for a moment to his father. "The purity of fighting for your country's freedom," he said, shaking his head. All he found inside him was a deep sense of injustice and a desire for vengeance. "Gandhi be damned!" he swore under his breath.

Hirok heard talk of their Leader visiting the camp and couldn't wait to meet him. The Leader had fought in the jungles with his men and travelled the length of the land extolling the benefits of freedom to his people. He learned to his surprise that despite his exploits and the devotion to the cause, few laid claim to have known the man. The Leader had never been photographed, and so nobody knew how he looked, but there formed in Hirok's mind the image of a man strong and powerful, one who had never known defeat nor lacked courage in the face of adversity. His was a face with sharp features, a stern moustache, hair that fell over his shoulders and eyes that shone with kindly light. He carried with him an aura of invisibility and possessed a voice that at once commanded and rallied his men, and put the fear of death in his enemies. But when Hirok saw him on the morning of their induction, he realized his imagination couldn't have been further from the truth.

The Leader was seated on a chair, a bunch of prisoners around him on the ground, their mouths gagged and hands tied behind their backs. The sun glistened on his bald pate and, from a face much wrinkled and scarred, he peered at them from behind thick glasses. The newly-trained men sat on the ground facing him. To show their respect, they kept their heads bowed and listened with averted eyes.

"All of you have a history of a life behind you," the Leader's voice rang out, "but you don't have a past. Learn from the lessons it gave you, listen to your past, but never repeat its mistakes. We have been exploited enough - all our lives, every part of our modern history. The Assamese are a hospitable people, but our guests have overstayed their welcome. It's time they leave so that we can make our own path in this world, be a nation with people that'd have been wealthy, but for the years of exploitation and neglect. We've a long and difficult struggle ahead of us, and many of us here today won't live to see it bear fruit, but we owe our mother this one, owe it to her to free her land of all the pests." He reeled off famous names from Assamese history: Lachit Barphukan, who defeated the might of the Mughals, the great Ahom kings, and so on.

Hirok heard about the exploits from Ai when a child, and read all about it in school when older, and so knew all the facts, but hearing it from the Leader, he felt proud to be an Assamese. At that moment, basking in the glory of history in foreign soil, he was willing to do anything for his land: die, bear the most horrific of pain, kill.

The Leader observed the eager faces of the men and knew he had them spellbound, and in his grasp. He continued in the same unshakeable tone: "You have been here for so few days now, but a day is a long time in this world. So many things change in a day. During your time here, the police and soldiers killed twelve people all over Assam. Thirty young people who chose to ride out time and stayed home were picked up by the military. I doubt we will see them again." He let his words sink in, noting the shocked expressions on the men's faces. When he spoke again, it was almost a congratulatory pat on their backs. "You've done well and should thank yourselves and god for making the right choice. You came here as boys so full of self doubts, but you are going back as men, and as freedom fighters." The men listened with their mouths agape, inspired and dreaming of greatness. The Leader watched with a pleased expression on his face. A smile pulled at the corner of his mouth. "Let's us find out how worthy you are of your mother's trust, let me see how deserving you are of your names," he said.

At a gesture from the Leader, two of the gagged prisoners were tied to bamboo poles at the edge of the clearing. Around them everyone in the camp sat in a circle. An aide read out from a file. The two men were charged with hoarding grain in warehouses to raise market prices. There was the more serious act of sedition for refusing a donation to the Sangathon's war chest. The aide closed the file, glanced at the Leader, and announced in a shrill voice: "The two accused men are guilty as charged. The penalty is death!"

Those in the gathering burst into polite applause. The two prisoners exchanged confused looks. Everyone looked at the Leader.

The Leader stood up. He gestured with his hands and the gentle hum of conversation ceased. He smiled his appreciation, nodding at everyone in turn. Gesturing at the newly-trained men, he said: "I'd be like to see someone from amongst you carry out the sentence."

For a stunned moment no one moved. Hirok's heart pounded and his arms and feet refused to budge. He stood like a statue. Two of the men stepped forward. They saluted smartly and checked out the two guns on the table. The forest grew quiet. The crowd held their breath. The two men raised their guns at the astonished prisoners, who struggled to free themselves. Fingers tightened on triggers, then slackened. The two men lowered their guns.

The Leader nodded. He understood how hard it was for a new recruit to shoot someone in cold blood with so many eyes watching their every move. But it was a necessary exercise, one the leadership favoured in separating the strong from the stronger - those that can be trusted to one day lead, and those who will always remain in the fringes and follow.

Two other men stepped forward. They repeated the drama, flinching at the last moment and returning their weapons with downcast eyes, seeking solace at the back of the crowd. Those in the crowd appeared disappointed. A few yawned while a couple of voices shouted about how they could do better. The two prisoners relaxed. When the last two men stepped forward, they calmly watched them raise their guns. The patter of nonchalant chatter died. A hush fell, this time with reluctance. Fingers tightened on triggers. The two prisoners waited for the fiasco to end. One gun fired. A red dot blossomed on a prisoner's forehead. The body sagged against the pole. The other prisoner screamed and pulled at his knots. The crowd pushed forward. Hirok paused, glanced at the Leader and shot the other man as well. Then, just to make sure, he shot them again. The other prisoners panicked and screamed. A couple of them fainted. Those in the crowd gathered around Hirok with adoring looks.

Those his age shook his hands; those older thumped his back. The Leader sat in his chair and heaved a sigh of relief. He rose from his seat and shook Hirok's hand. When Hirok touched his feet, he blessed him. In a moment of pandering, his transformation was complete.

It was finally too late to turn back, return to the life of his forefathers. For Manav Barua, the hard-working farmer-son of a Gandhian was already a life consigned to the pages of the past. He no longer existed, never lived.

In the clearing, everyone ate together, bound by their brotherhood of death and freedom. They sat cross-legged on the forest floor on cushions of fallen leaves, the two shot men still dripping blood in front of them.

Hirok ate a hearty meal that day, feeling ravenous and inspired, his mind fanned by the deed. After the meal, he was called to the camp commandant's office and given his orders. He left for home in a group of six that evening, shortly after the flies appeared in a noisy drone. The two bodies were untied and thrown into a pit at the edge of the camp, doused with kerosene and set alight.

Ai was lost in her work when she heard the gate opening followed by the excited barking of the neighbour's dog. Someone stepped on the verandah. The door opened and Hirok came in. He was wearing the torn trousers of a village lad and a tattered shirt hung over a muddy vest. His face was overgrown with a sparse beard and a droopy moustache hung over his mouth. There was a masked seriousness about his face, and the deep anguished look of a person who had seen something of the world and didn't like what he saw. He threw a plastic packet on the floor.

"My clothes," he said in a grave voice. "Jeans and shoes and some other stuff - wouldn't want to be caught in those with soldiers all over the place."

Ai had her back towards the door. She turned at the sound of Hirok's voice and a light spread over her face. Her lips trembled in joy and tears glistened at the corners of her eyes. She pored over her son, noting a thin scar on his cheek and the deep, unblinking eyes. "What has happened to him?" she thought, her mind full of unexplained anxieties. For a second, she said nothing, and he too stared back in silence.

Hirok broke the awkward silence. He nodded at Neal and grasped his hand when he stepped forward. "Good to see you," he said in a low voice.

"I was so worried," said Ai, finding her voice. "But I'm happy you are back." She stroked his hair and patted his cheeks.

Hirok pulled away from his mother, embarrassed by the show of affection. "I thought you'd be angry for leaving our fields, but you were wonderful," he said. "We're proud of you."

Ai smiled uncertainly. "We?" she thought.

Hirok noted the confused look on her face and smiled. "Our people, the Sangathon. I should tell you not to call me Manav anymore."

"Why? So they changed your name. You can tell them you will always be Manav to be. Doesn't matter how many names they give you," said Ai. But she was glad he had returned home to her - he hadn't forgotten his mother. She wanted to ask where he was the last few months, what he had learnt, but a sense of prudence warned her to be on guard. They always led silent and separate lives together. Now the time apart has brought them closer, and she wasn't willing to disturb the balance yet.

And in that hut, life flowed in a succession of eventful days. Each day brought something new. Nothing alarmed Ai, nobody surprised her. Complete strangers called at odd hours, whispering in anxious tones behind the house or in muffled murmurs in the other room. Then, like mysterious creatures from the forests behind the house, they disappeared into the darkness without a sound. Some of the people she saw once or twice and never again, only to be told later they'd been arrested by the police or shot by the military. A few visited regularly. Soon she learnt their names, where they came from, what they did. They were always in a hurry, always with another errand to run. She was conscious of the excitement inside each of them, the hunger for their cause, their deep commitment. Some were grave and reluctant converters, while others were gay and bursting believers, sparkling with youthful energy. All of them were confident and resolute. Not one was above thirty. Ai was in awe of each one of them. Few would consent to tread their long and difficult path; fewer understood their vision of a bright nation they had sworn to build for themselves. For people so young to sacrifice their lives for something they believed in, but also know in the back of their minds they might not live long enough to see it bear fruit, that alone made her feel as if they were like her children, of her own flesh and blood. They treated Ai with a deference and respect she never had before. There grew inside her a realization she was important to them and their cause, though she only had a vague idea how. When younger, her father was always after her, trying to get her married and rid himself of her presence. Her husband took her for just another piece of furniture, a living creature which made him food and washed his dirty clothes. Now, many people needed her, and this was a new and pleasant feeling, one that made her happy.

They often sat together on the floor under the watchful gaze of Gandhi's picture on the wall and talked or rested.

Mira, from the neighbouring village, would point at the portrait and think out aloud. "What if he hears us now?"

"What then?" said Nirav. He had this habit of sweeping the room with a suspicious glance before settling on a chair as if it was meant for him to fall. "In his time, he was a criminal to the

British, a traitor to their redcoats. He was no different from us. By the time the freedom struggle was over, he was a Mahatma. See how he ended up - father of the nation!"

"Well, he fathered a lot of problems," said Manoj, whose face was marred by long scars across his cheeks, which he was always hiding with his hands and only drawing more attention. "Comes from trying to bind everyone together in the name of nationhood when what keeps us together is a chicken's neck. We don't even look alike."

"If we are lucky, we should end up as worthy children of our mother," said Hirok.

Phukan was the one with the large brow and the shiny pate. He was the friendliest of the lot, and always the most circumspect. "Looks cannot justify a separate nation. Nor can religion or language. If we start to think on those lines, we'd be fighting amongst ourselves. All that matters is a common ideology."

"And plenty of will and arms to claim what is rightfully ours," said Hirok. "You try to be non-violent these days and the police will show you the end of their bullets."

"But the British never dared shoot Gandhi," said Phukan. "Amongst all the confusion and violence, he was their only hope, his was the only way."

"The British were clever politicians. They used him, dangled him a carrot and beat the rest with sticks," said Nirav. "These Indians - they are worse. They don't bother with carrots, they just go ahead and use their sticks."

"Systematic slaughter, that's what they are good at," said Hirok. "Gandhi would be more ashamed of his fellow countrymen now than us of them."

"Come to think of it," said Phukan. "Do you think we'd have to struggle had he been alive today? Fight and kill?"

In the village, the shock over Arun's death gave way to a blunt denial of the incident. The shraddha was thinly attended, and the rituals were carried out with uncharacteristic swiftness as if everyone wanted it to be over as soon as possible. There were other incidents too, a few beatings and a couple of bodies left by the roadside in the neighbouring villages, but everyone in the village pretended these never occurred and dismissed any suggestion to the contrary as heresy. There was talk of the Army being withdrawn and a return to the barracks in town. In the village, their patrols stopped. The soldiers disappeared from the roads. One of the villagers even saw a couple of trucks leave, but they remained in their camp outside the village and trained on the empty road or played volleyball with the policemen in the outpost.

The rain stopped for a change and the rising waters of the Dikhow ebbed. The sun shone and the humid smell went out of houses. Mud baked and the roads and gulleys became walkable. In the fields, the paddy burst out in a vigorous green.

Neal stopped hiding in the forest at night and slept in the house, losing himself in dreams that were strange and troubling and whose meaning he kept pestering Ai about. Hirok returned to tending the fields and Neal helped out in the guise of a distant uncle's son looking for work. Pale, sweating and exhausted, they came home every day at sunset. A hurried meal and they would be off again, returning bleary-eyed before dawn. Sometimes Hirok would be gone for a day or two, sometimes a week, and when Ai asked where he was, he always had one answer: "Work."

The only time they both stayed home was when it rained and the weather was as wild as a vile beast. Then, they helped Ai with her work, debating and discussing their life, and the struggle ahead, what the future held for them. Ai moved back and forth, bustling about the house with her work, listening to brief snatches of conversation. When her household chores were done, the doors locked and bolted and the lamps doused, she sat by their side and listened. Most times, they talked well past midnight, sometimes till dawn.

She often reached into her past and to her husband and his belief in the promise of independence, then sighing at the unfulfilled dreams, and the silent, shattered life he led till his death. The same path stretched out before them, winding through the barren waste of another struggle, but the inevitability of taking this path despite its promises of pain filled her with peace and eased her aching heart. Her fears and anxieties melted in the warm flow of their conversation and their optimistic rendering of the future. The gentle murmurs of their voices caressed her to sleep every night like a lullaby.

One such night, Neal watched as Hirok tucked a gun behind his back.

"What if Ai asks about you? She always wants to know why you have to go alone," he said.

"Tell her Assam is rid of another pest," said Hirok. Then, having another thought, he added: "No, don't tell her anything. She doesn't have to know."

"Where to now?"

"You know you shouldn't ask."

The murmur of low voices entered Ai's thoughts. She heard a door opening. Someone entered on stealthy steps.

"The forest is quiet tonight, not even a fox anywhere," a voice said. It sounded familiar. Nina? At this late hour? A pause. "Does Ai know where you are going or why?"

"She has no need to know," said Neal. "Don't make it harder for her by telling her."

"I won't," said Nina, and Ai sensed her nodding in tandem. "But these traitors, they deserve to die for turning their back on us."

"I follow orders," came Hirok's voice. "I do what is asked of me. The others - they are too weak, too forgiving. That's not the way to fight a battle. The government acts like a vengeful beast. Do you think the soldiers are angels? For them this is a jungle and we are game. For us it is our freedom, our rights."

"How right you are," said Neal. "Treat them like they'd treat you, put the fear of death in them."

Ai was wide awake now, staring into the darkness around her, listening intently, following every word. Her heart contracted with pity. She pitied Neal and Nina, pitied the value they put on life, but she pitied her son even more. And it's all her fault, all her fault. Where had she gone wrong? How could he turn out like this when he had such a noble soul for a father? His sins are now hers for she had made him what he was. How she had failed him, her husband, everyone. She sobbed in her bed and, when she couldn't bear it any longer, she ran all the way to the kitchen and to the idol in the corner, falling at its feet and praying for forgiveness.

Someone came in and lit the lamp. Hirok's eyes fell on Ai's tear-streaked face.

"You call killing work?" said Ai. "Have you realized what you've become?"

"I'm not a murderer, if that's what you meant to say. I'm a freedom fighter," said Hirok, but he lowered his gaze to the floor.

"By taking life you've sinned."

"There is nothing purer than fighting for your freedom – weren't those my father's exact words?" said Hirok. His eyes met his mother's. "I am no sinner. Those who suppress us, exploit us, they are the sinners."

"Your father, he also fought for his freedom. But he never hurt a fly, never abused another man. Do you know he even met Gandhi once?"

Hirok snorted. "He saw him when he came to Dibrugarh. Gandhi was good for his days. He won freedom for his country, for the Indians, not for us. Now the truth is twisted. The government hides behind a cloak of lies and broken promises. Things like hunger strikes and Satyagraha, it hardly makes the government budge. These are tools for cowards and the weak. If you want something you've to take it."

"That doesn't mean you kill whoever stands in your way," said Ai. "This is a free country, remember. Everyone is entitled to their opinion."

For a moment, Hirok stared at his mother. "But these people, they stand in the way of our struggle. They make life difficult for us. They take the side of the government and fleece the poor. They kill at every opportunity or use the military to do it for them. Nirav, Manoj, Mira - they are all dead because of people like them, turncoats who would tell on their mothers if they have to. They are leeches and suck our blood. For them what matters is money and power. For us it's freedom."

"It's ultimately the same thing," said Ai, looking away.

6

As the days passed, the villagers became more and more intrigued by the hut at the edge of the forest. Their interest was tinged with vague suspicions and muted hostility for the unknown, balanced between a curiosity for all the people who visited at night, and worked, as per village gossip, for the Sangathon, and fear of the wrath of the state and its military might. Whispers mingled with stolen glances and sharp ears picked up details about every visitor to be recounted later over cups of strong tea. There were hushed meetings everywhere, at street corners, inside every home and in gatherings at the village chowk. Events elsewhere in the state which never elicited a comment before now roused lively debate. Those younger appeared excited by the changing political climate in the state, while the elderly shrugged their shoulders and spat in anger, furious at having their way of life disturbed.

"Killings and bombs," said the elders. "Nothing will come of it."

"Troublemakers," they said. "Ought to be dragged to jail for ruining our peaceful lives."

"Sedition," said the grocer. "It's bad for business. They can't take care of themselves and they talk of freedom."

A few disgruntled voices emerged in the village. Led by the grocer, they met in the seclusion of his house in the evening or in a dark corner of the bazaar over a pack of bidis or a bottle of laopani. They swatted at the mosquitoes and hurled infamy and curses at Hirok and his lot in acrid undertones. The grocer held all the grouse and so did the most talking. Everyone knew him as a man with a heart as hard as the betel nuts that grew everywhere in the village, and a tongue as bitter as the Areca leaves with which it is eaten. He was the richest man in the village and thought himself the most influential. It was his advice the villagers sought in all matters. Now, few paid him any heed.

One rainy day, he stopped Ai on the road in front of her house. "How are you, mother?" he said. "And your son? Not working in the fields in such ghastly weather with his cousin, is he?" He peered into the gloom as if trying to catch a glimpse of the two men in the fields.

"I don't know," said Ai. "They have gone out on some work."

"Work?" he said, as if astonished by her reply. "I've to be frank with you, Ai. What work can there be for young people with no prospects other than the fields fate has given them? I've been keeping an eye on your house for some time - can't help it - I live practically next door. I noticed a lot of people come to your house at night when the whole world is in bed. Tell me, is that the time for people to visit? The word gets around and people can't help but think why they have to come at night and talk in whispers when the days are long and the road is in such good shape. Makes us wonder what's wrong, why your visitors need so much anonymity."

His speech was heavy with sarcasm, and his eyes gazed through the rain at Ai. "I don't believe in any other work than what you are destined for. I'd be marrying him off if I was you. A man keeps better with a family. A wife is like the mustard oil in your pickles. It will keep him good. These are bad times and you can't help but live carefully. Change is not good when it is forced. People are beginning to question their way of life. Too much loose thinking, too many loose morals, if you ask me. Girls moving at night, mixing with boys their age - what has the world come to? They keep away from us, sneak off into the jungle, visit when the world is asleep. Why so secretive? What

71

are they up to?" He paused to wipe the water from his face. "People have started talking about the Sangathon. Someone told me Arun is a good friend of this cousin and they were in that daredevilry with the Army."

Ai shivered in the rain, but kept her silence. "What do you think?" she said, finally.

"I'm not saying anything. The people in the village are saying it. The Sangathon, they mean nothing but trouble for us hardworking folks trying to make an honest living."

Ai laughed. "You should ask the same people what they think of your honest living."

The grocer glared at her. His lips quivered as he sought a suitable riposte. Finding no words, he turned in a swirl of wet clothes and walked away in a huff.

One her way back, Ai found Saikia, her next door neighbour, waiting for her. He hustled in after her, wet and barefoot.

"That fellow is up to no good," he said, coughing with the efforts of his words. "He sold me salt mixed with stones. Broke one of my teeth. And his lentils? Filth, I tell you." He settled down on the bench and scraped the mud from his feet. He bade her to sit by his side and said: "Your son - what's his name - Manav, he's a fine fellow. Him and his cousin and all the people you have over after the village goes to sleep."

Ai stared at him petrified, but the old man nodded, a smile on his lips as if to reassure her. "Look at me," he said. "Eighty years old - seen more of this world than anyone else in this village, but too old to dream. But your son, I think he knows what he is doing. When I was young all I used to think of was my fields, whether I'd have enough to eat and hoping I wouldn't fall sick, because we never had the money to buy medicines or take care of the doctor's fees. I led a nightmare of a life, always in botheration, trying to cope, scraping through till the sun rises again the next day and every day. I learnt too late that it's good to dream, live life for once."

"Would you like to eat here, khura?" said Ai, thinking she had to say something.

The old man shook his head. "I had my fill. That's what I have done all my life - think about what I'm going to have for my next meal or when." He chased away a fly perched on the tip of his nose: "Life has always been hard on us and it will be harder now. The agitation gave us nothing, just more excuses for the police to beat us up. What happened? Not a single Bangladeshi left this land, not a single one was found. Yet, I see them, everyday, everywhere. Why? Because the government is blind or pretends to be. And our leaders - once they became masters in Dispur, they forgot all about us, forgot the people who gave so much for them. Nonviolence is all right if it makes those with the reins sit up and take notice. But it never works that way." He pointed at the portrait of Gandhi through the open door. "His days are over. Nobody believes in him now. Now you must fight with guns and bombs, not truth or patience. More lives are lost, but there is a lot more noise and when you make a lot of noise, things start to happen."

Ai nodded. Somehow his words struck a chord within her. She had learnt enough from the debates and discussions in her home to follow his thoughts. "It's like treating a sick person. Everything needs to be shaken like medicine in a bottle. With Gandhi you will be dead before the medicine starts to work on you."

"Yes, time is important. Time is what we never had enough of, ever. But the government - it's clever - it uses it as a weapon. They drag their feet, dangle a few carrots and phuush...there goes another revolution in the making."

"Not if we have sufficient reason and belief," said Ai.

"Only reason can free man," the old man nodded. He

pointed to his watery eyes. "We have become blind. We hide behind our fears - just like my vision behind these cataracts. To think I just need an operation to see again."

"I know what you mean," said Ai.

"I'm sure you do," said Saikia. "We've too much hope riding on their young shoulders. It would break many hearts if they fail."

Ai listened to the old man grapple with the years that were past, speaking of times wasted and hopes dashed, letting loose his fury at a fate that had condemned him and his people to such a hard, unforgiving life. He left muttering about how things could have been different if only...

Ai reported these conversations to her son, but he only shrugged his shoulders while Neal laughed in his deep, soft way.

"But the grocer is right about the marrying bit," he said.

"Oh, come now," said Hirok with a grimace of disgust. "I don't have time to spare for such rubbish."

"Dear me," said Ai, shaking her head. "You think you know everything, but there are certain things in life from which there is no escape."

"Oh, there is, Ai," said Hirok. "There always is a way."

Neal sighed. "That's quite a thought, isn't it? But our Hirok is too committed to his cause. Look he's even changed his name. I don't think he is in a hurry to hang himself."

Ai glanced at his set face and hurried away to do her chores grumbling about the hard work she had to put up with. She was worried about Manav's frugal existence, the almost determined denial of the possibility of leading a normal life coexisting with his work. She squatted in the grain store and cleaned the rice for the evening meal, dusting the lot by throwing it in the air and catching it on a dola when it came down in a shuddering heap. She heard Neal pace the room. He stopped and spoke in a low voice.

"Ai is right, you know. Besides what else does she have to look forward to?"

Hirok made no reply.

"What do you think?" said Neal, almost in a whisper. "You know what I'm talking about - Nina."

"What about her?"

Ai chuckled in the other room.

"She would make you a nice wife." Neal whistled a merry tune. "You can sing her a nice Bihu song."

The whistling stopped. Ai sensed Manav must have glared at him.

"What would come of it?" he said. When Neal didn't reply, he persisted, "Well?"

"How can you expect me to make a stubborn ox see reason?"

"You don't see things as I do," said Hirok. "Supposing I get married, children will naturally come and you have to slave day and night to support them. Life will become a struggle for a mouthful of rice, and for the sake of the children, I'll be lost to the cause." He paused. When he spoke again, his tone was less accusing, but firm. "Better not think about it at all. You will only make it hard for Ai."

In the little room, Ai buried her face in her hands and wept for the family she could never hope to have.

One evening, Sarmani, her friend, knocked at the window. "Take care, baidew," she said, quite out of breath. "I just heard at the market. They've picked up all the young men from the neighbouring village."

Ai stopped her work. "They? But the military has been called off."

"Not the military, it's the police. Something must have happened. My son saw a truckload of policemen arrive at the outpost a couple of hours back. I think they will pay us a visit tonight."

"Tonight?" Ai said after her.

"I don't know. Perhaps...?" Sarmani darted a quick look behind her when she thought she heard the gate opening. "Better warn your son and his friends. That nice girl too - what's her name? Nina. And remember, I didn't tell you a thing." She met Ai's eyes, put a finger on her lips and disappeared into the gloom of dusk.

Ai closed the door and sank on the chair. If the police were planning a raid in the village, there was one place they'd definitely visit. And with Manav and his stubborn streak, things would be different from the last time around when she was all alone. What if he threatens the police, dare them to touch him, maybe lecture them a bit about being traitors? The policemen would beat him, even shoot him if he resisted. The realization of the danger threatening him brought her to her feet. She threw a chador over her shoulders and ran to Saikia. She found him on his bed, squinting at a medicine bottle, trying to read the label. He went pale on hearing the news.

"What do you want me to do?" he said, noting the scared look on Ai's face.

"I don't know. That's why I came here," said Ai, wiping sweat from her brow.

Saikia struggled out of bed. "I'll think of something," he said, a determined expression on his face. "You go home now and put the worries out of your head. They won't beat us. We're too old for their canes." He changed his dhoti, put on a tattered coat and hurried in the direction of the fields.

Ai went home, her mind in turmoil wondering whether she'd done the right thing in sending the old man to look for her son. Maybe he'd let the two hide in his house. She gathered all the newspapers and a few journals, tied them in a neat bundle and pushed the lot behind a sack of grain. She neatly arranged Neal's and Manav's clothes in a single pile and settled down to wait. As dusk turned to night and flicker of lights dotted the houses in the village, Ai became frantic. She paced the room, hustling from one corner to another, stopping every time she thought she heard the gate opening, craning her neck for a sight of the visitor, resuming her pacing when no one appeared. She expected Manav to rush home from the fields, but he didn't come and neither did Neal. At last exhausted, she sat down in front of the idol in the corner of her kitchen, hands folded together, lips moving in prayer, and there she remained, afraid to move, until she heard the shuffle of footsteps on the verandah.

"Didn't khura tell you?" she said, rushing out only to be met by Neal.

"Yes," said Neal. "Are you afraid?"

"Terribly. Why didn't you come earlier?" she said. "Where is Manav?"

"Some errand - he will be gone for a day or two," said Neal. He sat down by her side in the kitchen. "Anyway, you mustn't be scared. That won't help any. You weren't so scared the last time they came."

"Then I was too frightened to be scared," Ai smiled. "Besides, I didn't know they'd be coming."

"There's nothing to be frightened about," said Neal. He began to clean the stove. "If it's the police, it will be a lot like before, but only rowdier. They do this now and then to show they are more than just errand-boys for the military. They are a scared lot and they are more afraid of us then we are of them. They will come in a crowd, push and shove, make a lot of noise. They'll rummage through everything - look under the bed and inside the racks, smell the bin and steal a chicken or a few eggs. They'll get cobwebs in their faces and dust inside their noses. They'll sneeze a bit, cough up a storm and pretend to be angry.

They know what a beastly job they've with the risk of a bullet in their backs or a knife slitting their throats every time they come for a raid. The daruga will ask his questions, stamp his foot, hit you once or twice, never more. They aren't a clever lot - they are just tired and badly in need of rest, and the government is always after them. They must have talked to a dozen men that day and it can be quite frustrating repeating the same questions and receiving nothing in return for all the trouble. If they like the look of you, they will throw you in jail and hold on to you for a few days, then let you go because there are more in line. See, there is a queue here like in the ration shops."

"You talk as if you know everything," said Ai, finding comfort in his words.

Neal raised his face from where he was kneeling to kindle the fire and said, "I do. I've been there."

"And nobody ever hurt you?" said Ai, a look of incredulity on her face.

"Well, it's different if the soldiers take you," he said with a sad smile. "Then you wish you'd never been born because they really know how to hurt. But after a time, you don't fear it anymore and the pain ceases to matter. You learn it is true there is a soul inside you, which is something apart from your body. They can hurt your body, but they can rarely touch the soul."

"And you hate them for it?"

Neal shook his head. "They are only doing their job though I'm not sure it's the right way. You learn to accept. What can one do when people are like that? They become beasts, and one day, they will receive their fair share of pain. So it's better to move on." His words flowed smoothly, benumbing Ai's senses, driving away her fears and making her feel a lot braver.

She sighed, squatting before the stove to pour out the tea. "I never knew you went through so much."

Neal sat down by the door with a glass of tea. "It's going to rain. I don't think the police are going to come tonight," he said, glancing up at the sky. "They are afraid of dark, moonless nights. It'll save us the trouble of hiding from them."

"What if they come?"

"Let them. Who's afraid of policemen? They will sniff around a bit, ask all sorts of stupid questions. If you show them you're scared they'll think, 'Aha, there must be something in this house they don't want us to find.' So you stay where you are, let them look where they want, answer them sharply and they will leave embarrassed with their tail between their legs."

"What if they arrest you?"

"They wouldn't dare. I'll fight the lot. They are only policemen."

Ai looked at him in alarm. "You'll do no such thing."

Sixty kilometers to the east, two men sat in the smoke behind a tandoor in the noisy bedlam of a Punjabi restaurant in Dibrugarh. Sweat poured from their faces as they hunched over cups of tea, oblivious of the ruckus around them.

Hirok sat with his back to the oven. He tucked the photograph in his hands inside a pocket before turning to the man facing him. "Why him?"

"He will make the news, that's why," said Barman, watching the people in the shop through the haze of smoke.

"Who else?"

"Just him."

"His family?"

"They will be away at the time."

"Neighbours?"

"All his types. They won't bother you. They will hide under the bed when they hear the gunshots."

"How much time do we have?" said Hirok.

79

"Not much - three days at the most," said Barman. "You have to be home in time for the police raid. I can't risk you outside."

Hirok motioned to a passing tea-boy for another glass. "Why this sudden show of strength from the police? You'd think they were happy letting the military do all their dirty work," he said, blowing at his tea before taking a sip.

"From what I gather, Delhi doesn't like the way things are going in the state. They think the government in Dispur is to blame. The babus here are very insecure at the moment. There has been lots of activity the last few days - meetings, decisions. The end result is the police have instructions from their bosses to show themselves as competent as the military or else."

"So they think they can compete with the military. Bungling idiots," said Hirok.

"Can't agree more," said Barman. He watched a posse of CRPF personnel frisk people on motorbikes and scooters away from the light of a street lamp. "The police will be doing a merry-go-around of all the villages. Yours will be next. It is an opportunity not to be missed."

Hirok was lost in thought for some time. "How much?"

"One crore," said Barman. "Not bad for a man living in the poorest part of town, eh."

"And he agreed?"

"Actually we asked for a hundred crores. Gave us bargaining space - took him a week to whittle it down to one."

"Why kill him then?"

"So many reasons. Good riddance. Don't like his kind. Will teach his types to be careful how they deal with us. Moreover, he doesn't belong here."

"Enough reasons," nodded Hirok. "How bad is it going to be once the news breaks?"

"Pretty bad - he's big here. In one swift blow, you'd shut

down the very bank that funds these corrupt pro-Indian parties. That's why I think a police cell is the safest place for you till all this leaves the front pages."

Hirok pondered for a while. "Do you trust him?"

Barman laughed. "Do I trust a snake? Not him, no. But I don't think he will trouble us - he's a bit of a coward. He will do as told. He has deep pockets and people with money love themselves to death. There isn't a minister he doesn't know or helped with money one time or the other. He might be tempted to call in the police, but he'd rather trust us then risk them."

"So?"

"Watch your back. Make it back home by nightfall and everything will be in place to have you behind bars."

7

A couple of nights dragged by for Ai. She expected the police to come anytime now, but no one did. Evening came. Night set in. A cold rain swished against the walls and the wind rattled the doors and windows. Ai lit a lamp and placed it in the centre of the room, watching the shadow of the furniture play on the walls and the ceiling. She closed her eyes, tired out by her chores and the never-ending wait for the police.

There was a sharp knock on the door. Ai opened her eyes. She wondered if it was the police, then thinking why would they bother knocking on the door when they'd rather break it down.

"Ai, quickly!" A voice called out.

She threw a chador over her shoulders and rushed to open the door.

Phukan came in. He was followed by another man, a burly, thickset person, whose face was concealed by a cap pulled low over his brow.

"Is Neal in?" said Phukan. In contrast to his usual jolly manner, his voice was anxious and gloomy.

"He hasn't come back," said Ai. "Is something wrong?"

To her surprise, Phukan heaved a sigh of relief. His companion removed his cap to reveal his face. He was bald and a sad smile lurked at the corner of his mouth. From the way he talked and how Phukan treated him by standing a little behind, Ai guessed he was somebody important. He folded his hands together in greeting.

"Sorry we've to meet this way, but I must talk to you. It is very important," he said, introducing himself simply as Barman. He glanced at Phukan, who stepped outside.

Ai shook her head in surprise and stammered: "You must mean my son, but he hasn't been home the last few days. I don't know when he is coming back. If it's Neal you want…"

"I've met Neal," said Barman, interrupting Ai, "and your son should be home tomorrow." He bade her to sit down. When she obeyed, he explained. "Have you heard about the men arrested from the other village a few days back?" When Ai nodded, he looked surprised, but went on. "Anyway, they will be released tomorrow. All of them."

"That's good news," said Ai.

"It a way it is," he said, "but it means they will fill their lock-ups with those from this village."

"How can you be so sure?" said Ai.

"We've friends in the police," said Barman. "They are under too much pressure now that the military has been put on leash. They've to show they are as capable. Better them than the soldiers."

"You need not worry," said Ai. "Neal has been staying away from the house at night."

"No, no, that he mustn't do," said Barman. "To hide from the police will be an admission of guilt. Your son, he's a reasonable fellow and he has my orders. He will be home before the police arrive. Neal is a bit of an ox. He wants to fight them. This is not the time to fight. That's why we want you to talk to him. He will listen to you. Tell him to behave himself, go like a lamb with the police if they want him. If they don't, all is well and good." He paused and added: "Besides, it will be good for the lot. Gives them rest at the government's expense. They've been hard at work."

Ai listened with a confused look on her face. She thought about saying something, but held her tongue.

"We've lost many men in the last few months," continued Barman. "But we've managed to keep our work going and cannot afford to lose any more."

Ai nodded. "I understand. Dear god, now I'll be worried. What if they are beaten?"

"They won't be touched. We will make sure of that."

"What if they put them away for long?"

"They have no reason to."

"How can you be so sure?"

"Like I said, we've our way of knowing," said Barman. "The police, they belong here. The military, they are the outsiders." He rose to leave. "A man gets a good rest in jail and a chance to make new friends. People like us have no time to do either when we are at large."

After Barman left, Ai prayed in front of her idol as always for the people Manav had introduced in her life, and with whom she felt very close. When Neal came home for supper, Ai gave him a stern lecture, which surprised the usually reticent Neal. Reluctantly, he made his bed and settled down to wait for the police and his arrest.

Around the time Barman left his house, Hirok picked his way past the garbage on a narrow street not far from the tea shop where he received his orders. Some shops had downed their shutters for the day, and most of the offices near the cinema wore a deserted look. Beggars were settling down for the night on beds of rags and discarded newspapers. Those with stoves were cooking themselves a meal on the pavement. Even at this late hour, people jostled with each other for space, hurrying in an endless cycle of unfinished business. Hirok bought himself a cup of tea from a push-cart and surveyed the street. Nearby, in the dark shadows of a large Aahat tree, a police party randomly stopped passing cars and frisked their occupants. An Inspector sat on his motorcycle away from the light of a street lamp. He held court and passed judgment on drivers caught without documents and allowed them to leave for a bribe. Hirok watched the exchange of money with a smile before turning to the task on hand. He crossed the road and turned into a narrow bylane overflowing with water from a sewer. He stopped for a moment, overcome by the stench, giving the street a glance before taking the two flights of stairs at the corner building.

It was quiet except for a dog barking somewhere in the basement. For a moment, Hirok felt uneasy, even a deep sense of foreboding. There wasn't a guard on sight, and the collapsible gate leading inside was open. A door beckoned. Hirok paused and checked the gun tucked behind his back and was reassured by its cold touch.

He rang the bell.

A fat man with a thick neck opened the door, his obesity enhanced by his short stature. Hirok recognized the man from the photograph Barman had passed him. The man nodded at Hirok and ushered him in, his face betraying only a hint of apprehension.

"The money is ready and packed," he said, leading the way to the living room.

"Where's your family?" said Hirok.

"Visiting relatives," said the man.

"And the guard?"

"I've been told to give him leave for the evening."

"And leave the gate open?"

"And leave the gate open."

"I don't think you'll need the guard anymore."

The man stopped. His face clouded. "Good joke," he said after a moment's hesitation, a smile spreading over his face. "The government put him here to keep out people like you, but you know how stupid the government is."

"Foolish," said Hirok, "but you know better."

The man laughed, but it was a sad laugh meant to sound happy. He pointed to a briefcase resting on the divan. "Would you like to count the money?"

"How much?"

"One crore," said the man with a smile, eager to please. "I'm grateful to the Sangathon for being so considerate. Times are hard, you know."

"Not hard enough for you," said Hirok.

The man smiled sheepishly. "I work harder than others."

"We know all about your hard work," said Hirok.

The man made a motion to show him the money in the briefcase, but Hirok stopped him. "Don't you want to check?" he said, a little surprised.

Hirok shook his head. "I trust you." He knew the man wouldn't dare cheat the Sangathon and risk its wrath. He pointed to the sofa. "Sit down while I write you a receipt." When the man complied, he pulled out his gun and shot him in the head, the astonished look from the moment he saw the gun appear in Hirok's hands still on his face as he tottered and fell.

Hirok snapped open the briefcase to make sure before walking out, closing the door after him.

The police made their appearance the following night. All day it rained without a break. In the village, there was anxious talk of the Dikhow rising and the Brahmaputra flowing above the danger level. There was news of a breach in a dam somewhere in Arunachal; smaller talk about forecasts of more rain on the radio: all in urgent whispers lest the Dikhow hear and spate in spite. The swamp was a lake and no more the cramped muddy bog that everybody despised. Worried villagers gathered in front of their houses in clusters of umbrellas, full of huddled whispers, fear writ large on their faces. It was almost midnight when Hirok returned home with Neal. Ai was already in bed, and she heard the door opening and hushed voices. Someone approached on stealthy feet, hovered around her bed and left. Somebody else tiptoed across the room to the kitchen. There was the screech of the hand-pump winch and a bucket falling. The door was thrown open and someone stepped inside in a hurry.

"They are here," said Neal.

Ai jumped out of bed and snatched up her clothes with trembling fingers. Hirok appeared by the door. "Stay in bed, stay out of their way," he warned.

Ai looked surprised. "When did you come?" she said to her son, but he had already left.

There was the clamour of footsteps outside the window. Fists banged on the door. Hirok opened it, and a short, stout man in khaki with a large moustache, the daruga, pushed past him inside the house.

"Surprised? You were expecting somebody else, eh," he said.

One of the policemen pointed out Ai. "That's the mother, sir," he said. "And that's him," he nodded at Hirok. A man stood by his side, someone from the village, his face covered by a muffler. He nodded in confirmation.

The daruga looked at Hirok from head to toe. "Do you know someone named Hirok Hazarika?" he said in a loud voice meant to sound commanding. When Hirok shook his head, he nodded, twirling the ends of his moustache. "Thought so. Anyway, I'm here to make a search of your house and take you into custody."

A policeman opened the almirah and rummaged through the clothes, tossing them on the floor in a heap. Another returned with the bundle of newspapers from the grain store. The daruga raised his eyebrows and darted an accusing look in Hirok's direction.

"What are they doing here?" he said.

"When is it against the law to read newspapers?" said Hirok.

"You can't do this, can't do that," said Neal.

The policemen looked at him, and then at the daruga, who said: "Mind who you are talking to."

Neal laughed and bowed his head. "Oh, I forgot. Hail the Holy Emperor, Sycophant of the Soldiers and Torturer of the Innocent."

Ai tugged at his shirt. "Keep quiet now. You don't want to cause any trouble."

The daruga turned to Hirok. "Who reads these papers?"

"I do."

"Hmm, interesting," he frowned. "And what sort of interest might a farmer boy like you have in these papers?"

"News. I like to know what's happening."

The daruga sat down on the chair, glancing briefly at the portrait of Gandhi on the wall behind him. "Why, may I ask?"

"I told you. News."

"About how you harass innocent people in the name of the law everywhere," said Neal.

The daruga shook his cane. "You watch that mouth of yours - it will get you into trouble."

"I'm not scared of little turds like you," Neal said under his breath.

"I heard that, I heard that!" The daruga shot out of the chair waving his cane. He gritted his teeth in a curious manner. "Take the bugger out of here."

Two policemen stepped forward. They grabbed Neal by his arms and pushed him towards the door where he forced them to a halt.

The daruga turned to Hirok. "I heard a lot of people visit this place at night?"

Neal answered from the door: "That's right, too many to count."

A policeman burst into the room. "Nothing out there, sir," he said.

"Of course," said the daruga. "They think they are a clever lot. We'll soon find out." To Hirok, he said: "You are under arrest." To Ai, in a loud, stern voice: "Is it true there are visitors here most nights? Who are they? Speak up, woman."

Ai was overwhelmed by hatred for the man, but instead she smiled, and in that smile she showed her pity for him - pity for his apathy, the blindness of his sight. She sensed a soulless, selfish, evil man not much different from the contemptuous Army officer who ruined her home and made a mockery of what she held all along as inviolable. "You needn't shout. I'm not deaf," she said. "I don't know anything about visitors at night. I don't see how it is any business of yours. This is my house. Anyone can come and go. Let me see you stop them."

"Silence," said the daruga. At a gesture from him, a policeman cuffed Hirok and led him away. Neal followed with the two policemen by his side. The others fell in after them, jostling and pushing at each other. The daruga paused at the door, pointing at the portrait of Gandhi. "His must be a tormented soul watching your lot undo all his hard work from his perch on that wall. Don't you think he deserves better? If I were you, I'd put it away or cover it. Hide him, spare his soul."

The house was suddenly empty and silent.

Ai slid to the floor. Her eyes filled with tears of insult. She had cried all her life, most of it, but the sight of her son being led away in handcuffs like a common thief was too much to bear. "What would my husband think now?" she thought, horrified. "What have I done? How could I've let this happen?"

The door opened and a policeman pushed Neal inside. "Spare your tears, woman or you won't have enough left for the other boy."

Neal pulled free. "Better leave before my taunting turns

into something more harmful," he said, and the policeman beat a hasty retreat.

Ai stared at the chaos in the room. She expected trouble, but not the painful aftermath of helplessness, the sweet bitterness of doing something that had been asked of her, but seeing her son sacrificed in the bargain. "Do you think they will hurt him?" she said.

Neal shook his head. "I taunted them and they let me go. That's all the guts they have - they won't touch him."

Ai sighed. "One of these days, they will take you too if you keep on teasing them."

"I know they will," said Neal. "As soon as the government finds some excuse to release the military from the barracks. Then I won't be coming back."

Ai was silent for a while. "Is it real? Do they really treat people badly? Kill..." When Neal nodded, she said: "Manav?"

"Oh, he will be okay. But you never know. What if somebody comes from town and wants to interrogate him? Yes, it is something you'll have to learn to accept."

Ai looked away. She tried to keep her voice from breaking as she said, "I'm a mother. How can I?"

Ai couldn't catch a wink of sleep that night. Morning found her hurrying along the road leading out of the village washed clean by the previous night's rain. She hardly noticed the sun rise in front of her and a dark cloud coming out of nowhere to cover it. She shuffled ahead, full of worried thoughts: "Is Manav still at the police outpost? Did they give him anything to eat? What if they beat him? What if they took him away to town? What if the police turned him over to the military?"

The daruga stopped her in front of his office. "What do you want?"

The havildar, his deputy, came out and stood by his side.

"You've no business here."

"My son…he is here," said Ai. "I want to see if he is all right."

The daruga laughed. "Aha, the Gandhian's son! You are worried we beat him up? Of course, you can see him. How can I deny you your rights?"

A constable led her to an adjacent building, a decrepit structure with cracks on its walls and part of the roof missing. It was dark inside. The only light came from a ventilator, which shone like beacon near the ceiling. The smell of urine hung in the air, and the floor was cold and damp.

"A hole in hell if you ever saw one," said the constable with a smirk on his face. "No electricity, no dignity, only mosquitoes. And when it rains, plenty of water to wash." He pointed to his left. "See for yourself. He will be somewhere there keeping the rats company."

Ai craned her neck and blinked. All she saw was a depthless blackness.

Then, a strained whisper from somewhere to her left.

"Ai?"

"Hear that?" said the constable. "He's is alive. His time hasn't come, but it soon will."

"Watch your tongue, you son of a bitch." A voice warned from inside the cell.

The constable struck his cane at what sounded like an iron barricade. "Shut up," he said. "Any more of that and I'll cut off yours." There was much pushing and shoving in the darkness, and words of protests from someone who had his toes trodden. To Ai, he said, "Satisfied?"

Hirok's voice rang out: "You've seen enough, Ai. Go home now."

The daruga was waiting for her outside. "So, Ai," he said. "What do you think of our hospitality? It is the best we can do when the government has little money to spare." When Ai ignored him, he said, "Have you taken my advice? Have you hidden...Gandhi?"

Moments after Ai left, the grocer walked into the police outpost. The daruga was in the midst of his first cup of tea of the morning and was in a good mood for some reason. He looked at the grocer in surprise, noting the fresh bandages on his face and an arm in a sling. As the grocer spoke, a smile spread across his face.

"At least they didn't kill you," he offered his empathy without appearing very sympathetic.

"So you think I should be thankful to them for sparing my life," said the grocer in an angry voice. "Come, maksudas, break me up, cut me apart, but don't kill me." He paused waiting for the daruga to respond. When the daruga kept quiet, he added: "Well...aren't you going to do something about it? Find out the persons responsible, bring them to justice."

The daruga nodded in mock seriousness. "We will do our very best to bring the culprits to book, but we are understaffed, so it might take a while. If they are from the Sangathon like you said, you might as well forget about it."

The havildar poked his head into the office. "What's with you? Your wife beat you up?" he said, pointing at the bandages.

The grocer repeated his story.

"Robbers, most likely," said the havildar. "I think he is worried about his little secret. If it goes on like these, he will start suspecting his wife for being in cahoots with the Sangathon."

The grocer glared at him. "You think this fun," he said, pointing at his face. "After all I've done for you, for the police. I tell you, they were from the Sangathon."

"Oh, how can you tell?" said the daruga without much interest. "Did they show you their badges? Did they tell you they were from the Sangathon?"

"But who has heard of robbers in these parts?"

"Times are changing, Bora," said the daruga. "There's little work to be had and stomachs to fill. What can one do?"

"They didn't look like hungry people," said the grocer. "If they are poor, how could they afford the guns? Why didn't they take anything from me?"

"You had nothing on you."

"But the guns - explain the guns. I tell you they are from the Sangathon. They know all about me."

The daruga smiled. "But how could they know? How could they possibly know?"

Sarmani came to visit Ai on her way home from fishing, a jakoi hanging from her hips. She sat down on the verandah and brought out a couple of magurs from the basket. "They are good for you," she said, sliding the two into a pot of water.

Ai shook her head. "How can I think of eating when my son is in jail?"

"Oh, he'll be all right," said Sarmani. "He needs some rest from all the work he has been doing. Sometimes I think a police lockup is a safer place than being with these army butchers." She drew closer. "Haven't you heard? The grocer was waylaid by bandits last night. They couldn't find anything on him, so they beat him up. Everyone is saying they were from the Sangathon. Why didn't they shoot him then? Not that he doesn't deserve it for all the third rate groceries he sells us. Do you know he works for the military, sells them food and supplies so that they can come and break our bones?" She made herself a cud of betel nut and paan from the bota Ai brought her and continued her rant. "How dare the police come and take away someone like this? Where is the law? Do you know how many they took away last night from the village? Ten. Now we are ten men

93

short in the fields. They even took away the gaonbura's son, Rajen. And he is still in school and so little. What will happen now?" She let loose a tirade against the government and the police between spells of vigorous chewing. "All this will change, all this will not be for nothing. One day the people will come to their sense and rise. Then the police will be ours to do our bidding."

"Yes," said Ai, not really feeling like talking, wary of the two jumpy magurs.

"They're sick," Sarmani continued unmindful of Ai's anguish. "They're sick from all the power they have. What makes them do such things? There's no explaining it. It is us poor folk who always have to shoulder everything. Why is there so much injustice? And where is He now for whom there is neither rich nor poor and everyone is equal? It is times like this that make you wonder whether there is a god above us taking care of us poor people..." She clamped up when Ai glared at her. She mumbled something about remembering a chore left undone and left. "Can't even buy salt in this village..."

Ai passed the entire day in the shadow of gloom and anxiety. Her mind constantly darted to the dark cell and its numbing smell. Dusk fell. The sounds and stirrings of evening filtered into the house. Night brought with it rain and a flurry of footsteps on the verandah.

Ai raised her head. "Who is that?" she called out in the darkness.

"Phukan," a voice said. "Are you all right, Ai? Why isn't there a light?"

Two men came in. Barman sat on the chair and Phukan stood by the door.

Ai struck a match and lit the lamp. "What am I to do now?" she said. "They took him away like you said. I'm so worried."

Barman glanced at Phukan, who stepped outside closing the door after him. He cleared his throat and said: "Your son, he is well - we checked with the police. Everyone is safe and sound, though, as you saw in the morning, it's quite cramped. They should be released in a few days time. Nothing to worry about, of course." He paused for a moment. "The police are looking for someone called Hirok. They don't know yet."

Ai shook her head. "The police asked me about him last night. I told them there is no Hazarika in this village."

Barman nodded, pleased. "We'd like things to remain as it is. Your son is safer that way." He moved closer and said: "Ai, I need your help. I need you to do a couple of things for the Sangathon, for Hirok. And there are some things you need to know." He began to explain.

That evening, the grocer made a round of the village extolling his bravery in the face of two well-armed robbers. He held court in front of his store for most of the afternoon telling each and every customer, anyone who cared to listen, about the incident.

"Never heard of such a thing in these parts all my life," said Ai, when he came in late at night. "Anyway, how is it now?"

The grocer raised his face and said between clenched teeth: "How does it look?"

"Aagh," said Ai, recoiling at the sight of a lump of swollen flesh and angry cuts across the face.

He sat down and swept the room with a suspicious glance, stopping for a brief instant on Neal, who ignored him. "Bad, isn't it? The doctors said it will take some time for the swelling to go down. But no broken bones, thank god."

"Yes, you were lucky," said Ai.

"I know," said the grocer. "I don't think the same can be said about you. I heard they took Manav."

Ai shrugged her shoulders. "What can we simple folks do when the police abuse their power?" she said. She disliked him earlier; now, after what she learnt from Barman, she couldn't stand the sight of him.

He said nothing, staring dourly at her. He took out a pack of bidis from a pocket, fiddled with the lot, lit one and blew out the pungent smoke. "I heard they can be pretty rough sometimes," he said. "Bastards, if you ask me. It is better not to give them a chance. Nasty business all this, better to stay away from it."

"Why, of course," said Ai. Somehow she was feeling increasingly uneasy in his presence.

"Life is hard enough these days. Why make it harder?"

"The police are making it hard for us," said Ai. "Why don't they leave us alone?"

He glanced at her and closed his eyes. "You think it's really that? Don't you think it is the other way around?"

Neal let out a laugh. "What was that you said? Repeat that."

The grocer looked at him for some time. "I'm surprised they didn't take you."

"They couldn't bear to listen to me."

"You think it's that?"

"You know more?" Neal stood in front of the grocer, glowering down at him, who sat nonchalantly on the chair, wreathed in smoke.

"I know nothing," he said.

"Of course not," Neal said. "But I was wondering - did they search your place?"

"Why?"

"Just thinking…"

"You think too much. Ai will tell you the soldiers ruined my house for no reason the last time they were here."

"Oh, I forgot. But you don't hold it against them."

"You are quite a fool for someone with so many words. As for myself, I like to think I'm smart. You see, I'm a businessman and I have a contract to provide them with supplies. It wouldn't do me any good to hold any grudges against them, will it? Why should I cut off the very hands that feed my family?"

"You have such a sick soul, Bora," said Neal.

"No sicker than yours. You think what you are doing will put you in paradise, put your name down in golden letters for eternity. Myself, I like to see that paradise here, not in my dreams, not in a dream that will never come true." The grocer

97

fixed his eyes on Neal and waited, his teeth bared like a beast raring for a fight.

"No use arguing with a fool," said Neal, when he caught the grocer's hostile glance.

"I couldn't quite agree more," said the grocer. "You have caught a disease and a deadly one at that. All of us catch it sometime or the other. The strong ones, they hardly feel its passing menace, but on the weak ones, it takes its toll. When they become sick they become blind, so they can't see what they are doing. You, my friend, are ill. I think you need a doctor."

"Isn't it quite a coincidence I feel exactly the same about you?" said Neal. "But you and I can't argue - we're too far apart. You are too much in darkness to see any light."

The grocer jumped to his feet. "What do you mean by that?"

"Whatever you like to think," said Neal.

"Hmmph," the grocer grumbled and his face turned red. He stamped his foot and stumbled out.

Ai ran after him. "I made you a cup of tea."

"Later, later," the grocer called back.

"Don't worry, Ai," said Neal. "His kind always comes back even if it's for a cup of tea. His is a kind that never learns its lesson even from a thousand beatings. But I think he has more on his mind than a mere cup of tea."

The grocer returned the very next morning just as Neal predicted. Ai watched him dawdle by the gate, fumbling with the latch on the gate.

"Come in," she said, and the grocer stepped inside.

"Sorry about last evening. That boy gets on my nerves," he said.

"He gets on everybody's nerves, but he is a good one," she said, pointing at the bench.

"He isn't around..."

"You know he isn't."

The grocer lowered his glance. "Don't care much for him. But you and I, we've to live together in the village all our lives. We mustn't fight."

"Glad to hear that," Ai nodded. "Reason is so hard to find nowadays."

"True, true." He twitched his lips and did his best to put on a smile. "Ai, I'd like that cup of tea you told me about last night."

Ai nodded. Like all the genteel women of her ilk, she hurried to the kitchen to prepare the grocer the nicest cup of tea possible despite her loathing for the man. The grocer rose to his feet. He glanced inside the two rooms from outside to make sure no one was there. The girl - where was she? And that fat lard? "Up to no good, what else," he thought, and gritted his teeth in pain when he stepped on a stone. He went towards the back. In the cowshed, the lone cow swung its tail at a swarm of flies. The haystack looked undisturbed and the clothesline was deserted.

"I did my clothes yesterday. Won't get much time tomorrow," said Ai from the verandah.

The grocer pretended not be discomfited by her sudden appearance. He accepted the tea and sipped the hot brew. "Your cow needs some feeding to be done. Can't be helped when a son is in jail and the cousin doesn't treat this as his home."

Ai watched him for a while. "I'm going to town day after tomorrow. Dibrugarh - haven't been there in ages."

The grocer stopped slurping his tea. "Dibrugarh? Why?"

"One of my cousins. He's sick with cancer, doesn't have more than a few weeks. He is in the big hospital in town."

"How can you manage? You haven't set foot outside the village for so many years. You'll be lost."

Ai shook her head. "I'll be all right. Besides, I'll be gone only for the day. I have to visit the hospital and run an errand."

"Errand?"

"Oh, something for my son's friends."

The grocer choked in his tea. Despite his swollen face, Ai noticed the excitement gathering within him.

"What sort..." he began, but Ai cut him off.

"I don't know. They will let me know tonight," she said, taking the cup from his hands.

The grocer looked away. A bagful of questions cropped up in his mind, but he managed to hold his tongue. With great difficulty he excused himself.

Ai watched him leave, a strange emptiness in her heart.

"Barman is right about the grocer. He is guilty and he still hasn't learnt his lesson," she told Neal when he returned home that evening.

Neal grinned. "I told you he can't help himself. I'm sure he will be snooping around the house tonight."

"Let him come if he has so much time on his hands," said Ai.

"He won't come now for sure," said Neal, glancing at his watch and deciding he must still be at his shop. "Too busy counting the dirty money passing through his fingers. But he is about due for some more trouble."

Ai turned sharply. "What do you mean by that?"

"He is one of those who are to blame," he said.

"What is he to blame for? Our troubles?"

Neal nodded. "Everyone's. His kind keeps propping up our enemies. Without people like him they would be like thirsty men in a desert looking for water."

"Do you think he was responsible for what happened to Jogen kai and Molu ka?"

"Who else? I wasn't here, but all the people in the Sangathon blame him for Molu ka's death. And to think his poor widow is still waiting for him to come home one day."

"Do you think the Sangathon will punish him again?"

"They might give him another beating one of these days, break a few bones just to keep him at home," said Neal. "But they won't touch him, not for the time being, not when he can be used against them without his knowledge. We've some clever people out there."

"And when they have no more use of him?"

"Shoot him in the head. He deserves it too."

A man waited in the shadows of the jackfruit tree by the pond in the Barua's backyard. He sat still in the unending vigil of a snake waiting for its prey, his ears alert for the slightest sound. Every now and then, he swatted at mosquitoes droning above his head. All around him it was quiet except for the howl of a fox on prowl, and the call of a toad from the depths of the pond. A mile down the road, the grocer rushed through his ritual of closing shop for the day. He counted the money in the cash box, throwing the coins into a container with the rat-tat-tat of gunfire, then matched the amount with the register. He stepped outside and watched his assistant down the shutters. Satisfied the shop was secure for the night, he sent the boy on his way before turning the other way. He stopped a few metres from the Barua's gate and studied the road. He slipped through a gap in the fence and disappeared into the trees surrounding the house.

Neal came out from behind the Neem across the road. He opened the gate. With a song on his lips, he clambered up the steps and knocked on the door. Barman heard the loud rap and emerged from the darkness. He stepped inside the house. In the light of a lamp, he uncovered a plastic container from inside his jacket. He placed it on the table by the window and sat down on the chair. In a firm, deliberate voice he began to explain.

The grocer stood in the shadows of the house and watched

the visitor with interest. Ears pressed to the wall, he followed the conversation inside. He clung to every word. As the minutes passed, he was barely able to control his excitement.

"Do you think I'll be able to do it?" said Ai. "I'm just an illiterate village woman."

Barman's impatient voice interrupted her. "There is no reason why you can't."

There was no response from Ai for some time. Then: "What is it? What does it have inside? What are all these wires?"

"Does it matter? But if you like to know it's just a gift from us to them."

"Is it a bomb?" said Ai in alarm. "Should you be really doing this?"

"It has to be done," said Barman. "It's time these people are taught a lesson."

"But...but it will only kill innocent people."

"Can't be helped. This is a war we are fighting. In wars, innocent people die."

"How can you justify that?" said Ai, as if from deep conviction. "What have they done? Why do they deserve to die?"

"Death?" said Barman in a grim voice. "I don't decide who lives or dies. There is someone up there who decides that. I do my work."

"How...how cold you people are," said Ai. "I suppose I've a right to know why you picked me - an old woman. I'm no good for such things."

"It has to be you or no one else. The police won't bother an old woman like you."

Barman took out a piece of paper and drew directions. There were a few more snorted instructions and the hustled silence of obedience. As quickly as he came, he rose from his seat, gave the mother a last severe glance and disappeared through the door. The grocer heard the squishy-squashy splash of shoes, and then the wind rose and he couldn't hear a thing more.

Inside the house, Ai settled down on the bed with a sigh. "The rain, it never stops," she said. "Just like our troubles. It never ends."

"One day, a fair wind will blow the clouds away and everything will be fine," said Neal, trying to cheer her up.

"You think there will be such a day?" said Ai, a pained expression on her face.

"Yes I do," said Neal.

"When the dead pile up and the rivers turn red do you think it will be worth it?"

Neal made a swipe at a mosquito around his ears. "Change always demands its price, Ai, and freedom its blood. People will be happy and tired, but it is the tiredness that comes from doing good work, the exhaustion you get from plowing your fields every day. Nothing feels better than the pleasant ache of hard labour in the shoulders and the deep, restful sleep afterwards."

"Who is he?" said Ai. When Neal raised an eyebrow, she said: "Barman. I don't think that's his real name."

"He is somebody important."

"Who?"

"Must you really know?" said Neal. He swallowed his tea in one gulp and leaned forward. "Let's get down to business. If the police check your baggage and find the package, what will you say?"

"I'll say it's none of their business," said Ai, playing along.

"I'm afraid they won't agree with you," said Neal. "They will make it their business. They will shut you up in a closed room and keep asking for as long as it takes."

"I won't tell them anything."

"What if they arrest and send you to jail? Imagine that." Neal laughed out aloud.

"Let them. If they are up to it, so am I," said Ai.

The grocer decided he had heard and seen enough. With the feeling of suppressed excitement inside him, he jumped out of the bushes and slipped through the fence. Without a backward glance, he walked in the pouring rain to the police outpost. Neal gave the grocer a few minutes start. Then, cursing the rain and the grocer under his breath, he broke into a run. He returned home around midnight, humming a sad tune and dripping water from his clothes.

"Our friend didn't waste any time," he said to Ai waiting up for him. "But the police are such a lazy lot. They will not budge tonight." When Ai gave him a blank look, he explained: "Our daruga is a greedy pig. He needs his food and he must have his drink. When he has both, he must have his sleep. Over time, his men have picked up his habits, become him."

"So the grocer's complaint fell on deaf ears," said Ai.

"No, not deaf ears, lazy bodies. Thanks to the rain, the police will sleep in their quarters tonight and not make a fuss about it. But I'm sure they will send someone to accompany you to town."

"What happened to Bora? Did he come home?"

Neal shrugged his shoulders, hurrying outside to wash his feet. "I didn't wait to see. What can our poor helpless grocer do?"

Ai stared into the distance. Her eyes rested on the portrait of Gandhi on the wall, looking forlorn away from the light of the lamp. Her husband had followed his call to fight the British, given his everything. Now she was doing her bit, following her heart, fighting for her people. She smiled. Finally, she was making something of her life, playing a tiny part in a struggle that would change her world forever. She was still smiling when Neal blew out the lamp leaving the house in a swathe of darkness.

There was only one bus to town and Ai woke at dawn to be on

time. She left the house early and walked without haste. Ai imagined she was going on a fool's trip, carrying a plastic box to town to drop off at a garbage heap in the busiest part of town and meet someone for the first time in the last year of his life. It made no sense to her, but she knew from experience that nothing does, nothing ever followed the decreed path.

The bus was late and full. A mile down the road, it stopped to pick up another passenger, the havildar, who cursed his way inside. He found himself standing room behind Ai. When the seat behind her became vacant, he pushed past a lady with a child perched on her belly and settled down with a grunt of satisfaction.

Ai slept through the entire journey. In town, she took a rickshaw to the Civil Hospital, an hour's ride from the bus-stop and spent the entire journey trying to place the mustached rickshaw-puller, who appeared familiar. The invalid's family was surprised by the unexpected visit and Ai marveled at how good it felt talking to people she had never met in her life. Both sides kept up a lively pretence. Ai smiled at her new acquaintances and listened as they rued their misery at a life diminishing. Someone came forward with updates on those newly married and the antecedents of the girls acquired by marriage. Someone else gave her news about a dozen births and a couple of deaths. The invalid was well-liked and there was a tinge of sadness in the updates. She gave the family a warm goodbye and the patient a last glance, and she was on her way, this time to Graham Bazaar.

It was just a mile from the hospital and the rickshaw-puller took a short-cut, turning into a narrow lane cramped with shoppers. The stench of rotting vegetables and discarded food hung in the air, but people moved without a care. As they turned a corner, Ai saw garbage spilling on the road from a large concrete bin. She patted the rickshaw-puller's shoulder and he stopped.

"This will not take more than a minute," said Ai. She removed a box from her bag, sidestepped a pile of leftover food and placed it on the garbage.

"What was that?" said the rickshaw-puller, who watched with interest.

"Garbage," said Ai.

"You brought all that from the village to throw here?"

Ai said: "Our villages are clean. Let's leave it that way."

An hour later, she was on her way home, on the same bus that brought her to town, the havildar snoring in the seat behind her. The rickshaw-puller watched her leave from behind a nearby shed. When the bus turned the corner, he hurried to a public phone. He gave a sideways glance to make sure no one was watching and dialed a number. A girl answered the call at the other end. She put the call through to her superior. The rickshaw-puller spoke in an urgent voice.

Not much later, the police swung into action. They cordoned off the bazaar and evacuated everyone. A couple of scavengers were shown the end of a cane and told to rummage through the heap. They burrowed without a care and came up with the plastic box. The rickshaw-puller, now bereft of his mustache and turban, made a positive identification of the box from a safe distance. Two men from the bomb squad stepped forward. They picked up the box with a metal arm and placed it inside a metal-plated container; with a couple of escort cars in tow, they hurried for the empty spaces of Chowkidingee. They placed the box behind a barricade of sand bags and pried it opened. All that were inside it were bits and pieces of metal scrap, a couple of pencil batteries, some wires and an old torchlight.

Several miles away from town, the policemen manning a check-point tightened their grips on their guns as a bus rounded a bend in the road.

"Careful now," one of them said. "She could be dangerous. If she tries to escape, shoot her."

A policeman raised his hands and gestured at the driver to stop. Two policemen went on either side of the bus. The radio crackled to life. The policeman identified himself to his superior.

"We have the bus surrounded, sir," he said.

A broken voice barked an indignant order.

"Sir, but…"

"Do as I say, you buffoon. Do I have to repeat everything?"

The policeman signed off. "Let the bus go," he said to his men. They turned to him in surprise. "Do I have to repeat everything?"

As the bus rumbled off, the men gathered around him.

"What happened, sir?"

"I saw her inside."

"Seems like a nice lady. She doesn't look at all scared. She even smiled at me."

"Why should she be scared?" said the policeman. "Somebody fed us wrong information. There was no bomb."

In the midst of the hullabaloo, a girl rode into town in a scooter. The policemen at the checkpoint waved her through and crowded around their officer. They listened to the wireless and passed on news about the bomb at Graham Bazaar. She took the first right turn towards the Kachari, the area in town where the government offices were clustered around those of the Deputy Commissioner and the Superintendent of Police. It was well past noon, and the usually bustling area was deserted save for a few scattered policemen. The girl drove straight to the SP's office and parked near the gate.

A policeman hurried out waving his baton, frowning at the girl.

"You can't park your scooter here," he said. "SP sahib is

107

leaving any minute now. I can't have anybody blocking the road."

The girl hesitated. "I...I'm sorry, sir. It will just be a minute."

The lowly constable smiled, pleased the girl had called him 'sir', but insisted. "Please, please," he gestured with his baton, trying to push her back.

The girl held out the paper in her hands. "I need to have it signed," she said, pointing at the DC's office. "It's very urgent."

Someone from the guard tower called out: "Sahib will be out soon."

"No, no. I can't allow it. Take your scooter away. Go," said the policeman to the girl.

"Please, sir," the girl pleaded. There were tears in her eyes. "It will take only a few minutes."

"I don't know..." The policeman hesitated.

The girl nodded and hurried away.

"Sahib is coming out," said the policeman in the guard tower. "Why did you let that bitch park the scooter here?"

"I didn't...," mumbled the policeman, staring after the girl. He glanced at the scooter: the peeling paint, the ramshackle condition, oil leaking - good enough for the scrap dealer. Such good clothes, but such an old scooter. Ah, well, it's only a few minutes, and when she comes back, he will teach that girl a lesson in obedience. But you never know with young people these days. They look all the same. What if there is a...?

The distant wail of a siren broke into his thoughts.

"Sahib's on the way," said the policeman in the guard tower. "He is not in a good mood. They've found a bomb at Graham Bazaar."

The policeman breathed a little easier. If they found a bomb elsewhere, there won't be another here, not when there were policemen in sight every few metres. Those in the Sangathon are brave, not foolish. And that girl - she doesn't have enough common sense to take care of herself. What harm could she possibly do? He chided himself for letting his suspicions run away like the wind and hurried to remove the scooter.

"Damn that bitch," the policeman swore when he found the scooter locked. "Why can't she leave the keys behind? We are thieves, is that it. Let her come back." He suddenly noticed the keys on the footboard. The lead Ambassador with the red light on top turned the bend in the driveway. "Damn, damn," the policeman fumbled with the key. His palms were clammy and sweat bristled on his forehead. "Oh, he is going to miss his salute. What will sir think?" He pushed hard at the handle. "Why not break it to teach that bitch a lesson about parking in proper places." The first car of the three-car convoy was almost upon him. The key slipped into the lock. The policeman sighed in relief and turned the key. The explosives cramped inside the dickey erupted with violent force.

The policeman died instantly. The first car caught the full impact of the blast and turned over like a plastic toy, bursting into flames. The second car with the SP inside careened out of control. The driver tried to avoid the ball of molten metal in front, but the road was narrow and the tree-lined driveway gave him no space to maneuver. It crashed into the rear of the first car sending it spiraling across the road. Only the third car escaped undamaged. It screeched to a halt, hitting the brick wall attached to the guard tower, stopping metres away from the crater left by the blast. Inside the guard tower, the policeman cowered under a table and bore the shower of brick and mortar landing on his back.

A mile away, walking towards the bus station humming an old Assamese tune, Nina heard the explosion and sighed, a dull ache in her heart.

9

By the time Ai reached home, it was close to evening. The sun had long gone down and she walked with her head down, watching the road in front of her in the dim light, picking a dry path on which to tread through the mud. A brisk wind was blowing and the long winding road past the swamp seemed longer than usual. By the time she reached home, it was dark. The light from a lamp flickered in the breeze, which carried the murmur of several voices to her ears. She opened the door and stopped.

Hirok sat with his back to the door. He turned and a smile broke over his face.

"They let you go?" said Ai.

"They are letting everyone go," he said. He looked pale and smelled a bit. There were stubbles on his chin and an overgrown moustache drooped over cracked lips. His voice was weak, but his eyes still had the same fierce determination.

"They are releasing them one by one," said Neal. "They don't want a stampede on their hands. Do you know why?" When Ai shook her head, he said, "The Dikhow has been rising all day and they are afraid the water would enter the outpost."

"At last we've some use for this infernal rain," said Hirok.

"You look hungry," said Ai, examining him in the light. All she saw was a woefully thin son in need of food and rest.

"That I am," said Hirok. "All they gave us was rice and dal. The rice was too sticky and tasted like plaster. The dal was too watery - a fish could live in it. Sometimes there was too much salt in it, sometimes so little. I hardly ate anything, just enough when I couldn't help it. In the darkness you don't know what you are eating with your food - cockroaches, caterpillars...rat shit."

Ai was silent for a while. "It must have been horrible."

Hirok laughed. "Not at all. We were all together after a long time. For a change we could safely discuss and make plans instead of meeting secretly in the forests or by the river at night. We were above suspicion of any wrong doing during the time we were inside." He paused. "The darkness helps you rest and collect your thoughts once you get used to the smell. But the mosquitoes - at times it felt like they've been trained by the police to bug you till you are bursting to tell them everything just to get away from them."

"Were they hard on you, my son?" said Ai.

"The police? Did they beat me up? Is that what you meant?" said Hirok, laughing and shaking his head. "But they asked a lot of questions, the same questions over and over again."

"About what?"

"Everything. From what I think about politics to how many visitors to our house. They want to know everything."

"And?" said Neal, a smile on his lips.

"We told them, of course. Everything they needed to know and much more. I'm sure they will find the information useful," said Hirok, and both men burst into laughter.

Ai told Hirok about her trip to Dibrugarh and the story they fed the grocer.

"You are clever, Ai," he said. "Now we can feed him all sorts of rubbish."

"You can't feed rubbish to a man who is garbage," said Neal. "I wonder how he manages a good night's sleep with that dark soul of his."

"Well, he has only one faith - money," said Hirok. "He'd sell his mother if he gets the right price."

"Is he really that bad?" said Ai.

"Much worse actually."

"I've been thinking," said Ai, "and it's little else than a matter of faith. He believes in something which is different from what we follow. There is bound to be a clash somewhere as both sides pursue what each believe is right."

"There can't be anything right about what he believes in when people are taken away at night by soldiers to be tortured or shot. We mustn't forget what happened to Jogen kai and Molu ka," said Hirok. "We are fighting against a big beast and he is a tiny part of that beast."

"Bora is a dog," said Neal. "I'm sure he will drop in as soon as he gets Hirok's smell and make a saintly sermon. Besides he has to know how Ai's trip to town went so that he can get the bah-bahs at the police station."

Sure enough, there was a knock at the door that very night about the time the food had been cooked and put away till dinner, and the two men had gone out on an errand. Ai started when she heard the low, hesitant knock.

"Who is there?"

"Bora."

Ai opened the door and the grocer came in wiping sweat from his face and shaking the water from his umbrella.

"You always kept your door open for anyone one who cared to come in," he said. "Now you keep it locked."

Ai motioned him to the chair. "Times are changing, Bora. Now I fear people, fear their motives." She settled down on the bed facing him. Despite her dislike for the man, she was glad to be talking to him. Her world was divided and talking to him felt like talking to someone from the other side of the chasm. It was an opportunity to learn more about him.

He sat down and looked around uneasily. "Your son isn't here..." he said. When Ai shook her head, he said: "I saw him when he was coming home. He looked pretty thin and worn out. Jail food - it really does a man in, teaches him a few lessons..."

"Lessons?"

The grocer gave Ai a sharp look that filled her with vague fears. "About everything," he said. "People, life, beliefs. If you are in long enough you even know the straight path through life."

"And you know this 'straight path?'"

The grocer stared at the floor. "Do you think your son would've been in jail had he stayed on the right path and not strayed? Where he is going there is only more pain and darkness. It is like the blackness in that cramped cell with a thousand mosquitoes. Only it gets worse and instead of mosquito bites, he could find himself at the end of bullets."

Ai let out a low laugh. "You know everything and you have judged everyone. It must make you feel very happy to be able to do that."

A flush spread across the grocer's face. He shifted on his seat. "I was only trying to be helpful," he said. "You've been kind to me, the village has been kind to me. I don't want to see any of it ruined, our young ones killed or taken away in the dead of the night without any hope of seeing them again. Do you think it's worth the pain and effort? Do you think even a single life is worth all this trouble? All this talk about change and revolution, all it has done is divided us, divided our homes, divided this village, people turning against each other. Is this right?"

Ai blinked her eyes. "What do you think?"

"Does it matter?" he said in a sad voice. He cheered up a bit. "You went to town? How was the trip?"

Ai laughed her soft, gentle laugh. "I slept through most of it. A kindly rickshaw-puller took me to the hospital and we

113

hurried back because I had the bus to catch."

The grocer shook his head. "Then you don't know?"

"About what?"

"The bomb explosion in town? It killed four policemen, damaged three cars, badly injured the SP and threw the entire town into chaos." The grocer noted the startled look on Ai's face. "The police were looking for a bomb at Graham Bazaar. The entire police force had to be summoned to clear the area of all the people."

"And?"

"The bomb squad took away what they thought to be the bomb to Chowkidingee to defuse it, but it was a dude, a decoy, to draw the attention away from the real bomb."

"You mean..."

"Yes, yes," the grocer nodded. "While the police were concentrating their attention on the box at Graham Bazaar, they sent someone over to the SP's office because they knew he had to come out. The bomb was left in a scooter by a girl."

Ai straightened in her seat. Her eyes showed the alertness of old people when something held their attention. "You said the police were looking for a bomb at Graham Bazaar. You said it was a decoy. You know about the bomb in the scooter and the girl. You know so much," she said, and the grocer nodded, chest puffed up. "How do you know...everything?"

The chest shrunk, but the grocer managed to regain his composure. "Just like you pretend not to."

Ai smiled. "See, we understand each other perfectly."

The grocer sprang to his feet. "I've been tricked and I can sense the treachery here. You folks, you think you are clever. But you are wrong just like you think I am. I know what is right, I understand it and I follow it. I'm not going along because most think like you." He stood in front of her, glowering down at her timid form on the bed.

"I didn't understand a word of what you just said, Bora," said Ai, ignoring his furious look. "But I've a conscience. Do you have one? Don't talk about right or wrong when you don't understand it yourself."

The grocer lowered his voice. "Ai, try and understand me once. Don't believe me, hate me if you like, but look beyond me. Your son and his friends, they are good people who have gone astray. They don't know it yet, but they will. Their beliefs, their faith cloud their vision at the present. They don't realize they are being used, that their actions are putting a lot of people in peril - you, me, the entire village. Behind them stand other people, people who are interested only in their own good. Nothing will ever come good of all their troubles and sacrifices. They are being used just like they used you."

"Why don't you talk to them yourself, show them the right path?"

"Me? But they don't trust me."

"Nobody does," said Ai, pointing at the door.

The grocer became moody and silent. He dropped his head and was lost in thought. Finally, he stirred in his chair and rose to leave. He pointed at the portrait of Gandhi on the wall. "He deserves better. This country deserves better. And your husband - what must he be thinking now? Such a good man and to think his house has been turned into..." His voice trailed off. He paused at the door. "This'll be the end of you, Ai. You and your son, his friends."

Ai sat on the bench in the verandah turning over the grocer's words in her mind and listening to the doubts in her own heart. The darkness grew around her. She watched the people on the road for a while. They spoke in low voices and sometimes not at all as they slouched for the shelter of their homes. As the hours passed, the road emptied. The village fell silent.

Behind the house, beneath the jackfruit tree by the pond, two eyes scanned the darkness through the rain. A short, lithe figure leaned against the tree, chest heaving in laboured breathing, tired feet having a respite from a long walk over rough roads. Sweat dripped from the forehead, while her skin, ripped from running through the forest behind the house, burnt like pricks from hot needles. A moment later, head bowed, she scampered past the kitchen light and stole into the house. Still keeping to the shadows, she paused at the front door and coughed.

Ai was lost in thought, listening to the rain and feeling the wet kiss of the wind on her cheeks. She started and turned around. A look of astonishment came over her face. For a moment she couldn't recognize the figure in front of her. She was wearing clothes that were drenched and torn. Her feet were bare. Her hair hung over her forehead and her face was smudged with mud. As Ai watched, she sank to the ground. Her head leaned against the wall, her arms fell by the side and feet stretched forward. "Nina!" said Ai, rushing inside. "Are you all right?" Her eyes ran over her body, noting the cuts on her arms and the blisters on her feet. She looked exhausted and her forehead burned with fever. She breathed in short, greedy gasps. "Let me get the tincture and a towel," said Ai, hurrying off. She returned shortly. With a gamocha, she wiped Nina's hair dry. "You shouldn't be out so late, and in the rain too - now you are running a temperature."

Nina opened her eyes. "The police, they saw me," she said. "I think they are looking for me."

"Why should they be looking for you?" said Ai.

"The bomb at Dibrugarh - you must have heard about it," said Nina. Tears streamed down her cheeks and she wiped them away with the back of her hands.

The grocer's words rang in the mother's ears. "The grocer

told me. I was the decoy there."

Nina gave her a blank look. "One of the guards survived the blast..."

"And he saw you when you parked the scooter..."

Nina looked at Ai in surprise. "They know me well, but I'm not scared of the police." She paused for a moment. "There were seven bomb blasts today all over the state. Enough excuse for the government to do as they please. They are going to call out the Army again."

"You are afraid of the military?"

"This time around they will be in charge. The police will be their guides. They'll have powers to kill anyone on suspicion."

"Don't they have laws anymore?"

"Not for them. They will interrogate every prisoner, kill those they think are dangerous."

"And you are one of those?"

"I'm an expert with bombs. I suppose that makes me one," said Nina. She looked at Ai with tear-streaked eyes. "How many more of them do I've to kill before I can beg my parent's forgiveness for what they did to my sister?" She lowered her eyes and sketched a vague figure on the floor with a toenail. "They are beasts. They kill without compunction and they treat women like garbage. They use you and take your soul, and then they kill you. If they can't find you, they will take it out on your family, anyone. My sister, how is she to blame for what was happening in another village? They...they raped her in front of my parents, and when they were done, they put a bullet in her head."

Ai shivered with fright. She patted Nina and held her hands. "What will happen now?" she thought.

At dawn, Hirok and Neal returned home.

Ai rushed out when she spotted them. "What happened?

Where were you all night?" she said, noting the harried looks on their faces.

"Where is Nina?" said Hirok in a grim voice. His hair was unkempt and clothes disheveled.

"She is sleeping," said Ai. "She has fever. She was in a bad way when she came home last night."

Hirok brushed past her into the house. A sober Neal with a slack smile on his lips explained to Ai.

"There has been trouble, Ai. Lots of it," he said. "The police are looking for her. If they catch Nina, they'd have to turn her over to the Army. It will be the end of her."

"How do you know? How can you be so sure?"

"We know…"

"So…"

"It is not safe for her to stay here anymore. She has been seen here."

Inside, they found Nina and Hirok in the midst of a fierce argument.

"Think it over," said Nina in a determined voice. "I'm familiar with this place. I feel safe here. I can hide somewhere if I see them coming."

"What if you don't?"

"I've good instincts. I'll know."

"Your instincts doesn't count, not when your safety is our primary concern," said Hirok. "We need you alive and well for another day."

"Then I'll go far away and for a long time," said Nina with tears in her eyes.

"As long as it is away from the police and the military," said Hirok. "Nothing can change my mind, not even tears."

Ai felt the pangs of desperation in Nina's voice. "Why are you pushing the sick child?" she said to Hirok, holding her hand. "Let her stay here. We'll think of something."

"No," said Hirok. "You know as well as I do it is not safe for her here any longer. She has to leave today, now. She has her orders." To Nina, he said, "Pack your things. We don't have a moment to waste. You know where to go."

Nina glared at Hirok, but obeyed. She pulled free from Ai's feeble grasp, and when tears started rolling down her cheeks, she wiped them away. With a sullen face so much like the gloomy weather outside, she gathered her clothes in a plastic bag, stepped into her sandals and turned to leave. She stopped at the door and thought of saying something. A quick glance and she scampered out of the house. Hirok went after her, but Nina wouldn't pay any heed to him. She rushed down a narrow trail into the forest and was gone.

Ai's heart contracted with fear. She couldn't quite understand her son's insistence on Nina leaving as soon as possible. There were plenty of places around the house for her to hide if the soldiers came. They'd never dare go into the forest, not even in their hundreds. And the bamboo thickets were impenetrable. Not to forget the dense foliage in the swamp or the areca plantations on the other side of the village. Tears surged in her heart and she had a premonition of a great misfortune befalling Nina.

Hirok returned a few minutes later, his head bent and shoulders drooping. When he looked at Ai, his eyes betrayed the burden of a man in the midst of some turmoil. "What else could I've done?" he said in a small voice. "I was worried about Nina. I thought she wouldn't leave. She has such a stubborn streak."

Ai patted him on his shoulders. "You were right and you were only thinking of her good, but sometimes it is better to speak with more understanding. It wouldn't have harmed if you had spoken to her gently, made her see your point."

Hirok didn't reply for some time. "Ai, I know I was wrong.

When I was firm with her, I was being adamant with myself, everyone. You don't want emotions to hold you back, ruin the very cause you are fighting for."

Ai turned away from the window. "Everything's changed," she said in a sad voice. "People are getting angrier, wanting this, wanting that. The weather, its gets worse. The rain never stops, the sun never shines. People lie to you, people use you...when will it all end?"

"I understand your feelings, Ai," said Hirok. "But these are hard times. Things will only get worse now. That's why I need you to understand. Trust."

Ai glanced at her son. Her face was flushed with anger. "Don't use words you don't understand," she said.

"Listen to me, Ai," said Hirok. "There is a way we could help Nina."

It took the police three days to come looking for Nina. In between, Ai lived in the shadow of doubt, fighting worries and spending sleepless nights. She went to bed every night certain her wait would end before midnight and Nina would be safe to come back, but nothing happened. All day, Hirok wandered about tired and gloomy with eyes that were searching for something. Ai noticed this.

"What's the matter?" she said.

"I've got fever," said Hirok.

"Why don't you go to the dispensary? Neal will take you."

"To a dispensary where there never has been a doctor. No, I'm all right, really," he said. He paced the room. "Why aren't the police coming? Why are they so slow?" he said with a measure of impatience. "That's why this country has never seen progress - so many days to do a small task. The longer they take, the more I'm worried about Nina."

Ai sought to comfort him. "Don't worry, she will be all right.

God is with us."

"I hope you are right, Ai," he said.

When the police came, a new day was already beginning. Ai was asleep on her bed. On the floor, Hirok lay mumbling in feverish incoherence, while Neal was lost to the world. They surrounded the house and forced open the front door. When the three startled occupants opened their eyes, they found the daruga sitting on the chair, one leg over the other, rapping with his knuckles.

Ai sat up on the bed, her eyes on her son, who shivered under a blanket.

"Malaria," said the daruga, watching Hirok with narrowed eyes. "Or is it encephalitis? Comes from hiding in the jungles and spreading sedition. I'd suggest another spell in a police lock-up."

Ai kept her silence. A policeman emptied the contents of the almirah on the floor. Another came in with a pile of papers on one hand and a number of photographs on the other. The daruga leafed through the pile, tossing those on the floor that didn't interest him. Finally, there remained only a photograph, and he examined it with great interest, lifting the lamp and peering into the picture of a girl. He produced a sheet of crumpled paper from his pocket and compared the two.

"What do you think?" he said, holding it up and asking the havildar by his side.

The havildar scratched his head and shifted on his feet. "Can't be, sir," he said, after a moment's consideration. "They look miles apart."

Neal yawned and pointed to the papers and photographs on the floor. "Why must you always ruin everything? Don't you have any respect for other people's things?"

"Quiet," said the daruga. He straightened in his chair and laid out the sheet on his thigh.

Ai craned her neck and could make out the sketch of a face with long hair and a sleek nose.

"Hmm-m," the daruga drawled, picking his nose. He turned to Ai, pointing at the photograph: "Who is this?"

"My niece, Nina," said Ai. She had never seen the photograph before her son gave it to her the day Nina went away.

"Nina?" said the daruga. "What happened to your brother that she stays here?"

"She doesn't," said Ai. "She visits us sometimes and then I don't let her go, and she stays a few more days just to please me."

The daruga handed her the sketch. "Then who is this girl?"

Ai studied the penciled image. It was just a vague face, poorly drawn with no resemblance to Nina. The policeman in the guard tower wasn't very observant. "She could be anybody," she said, shrugging her shoulders.

"So you don't know her."

Ai shook her head. "She's not as pretty as my niece."

"Very well." To Neal, he said: "You there, have you seen her before?"

Neal took the paper and handed it back after a quick glance. "Yes, I have. In my dreams."

The daruga shot out of the chair. "You, you watch that mouth of yours. Someday, I'll break it into pieces and by the time you join them together, the girl in your dreams will be long gone."

"Then it will be a nightmare," said Neal, under his breath.

Ai caught Neal's eyes and shook her head, placing a finger on her lips. "Why are you looking for that nice girl?" she said. "Is she lost?"

The daruga gave her a scornful look. "She is as innocent as you are, woman." He paced the room, his cane dragging behind him. The other policemen crowded around the door, their eyes following the daruga. He stopped and turned to Ai. "Your brother. Quick, give me his address."

A policeman hurried forward with a pencil and notebook.

Ai fed him the lie Hirok made her memorize. She made it sound as vague as possible. "He's very poor. The floods, they ruined his entire crop. He had to sell his land and shift his house." Nodding at the policeman, she said, "Yes, yes. Write it down. Kumud Barua, village Nagoan, district Barpeta. His house is close to the fields. The last time I saw him was twenty years back. I'm too old to travel now. He is older."

"Yes, yes, enough," said the policeman, gesturing with his hands. "I want his address, not his life history. Tell me the postcode."

"What?"

"You write letters to him, don't you? You need the postcode to send him letters."

A smile broke over Ai's face. "No, no. I've no need to write. Nina, she tells me all the news and we get along with that."

The daruga yawned, sending a tired look in Ai's direction. He turned to leave. "You still haven't taken my advice," he said to her on his way out. When she gave him a blank look, he explained: "Gandhi. Hide him. Spare him the torment."

Outside, the rain fell in a thick sleet. In the thickets, the bamboo creaked with every gust of wind. The daruga accepted the paper with the address from the policeman and stepped into the drizzle. One or two households were already stirring to mark a new day. He lit a cigarette, hiding the flame in the palm of his hand, nodding as his men passed him one by one and disappeared into the gloom. He slowed his pace and watched the last man disappear. He took out the paper and tore it into pieces. He rolled them into a tight ball and with a swing of his arm, threw it into the murkiness of the swamp. Then, contemplating the words of his report to the SP, he followed his men.

10

The rain stopped after a couple of days. In the Army camp a few miles outside the village, the first truck arrived with a fresh batch of soldiers. People huddled inside huts and in courtyards and discussed with friends and relatives, anyone they could trust, and talked of past experiences:

"So many soldiers. Is it a war they are fighting?"

"They are not going to spare anyone this time. It is blood they want."

"Remember the three men they took away last year? We heard their screams every night from inside the camp. Then mercifully the screams stopped, but they never handed over the bodies."

"How can we forget what happened with Molu ka? And Jogen kai - his pain gets worse every day. They scarred him for life - much worse than death."

"Why do they take it out on us innocent people? What've we done to harm them? Don't give a damn for these Sangathon fellows either."

"They treat us like cattle, making us stand in the rain like thieves."

"I tell you, they are more scared of us then we are of them. Have you seen a single one of them move about all alone? Cowards."

Despite their outrage, the villagers remained very much afraid. The past was a painful memory, but it was the present that worried them. They knew the situation elsewhere in the state was worsening, but would the soldiers beat them because of trouble in another town? There was some suggestion about all able-bodied men of the village hiding in the forest at night, but since no one knew for certain when the raids would start, everyone decided it was prudent to wait.

A pall of fear enveloped the village.

Inside the Barua's house, Hirok sat on the floor, the day's newspaper spread in front. "Not a word about President's rule or any operations and yet we see soldiers in their hundreds."

"The government has to do something," said Ai. "It just can't let everything run out of control."

"The point is which government," said Hirok. "Delhi or Dispur?"

"Those in Dispur are chicken-shit - who else but the babus in Delhi," said Neal. "They are the ones worried about their sweet little country breaking up. They could behave themselves and let things be under our control. That's the whole point of the struggle, isn't it?"

Ai gave him a sharp glance. "I thought this was a struggle for liberation. When did it become one for power?"

Neal smiled. "It's the same, isn't it? You need either of the two to have the other."

Their conversation was interrupted by urgent knocking on the door. Barman entered in a rush, a harried look about him. He glanced at everyone in turn and sat down on the chair.

"I just got news - bad news, in fact," he said, quite out of breath. "The Army's going to move into the village tomorrow. All of you must leave."

The house filled with silence. Ai listened with a frozen face. Hirok maintained a stoic expression and Neal scratched an itch on his arm.

He looked at their faces and grinned. "The battle begins," he said; as usual he was seeing something funny in adversity.

"They've been here before," said Ai, taken aback by Barman's anxious face.

Barman shook his head. "This time it's different. This time it's going to be worse."

"How?" said Ai.

"If our information is correct, they've strict orders not to take any prisoners. All suspects are to be eliminated. We are to be wiped out, destroyed for all time to come."

"What about the police?" said Ai. "Won't they be along with the soldiers?"

"I doubt it," said Barman. "The military doesn't trust them or share information with them. They will be just errand boys, I guess." He paused for a moment. "Which is why we think they will not be making any arrests. Now you know why I'm so worried. This house must be empty before they come. Everyone must stay out of harm's way - both of you. You too, Ai."

"What about Nina? She shouldn't be in the forest alone. What if the soldiers go there?" she said.

"She has my orders," said Barman. "She knows where to go. She should be safe."

Ai looked away. She was angry for being sent on an errand whose purpose she knew only vaguely about. "I'm not leaving," she said. "No Army is going to chase me out of my own house. How dare they?"

Hirok turned towards her with a look of alarm. "You are coming with us." He tried to speak in a commanding tone, but his voice was weak and hesitant and didn't convince Ai at all.

Neal said: "Ai, this is not the time to be stubborn. You've to understand. If not for your sake, at least for us."

"Leave the village for sometime - a few days, a few months, a year. Go with Hirok if you want, for as long as you wish. We'll make all the arrangements," said Barman.

Ai shook her head. "No, I won't leave my home, not even if all the armies in the world come. I belong here, can't you see?

I've lived here all my life. I can't be like you, going everywhere, anywhere. Your writ doesn't run over me - I don't follow orders. I do as I please." Besides, she was too old to run away and so she must make a stand, show these outsiders how brave the old were in this land in spite of all their guns and black laws, and the promise of pain and death. Barman made a motion as if to interrupt her, but she brushed him aside with a dismissive gesture of her hands. "Don't you dare argue with me," she said, and she was happy to see him squirm in his seat.

"Maybe it is for the best," he said with a crestfallen face. To Hirok and Neal: "You two are coming with me."

A tall figure crept barefoot along the walls of the house. He crouched in its shadows, away from the verandah where Phukan sat on guard. He listened to the conversation inside with great interest. "Hirok?" he thought. "Where has he heard that name before? Isn't he the one the police are looking for?" He counted the people in the room. "Four? That fat bugger, Manav, the cousin, Ai. Hirok? Is he that fat person?" His ears caught the bit about the men moving off that very night. "I must hurry," he told himself. He slunk away through the thickets, startling a lone fox, picking up his sandals where he had left them by the bushes on the road. In the night, under a star-draped sky, he walked as fast as he could to the police outpost.

A couple of miles away, the daruga was sitting down to dinner. It struck him he never had a meal in peace or a sound night's sleep ever since the insurgency broke. He was in a foul mood after a mob in one of the nearby hamlets lynched a dacoit and beat up two others of the gang. He hated the idea of people taking the law into their own hands and liked to keep things tidy in his area. Now, there were a dozen villagers in his custody and nobody was telling the truth. Well, he wouldn't blame them, not after the harrowing time at the hands of the dacoits. He settled down to eat, one eye on the elich in mustard, when the doorbell rang.

His wife returned and told him the grocer has made his usual unearthly appearance and wanted to see him immediately. "He said it's important."

"He thinks his rubbish is always important," said the daruga. He resented the fellow, but he was still in uniform and duty beckoned. The food would have to wait for the time being. The elich with its delicate bones and lingering taste needed to be relished at leisure, enjoyed over a fulsome dinner conversation with friends or family. With a scowl of annoyance, he covered his food and pointed it out to his wife. He found the grocer chatting up a couple of constables and passing around a pack of cigarettes. "What is it now?" he said, brushing past him into his office.

The grocer followed him. "I've news for you."

The daruga gave him a skeptical look. "I know what that means. You only create more trouble for me."

"No, no, no trouble. Not this time," said the grocer. He leaned forward and whispered in his ears.

The daruga gave him a wry smile. "Really? How can you be so sure?"

"I saw him. He is a big man, bald and fat and quite important."

"Important?"

"He has a bodyguard with itchy feet outside. You must take my word this time."

"I've taken plenty of your word. For you everyone is suspect. Every girl makes bombs, every old woman is a carrier for the Sangathon, every young man an assassin. I'd be better off arresting your imagination."

"They fooled you," said the grocer. "That old hag, she fooled you with her clever stories. You always underestimate her."

The daruga glared at the grocer. Now he had to humour the idiot, follow up on his information. He gestured at his men. "Three of you, come with me. Let's test our friend's eyesight. Otherwise we take them out." Twenty minutes later, he was seated on the only chair in the Barua's house. Ai sat on the bed, a startled look on her face.

"What is it now?" she said, wiping sleep from her eyes.

"This is most inconvenient," said the daruga. "Do you know I haven't been able to finish my dinner this evening? All because of people like you."

"Would you like a cup of tea?" said Ai before she could help herself.

The daruga was surprised by the offer. In a nook of his heart, he was touched by this gesture of kindness from a woman towards whom he had always behaved rudely. "I'm not here to take your tea," he said in his stern police-voice. "I'm looking for a man. His name is Hirok Hazarika. I've reason to believe he was here this evening along with a number of other undesirable elements."

"I don't know what you are talking about," said Ai. "But you are turning out to be a bit of a bother, coming whenever you like, barging into my house without reason."

"So we are bothering you, is it?" said one policemen. Another returned from outside. His stamping feet and crisp salute deposited mud and grass on the floor.

"Nobody anywhere, sir," he said in a voice that conveyed "Can we go now?"

The daruga rose to leave. "You can't hide things from me, see. I know what's going on here, the people that come here, the things you do. I'll catch you one of these days."

Ai glared at him. "Please leave," she said, exasperated.

The daruga thought about saying something in reply, but kept his tongue in check. He was tired and longed for his bed, and a good night's sleep. There was also the small matter of the elich waiting for him. Back in his quarters, he was sitting down to dinner when the doorbell rang again. His wife made a sound of impatience and rose to see the caller.

"Can't we have our food in peace?" she said. She returned a minute later. "There is a girl to see you. I wonder what she wants at this time of night."

The daruga swore under his breath and went to see the visitor. His wife remained at the table and held her head in her hands. From the other room came urgent voices and hushed whispers:

"You have placed me in great peril by coming here."

"I know, but I don't have anywhere else to go."

"You were supposed to get far away from here."

"You were supposed to make it easy for me."

"I sent my report and made the calls. I don't know what else to do. I heard everyone is making for Lakhipathar."

"I tried, but it is impossible to travel. The soldiers are everywhere. What if they arrest me?"

"Did anyone saw you come here? The grocer…"

"He's a fool."

"He is cleverer than you think. He saw you at Ai's, and he knows about Hirok."

"Pig."

A long pause. More hurried whispers.

The door opened and the daruga entered followed by a short, slim girl with freshly trimmed tresses. She sat on a murrah and kept her glance on the floor.

"You said you wanted a maid," he said to his wife. "So I got you one."

"Now? Do you know what time it is? Why didn't she come during the day?"

"Does it matter?" said the daruga, raising his voice. Then in a gentler tone, he added: "She has travelled a long way. You know how difficult it is to find a good maid."

The wife looked her over. She liked the look of the girl - the downcast eyes, the shy demeanour, the mumbled replies to her pointed queries. She nodded, pleased: the girl had obedience written all over her. But she has to talk to her, find out more about her - you never knew with girls these days. It was getting late and all that would have to wait till morning.

The daruga and his wife finally sat down to dinner. The new maid ate in the kitchen, sitting on the floor with only the head of the elich for company. For some time, peace reigned in the household, broken only by the sound of merry munching and careful sucking of succulent fish.

In the dining room, the daruga leaned back in his chair and patted his stomach, a contented expression on his face. The wife gave a pleased smile and burped. The maid came to clear up. The wife rattled off instructions - where to throw the garbage, where to wash. She left her alone to close up for the night.

In a corner of the kitchen, Nina twitched her nose in disgust and cleared the dishes of leftover rice and fishbone. Humming an old Bihu tune, she soaked a sponge in Surf and began to wash the dirty dishes.

Something struck Ai on her chest. When she opened her eyes, they stung from a fierce white light. It went away, and the light from a torch swept the room. A tall soldier with a beard stared down at her, and deep-set eyes glared from a menacing face.

"Get up, woman," he said.

Ai started and jumped out of bed. Behind him she made out the silhouettes of more men - soldiers - with guns pointing at her. A soldier was emptying the contents of the almirah on the floor. "Who are you people? What are you doing in my house?" she said, watching him search through the pile at his feet.

A photograph fell from one of the shelves. The soldier picked it up, took one look and threw it away. Ai bent forward to pick it up. The soldier stepped on her fingers. "Move away, I tell you, move away," he said, and pressed down with his boots. Ai screamed with pain. To the others, he said: "Her old man, I think."

Ai swayed on the verge of fainting. The pain gnawed at her fingers as if in a vice and the darkness closed around her. She struggled to breathe and fell on the floor.

The bearded officer stepped forward. "Poor thing, suffering this way." He grabbed her hair and pulled. "On your feet," he ordered. Ai struggled to her feet, her head feeling as if somebody had run a hot knife through the scalp. She stood unsteadily in the middle of the room. The officer walked around her. "So you are Hirok's mother or whatever his name is. I've heard of you."

Ai shivered with fear, but shook her head. "No, no, I don't know anyone by that name," she said, frightened by the roughness in the man's voice. "My son's name is Manav. Everyone knows him. Ask the daruga, ask the gaonbura, anyone in the village."

The officer ignored her. "You and your son gave shelter to two known offenders - Nina Barsaikia and Neal Choudhury. I daresay you haven't heard of them either."

Ai shook her head. "My house is small and we are poor and have enough trouble feeding ourselves. How can we provide for others?"

The officer watched her for some time. "I've been told to expect something like this. But an old convert..." He shook his head. "You should be ashamed of yourself, using your age to spread sedition and help criminals - people who plant bombs and kill innocent people."

"God sees everything. God will punish me if I've done anything wrong."

"I'm god here. I'll punish you."

"You are someone with a gun in his hand…"

"That is god in my book," the officer smiled. He was quiet for a while, as if in contemplation. "I'm told your husband was a Gandhian and even refused a government pension," he said at length. "Such a tragedy to see the wife and son throw water on the very freedom he fought so hard to give you."

Ai kept quiet. How dare he talk of her husband and his life? He doesn't owe this country one paisa. Freedom to her husband always meant liberty from servitude and poverty. How dare this officer, who wasn't even born then, use her husband as an example? Who is he but a brute let loose by his masters, who told him this freedom was his to abuse, and the law an extension of their powers over the poor and helpless? She glared at the officer and past him at the others in the room.

"Please leave my house," she said. "I've heard enough of your nonsense."

The officer lit a cigarette and watched the portrait of Gandhi on the wall in the flame of the match. "Why have Gandhi at home? Is that what you think of your husband's work? Nonsense?"

"Please don't take my husband's name. You are beneath him," said Ai.

A soldier stepped forward. He swung his gun. The butt hit Ai on the stomach. She collapsed on the floor in a heap. He spat on her. "That's for being rude to your guests."

One of the men hurried outside. He returned with a bucketful of water, which he emptied over Ai. She sat up gasping for air.

"Feeling better?" said the officer. "Perhaps now you can make better sense of what I was saying? What your husband fought for, why you shouldn't abuse your freedom?" To his men, he said: "Age does crazy things to people's minds, but she has more guts than all the men I killed – I'll give her that."

A soldier struck Ai on the face. She fell backwards and her head struck a wall. The others joined in, hitting her with their guns and kicking at her. The room swam in front of Ai's eyes. Everything blurred in a cocoon of darkness. She struggled to breathe. Her body grew heavy and the knees gave away. At a signal from the officer all the men dispersed except for one. He prodded Ai with his gun. "Okay, you old hag, you better hurry outside. You won't like it here, I can tell you that."

"What are you going to do to me? What are you going to do to the house?" said Ai, dark fears clutching at her throat. She grabbed the bed post.

The soldier struck her on the hand with his gun. He grabbed her hair and pulled, mimicking in a coy voice when Ai cried out in pain. A shove sent her sprawling across the room. The soldier followed her, kicking at her. Screaming and crying, Ai stumbled out on the verandah, falling, crawling, trying to get away.

A village alerted by the gruff voices and Ai's screams watched in horror.

"There she is."

"What are they doing to her?"

"They are going to set fire to the house!"

A crowd collected outside the fence. Part of it collapsed under their weight. They moved closer. As they watched, the soldier hit Ai again and again. She remained where she fell and when he prodded her with his boots, she crawled out to the courtyard. A chorus of oohs and aahs rose from the crowd. Hearts pounded in fear. Lips moved in prayers. There were calls for providential intervention from the women. The men shouted in anger:

"They think they are brave soldiers, but they are just dogs, dogs we kick everyday in the bazaar."

"Beasts, don't they have mothers?"

"The guns - that's where their bravado comes from. Take them away and they are like dogs with tails between their legs."

Two soldiers approached the crowd.

"Break it up. Go away," said one. "You've no business here."

"What business do you have here?" someone called out from the back of the crowd.

"Watch your tongue," said the other soldier, "or this whole village will go up in flames."

An angry silence descended at the threat of arson. There persisted a buzz of discontented murmurs. A few of the men left with their wives and children.

Ai tried to rise, but found she couldn't move. A racking weariness rose from within her and made her giddy and weak. The pain was everywhere, with every breath, every turn and contortion of her body.

"You beasts," said Saikia, her neighbour, rushing forward to help. "Don't you have any shame treating a woman like this?"

"Who is this?" The officer materialized from behind a bush.

"Her Majnu," said one of his men. Her lover.

The old man shook his fist and gave a mighty oath.

"The old bastard has got some fight in him too," said one soldier.

"Something to do with the weather here - it breeds heroism. We'll soon put an end to it," said another. He rushed forward swinging his gun at the old man. There was a crack and Saikia fell like a stone. He tried to get back on his feet, but the soldier brought down the gun with tremendous force on the back of the head. Saikia collapsed in a heap beside Ai. She opened her eyes and saw a trickle of blood ooze out of Saikia's nostrils. She tried to scream, but all that came out was a whimper. Tears welled in her eyes and then it all became quiet.

The crowd grew restive and pushed closer. More soldiers

rushed forward with guns drawn. The officer stood near Ai and smoked a cigarette. One of his men doused the roof of the house with kerosene. He lit a match and threw it on the roof. It burst into flames. Someone in the crowd picked up a rock and threw it at the soldiers. It struck one of the men on the head. More rocks and stones come pouring out of the darkness. The officer ordered his men to step back. He pointed his gun at the sky and fired a shot. The crowd stopped, surprised.

"Run. They are firing." A voice screamed in panic.

"Run for your lives."

"They are shooting at us. Save yourselves."

Children wailed. Women screamed in terror. People ran helter-skelter. Some fell in the mad rush. Old people were shoved aside. The women were overtaken. The men ran away.

The officer watched the comic dispersal with a smile on his face. He turned to watch the roof collapse in a shower of hissing bamboo and sparks.

Ai remained where she lay, unconscious and quite unaware.

The old man died.

One of the soldiers rushed forward.

"We have two injured, sir. One badly."

The officer nodded. "Call for reinforcements. Surround the village. Make sure no one escapes."

11

Ai woke up in a cold sweat. The sky was a deep gray and an eerie stillness hung in the air. She turned her head and her eyes fell on her dead neighbour, a crow scampering over the lifeless body. There was a pain in her heart as if a heavy hand had seized her heart in spite and was squeezing it hard. Her head throbbed with a sort of pain she never imagined possible. Her body tingled with a dull numbing sensation and when she wiped her face, it was wet with morning dew. She raised her head. The courtyard was empty. The fence was trampled and broken in many places, and the gate hung from its post. Behind her stood the burnt out shell of the house. Everywhere it was quiet as if the people who protested with their shouts and stones had lost their voice in the melee, covered themselves in a pall of silence.

Ai rose to her feet, grabbing a piece of bamboo lying nearby for support. Her heart pounding, she hurried to the cowshed. The haystack was a mound of ashen straw, but the cowshed was untouched. Overwhelmed by the events of the night, she sat down by the pond. She held her head in her hands and a stifled sob rippled through her body. The shuffle of footsteps behind her startled her out of her stupor.

"Why have you come?" she said, observing a disheveled figure emerge from behind the thickets. "Nina?"

"She's safe," said Neal.

"You shouldn't have come. They'll kill you if they see you."

Neal gave her hand a squeeze. He squatted on the ground beside her. "They won't, not when they are busy rounding up all the men in the village."

Ai turned to him sharply. "Is that why it is so quiet?"

Neal nodded. "There has been a search, Ai. They've broken into every home in the village save the grocer's, rummaged through everything without shame or conscience, broken what they liked, hit anyone who opposed them."

"Why?" said Ai, a look of confusion on her face.

Neal let out a sigh. "You don't know? How could you? After they dragged you out and killed Saikia, the villagers got angry and started abusing the soldiers. When they torched the house, they started pelting them with stones, sticks, whatever they could lay their hands on. They injured two of them. This is their revenge."

"This is revenge? Picking on unarmed people?"

"This is the honour they gloat over. You'll read in the papers they were provoked."

"Why doesn't somebody tell the truth?"

"This is the truth because we've become lies - terrorists, bad people. By the time they are finished with the men, you'll read that the soldiers were forced to retaliate killing three suspected militants. Maybe they'll put a couple of AK-47s in their hands and photograph them to show they aren't lying."

"What are AK-47s?"

"Guns. They let off a hundred bullets with a single pull of the trigger."

"So many. They're really going to shoot them then," said Ai, horrified. She recalled the tales of torture she'd picked from her son, Neal, their friends, every visitor.

Neal read her mind. "Too many prisoners. They won't shoot them. If the truth gets out it will be bad for them because people will come out on the streets. They'll question them, beat whoever they like, beat them badly if they feel like it, and let them go in a day or two. They'll have their revenge and feel good about teaching the villagers a lesson for allowing us to stay here." He rose to his feet. "Enough talk. Come, Ai. We've work to do and a body to burn."

Less than a furlong away, the soldiers ransacked the houses in the village one by one. They kicked open the flimsy bamboo doors and rushed inside in twos and threes. A brief struggle, shrieks of terror, children crying and grown-up daughters wailing, and a man or two was dragged outside at gunpoint followed by a screaming woman - a wife or a mother, tears in their eyes, voices hoarse with fear. They were made to kneel by the side of the road, and there they remained until all the men in the village were rounded up. The bearded officer walked up to them with a bored expression on his face. He pushed away those that were old, nodding with an expression of satisfaction at those that were not. They were lined up in single file and led away. They were marched to the Army encampment, stripped of their clothes and hustled into a tent. Young sons huddled with fathers and neighbours and stared at each other's naked bodies, united by a feeling of fear. Some sat silent, shocked beyond despair, some passed a few whispered words of solace to those sitting beside them, but most were lost in their own thoughts and the possibility of impending pain.

They didn't have to wait long.

Two soldiers rushed out of a small building, what remained of a school, and escorted the frightened men one by one to a windowless room. Their privates hidden in the clasp of their palms, they stood beneath the solitary bulb hanging from the ceiling, eyes downcast, thin, shriveled bodies shaking with fear. Two men sat in the shadows away from the light. They appeared like apparitions out of the darkness and took turns questioning each villager. They walked around the prisoner asking questions within their limited grasp of the local language, the villager answering them when he could, neither understanding the other, both pretending to. Every now and then, they tapped the villager on his shoulders with a cane to keep reminding an interrogation was in progress. Sometimes, when an answer didn't satisfy them or its meaning completely eluded their understanding, they gave a hard blow or two and smiled at the cry of pain. A couple of times, they lost their tempers and flogged the unfortunate villager for no reason until he lay quite still or unable to move. A soldier would hurry forward with a bucket of water and empty it on the fallen figure. When the villager woke up, he was hit again, more severely than before and he would fall silent once more, this time quickly.

This went on the whole day. When it was finally over, it was dusk. A wind was blowing and clouds heavy with rain hovered overhead. A soldier approached the prisoners in the tent. He opened the gate of the enclosure and nodded at the villagers. "Leave now," he said. "Go home."

Not far away, on the banks of the Dikhow, on a bed of sand lapped by its cold waters, the old and those who were spared in the village crowded around a bamboo pyre. Neal, a tired look on his face had taken on the mantle of a son for the widower and childless Saikia. He lit the pyre as the first drops of rain fell on his face.

The village remained in shock for a day or two. On the third, the first murmur of dissent emerged. The grocer held court in front of his store under the shade of an Acacia and the gaze of a couple of resting cows.

"Really? This has gone far enough," he said in his high pitched voice. "Isn't it a slap on our face, someone from outside doing the last rites of one of the most respected members of our society. A slur, I tell you."

Six or seven persons sat on the narrow bench in front. They

had no bearing on village affairs, but age was on their side and, so it was believed, wisdom too. They had observed the recent happenings in the village with feelings of reticence and lost hope and each knew or had someone close who had borne the brunt of the soldiers' brutality. Age and a weak constitution spared them the agony of those younger, but they suffered from the increasing frustration of the weak and the helpless. They shifted in their seats and the bamboo bench squeaked in protest.

The grocer gestured at his assistant to put out a chair and the odd man out at one end nodded gratefully in his direction. He decided he must say something and so became the first man in the gathering to air an opinion.

"But what can we do?" he said with a helpless shrug of his shoulders.

The others found their voices:

"The Army took away all the able men - anyone capable of lifting a spade."

"They beat them, broke their bones, tortured them for no reason."

"Such power. How can we fight them?"

"Can we forget what happened to Molu ka?"

"And Jogen kai? He is better off dead. What can we do if they decide to kill somebody?"

"All our fault, all our fault," said the grocer. "We allowed things to drift, we allowed outside influences to corrupt our people, we whispered things like independence and freedom and rights. Now see the fun."

"What is wrong with talking about such things?" said one man from behind thick glasses. "Someone has to. Better them than us."

"Someone has to?" The grocer shook his head as if aghast at the idea. "If someone has to, then bear the consequences. Don't discuss the pain of your suffering and the broken bones and all the terrible trouble that is going to keep on coming. Have you any idea what they might do next?"

"Yes, yes," said another man. "Bora is right. We were poor before, poor always. We were busy with our lives, struggling to make ends meet, feed ourselves, somehow keep alive. At least there was no trouble. The village was peaceful and things were better before than now."

There was a hum of approval and vigorous nods. The grocer smiled. A few more people sauntered in. The grocer arranged tea for everyone and tore off packets of biscuits. Those present felt their hostility towards the man diminish. A few found him likeable and concerned. More people arrived at the promise of free tea and crunchy biscuits. The grocer obliged with a smile. When everyone had a glass in their hands, he came straight to the point: "Have you realized the real culprits - those who brought us trouble - have gone, left us to face the consequences of their actions?"

"What could they do?" said someone from the back. "The soldiers would have killed them without a thought. And they'd have still taken us in."

"At least we could've told them something, spared ourselves the blame," said the grocer.

Another voiced spoke up. "These military fellows - they can't be trusted. All they want is to kill. They've the sickness of death inside them, I tell you."

A babble of sighs and nods followed the observation. A few debated amongst themselves. Several women came looking for their husbands. They left when they found the reasoning beyond belief.

The grocer raised his hands. "No, no, we must try and understand their position. They're strangers here. For them this is a foreign land, where everyone is an enemy, every face a threat. These Sangathon people don't move around with badges, so they must flush them out from amongst us. Unfortunately, sometimes things go wrong."

A sputter of claps followed the grocer's explanation, accompanied by sarcastic sniggers. One man stepped forward. He was short and heavily built with a bald head. The grocer stared hard at him. Where had he seen him before?

"You know a lot, Bora." His voice cut through the grocer's thoughts. "You know so much about them that some of us are beginning to think you work for them." The brief statement had a remarkable effect on the grocer. He stammered and looked around uneasily, then laughed uncomfortably in denial. "Too much knowledge can bring trouble these days. These Army people - these strangers, as you choose to call them - they've no business here, to take away what is ours, beat or kill our people."

This opinion found greater acceptance:

"Yes, these Sangathon people are better than those Army fellows," said one man. "They never bother us. In fact, I've heard of instances when they've gone out of the way to help people - people like us, people without a voice, people who are poor."

"Yes, yes," said another man. "Have you seen how that fellow - what's his name - Neal, how he has taken it upon himself to cremate the old man, complete all the rites."

"Have you realized the risk he has taken?" A voice said from the back of the crowd.

"Risk? What risk?" said the grocer, craning his neck to catch a glimpse of the speaker.

"Now he can't leave until the shraddha is over," said the voice. "He's told everyone he is going to complete the rituals come what may."

The grocer tried to pinpoint the face behind the voice, but it was lost in the uproar that followed.

"Quite an unselfish thing to do," said the old man on the chair.

"What an enormous risk. If the military or police get the news they'll surely arrest him," said the man by his side.

"Does he really belong to the Sangathon?" said another.

"It is common knowledge. You must know it," said someone at the back.

The grocer shook his head. The meeting hadn't gone the way he expected, and public opinion had veered from the path he hoped to show the people. "It's just an old trick to gain our sympathy," he said. "But that's what we're not going to do - succumb to their petty politics. Does everyone understand me?"

"I'm not so sure," said the bald man. "We mustn't forget the soldiers killed Saikia. And have we forgotten how they treated Ai - kicking her, dragging her out of her house like a thief. What reason could they possibly have for setting fire to the house?"

The grocer swore under his breath. "She deserved every bit of it," he said in a low voice, and was glad nobody heard him.

"We should be ashamed of ourselves," said another man. "Saikia was brave enough to defend the mother, rush to her aid. We ran away, threw stones and swore at them. Nobody amongst us tried to help her, not that night nor the next day."

The grocer looked on in frustration ignoring the hostile faces around him. He was beginning to have doubts about how right he was in entertaining everyone to tea and biscuits.

"Too bad, Bora," said the bald man. "People here don't seem to agree with you."

"Really," said the grocer. "Who are you, by the way? I don't recall seeing you here before."

"I belong here," said the bald man. "I'm an Assamese. You're an Assamese too, but you think like them. You'd sell your mother if you could. The way you were talking today, the people here think you've more of their interest in mind. Who do you belong, my friend?"

Bora shifted in his sandals. The eyes in the crowd turned him over, looking at areas he had kept hidden all his life. His heart beat in alarm and he began to perspire. Words deserted him. He found he couldn't think, couldn't remember...

"Enough of this nonsense, people," said someone.

The villagers moved away in small groups. One man came forward to the sales counter and placed an order. The assistant handed over the items and he walked away, waving the brown paper bag in the grocer's face.

"Put it on my account," he said.

"No more credit for you people," said the grocer, snatching away the bag. "If you want something, pay in cash or you get nothing."

The man watched astonished. "If you start behaving like this, you will be ruined," he said.

"So be it," said the grocer, turning his back on the man.

Dusk descended. Evening set in. Lamps were lit. In houses with electricity, lights were switched on. Bulbs flickered, then dimmed and went off. As usual the electricity had been cut and so more lamps had to be lit.

The grocer sat in his shop, lost in a haze of smoke from a bidi between his fingers. He was tired and crestfallen and wanted to go home and rest. The meeting had gone badly, and now, he was in a terrible position in the eyes of the villagers. Oh, what had he done? He'd tried to be clever and, instead, thanks to that bald man, he had taken the bait, played into his hands. He'd lost whatever esteem the villagers held him, the respect his money gave him. The bald man - he had seen him before, seen him somewhere near - yes, yes, he was the one who visited the mother's house at night, the one with the bodyguard. Hirok! He kicked out at his assistant, who yelped in pain.

"What did I do?" he said.

"Nothing," said the grocer. He lit another bidi to calm himself. So they'd come back to the village to keep watch, take care of Neal and make the funeral arrangements. Well, that boy, he was done for. He couldn't run away now, not when he'd committed himself in front of an entire village. He would get him, get the whole lot yet. He'd show these damn villagers, show them what he is capable of.

He said to his assistant: "Close the shop. I've work to do."

The dead man's house became the focus of attention in the village. People came in swarms of onlookers and well-wishers. Some were eager to catch a glimpse of Neal; others arrived with packets of food as was the custom, mostly rice and fruits, sweets and fresh milk. Neal sat on the floor, a single, white loin cloth wrapped around his waist. Every morning, he bathed in cold water in the simple cloth, then shivered and sat in the sun waiting for it to dry. A day of fasting followed. At sundown, he'd eat his lone meal for the day: boiled rice and vegetables with ghee, and a slice of ginger mixed together in a lumpy mass on a plantain leaf.

The light from a lamp cast a feeling of camaraderie amongst the visitors. Despite the events of the preceding days, there was a smile on everyone's face and laughter cascaded through the house. The young people were invigorated by the debate of the afternoon. They disliked the grocer and were envious of his prosperity. Somehow in that far-flung village, where he'd become the epitome of the rude and well-off, the putdown was an opportunity well taken. What they enjoyed more was the free tea and biscuits: it made the tea sweeter and the biscuits crisper. Those older were, however, less convinced. The accusations flung at the grocer rekindled dormant thoughts and poked at their beliefs. The simple act of solicitation with the tepid tea and biscuits hadn't gone down well with them. Afterwards, they met at the gaonbura's house and resumed the discussion. Then, having decided what was right for everyone in the village, a delegation of three men was entrusted with the task of conveying their opinion.

Inside the house, Hirok, who had been hard at work rebuilding their hut, listened to the chatter of his friends and laughed at the jokes they threw at Neal. The appearance of the three elders put an end to the racket. They made space for the three men to sit facing Hirok and Neal, and their friends, who tucked their guns under them.

"How are you?" said the gaonbura. It was a cursory greeting and Neal nodded, casting a glance in Hirok's direction.

Khanindra, a brooding, heavily-built man sat next to the gaonbura. "There is something important we must discuss with you people," he said.

Soumen was the third person in the group. "Look," he said. "We appreciate what you young people are doing for Saikia. It's no joke because taking up responsibilities are easy, but it's harder fulfilling them and you boys are doing more than your bit."

Hirok's eyes narrowed. "What is this about?" he said, a confused look on his face.

Soumen glanced at the two men by his side and cleared his throat. "Please, don't misunderstand us. We're poor people and we'd enough trouble feeding and clothing ourselves and sending our children to school when we could. We know what terrible lives we lead, but in spite of everything, once you learn to live it, it's a life full of peace and contentment. Our forefathers lived the same life we lead now and we don't see any need for change." He paused to catch his breath. "We've been talking and our view is that we invited the wrath of the military and the police, and we've only ourselves to blame." Hirok glanced at Neal and their friends, and then at Soumen, who continued: "We're simple people and we lead simple lives. We know the world is changing, but whatever is happening is too fast for us. We are not even sure what we want is right or what good will come of it. And us poor people, did we ever have a choice?"

"You've now," said Hirok. "We've always followed. Don't you think it's time we claim what is ours as a people?"

"I don't know what you mean," said the gaonbura, "but we know this much - we are afraid for our people, afraid of the harsh consequences of your action. We've already seen it happen, and we are scared to imagine how much worse it can get."

Hirok rose to his feet. He realized what the three men were about to tell them. He was seized by a desire to offer his heart, bring them over to his side, make them understand. "We've done no harm and we have taken it upon ourselves to help anyone we could. We've a dream and we dream for everyone and we need your support to make it come true. We've worked hard all our lives, every single one of us, toiled our fields under the hot sun, braved the rain, fought floods - for what? To feed us, feed everyone, and in return what have we got? A wretched life, a life spent in poverty, and worst of all, no justice. This struggle is for what we believe is rightfully ours. Tell me, which one amongst us doesn't feel that way?"

Hirok's words found favour among the young people in the room setting off loud exclamations. More people entered the room. Their voices merged in a roar and drowned out the protests from the three men in front.

Hirok nodded, pleased with the support. "Who has ever done anything for us? Remember the drama during every election? How we've been cheated all our lives? How we've to fend for ourselves come the floods? We've always paid our taxes, given our share when asked, yet we don't count, our lives don't matter. The soldiers shot dead Arun and nobody cared, not even in the village. We forgot our tears too soon, even before they dried. And Molu ka. Does anybody cared what happened to him, whether he is alive or dead? Does his wife not deserve an answer, justice? They made life miserable for us and when they beat us, broke our bones, bruised our bodies, has anybody cared, has anyone asked how we are, how we managed? There is not even a doctor in the village, not even a decent bus to town or a good road. Do we matter? Does anyone look at us as human beings? NO!"

More cheers and whistles. A smattering of claps.

"I don't know what the grocer said today," continued Hirok, surveying the eager faces. "I wasn't there, but I've heard bits and pieces. What he said must have sounded like the truth to our elders - to some of you at least, but it isn't. It is just a promise of falsehood, a peace and quiet that is never permanent, and a happiness that always has too much sorrow hiding behind its smile." He stopped to catch his breath. "We're all in this together and we'll never succeed unless we realize that."

Soumen tried to interject, but someone from the back shouted him down.

"Don't interrupt, khura."

"Yes, let him continue."

The three elders frowned. They whispered amongst themselves.

Soumen rose to his feet, a look of exasperation on his face. "We came here to talk to Manav and his friends," he said in a stern voice. "I don't believe the others in the room have any business here. Not when they behave like monkeys and make a nuisance of themselves. Have they forgotten how to behave in front of their elders?" A few heads dropped. The murmur of voices died down. When Soumen spoke again, everyone listened for a change. "We agree with every single word of what Manav said. We agree with his beliefs, his dreams, his passion and his willingness to sacrifice himself for it. But we're far too old for this sort of thing. Our life has been a struggle enough and we don't have the strength for any more fights. More than that, we're scared for you. The soldiers, they'll look at us and spare us because of our age, but what about you, our sons, our daughters?"

A bedlam of disagreement burst forth:

"Don't forget what happened to Ai."

"They dragged her out of her house, beat her, burnt her house."

"At the moment we're sitting in the house of the very man they killed."

"What about Molu ka?"

"Age? They're here to take lives. It doesn't matter if that life is young or old."

Soumen stood frozen like a statue. His argument had no standing in the face of the events of the past week. He turned to Hirok. "Your father was such a brave man, a Gandhian, who faced British bullets without batting an eyelid. Have you realized what you've become?"

"I'm a freedom fighter just like my father," said Hirok.

"Your father never hurt a fly, never said a bad word about another soul."

"Those days were different. Now if you are meek they will smash you to pulp without a moment's thought."

"That's no excuse to pick up a gun, kill."

"Sometimes death becomes a necessity. Remember what happened to Gandhi, how he died. The meek have no place in this world."

"So you've taken to killing?"

"I'll do anything to free this land from its oppressors."

"How many have you killed?"

"Everyone who deserved to die," said Hirok. "But there's more left."

"There's always more left," someone grumbled at the back.

"So you've become a killer, an assassin, a murderer, an outlaw in the eyes of the law," said Soumen.

"What law?" said Hirok. "The law is what is right, not what is written and touted to be legal."

"You've the blood of the dead in your hands. And Saikia's too. He would've been alive today if you haven't brought your dreams here - that and your friends."

"In struggles people die. There is a price to pay for peace and change."

"There is god above us. You'll suffer for the deaths you have caused just like those Army bastards."

"I'll worry about that when the time comes. My hands are bound by my oath to this land. I don't even own my conscience. I gave it up when I swore to fight on her behalf. I believe it's god's wish we fight for our just cause."

"Your soul is free, my son. Your soul will suffer."

"What good is a suffering soul in a bonded body?"

"It's no use arguing with you."

"Khura, I don't have the power of penitence because I'm not free. The saddest thing is you think you are."

"Enough!"

"Time is a cold blooded killer. It will get us one way or the other. Let's make something of our lives while we can."

Soumen sighed and sat down on the floor.

The gaonbura rose to his feet. "Enough talk," he said, gesturing at Hirok to sit down. "We're not here to argue with you. We're here to ask you to leave this village once the shraddha is over."

12

In the village, the grocer kept his shop shut and people ran out of sugar and salt, soap and tea. Hirok left for Dibrugarh in response to urgent summons. The villagers returned to the fields in groups of threes and fours, half afraid they'd find the soldiers waiting with guns and knives. But the fields were fallow and bare and waiting for them to get to work.

At noon, not many days later, they saw a cyclist pedal down the road. As the khaki dot drew nearer, the rider became visible. When the cyclist turned into the narrow road leading to the village, his purpose became apparent. The policeman pedaled as fast as he could. Sweat poured from his face and a red cap bobbed on a thinning pate. He was unarmed except for a stout cane clamped to the cycle's carrier, which stood out at the back like an unkempt mustache. Those working in the fields stopped and stared and told themselves not to worry. There was no other policeman behind him and he was, therefore, on some errand, a harmless one at that with only a cane for company. They shrugged their shoulders and went back to work.

The policeman pedaled past the fields, mellowed by neglect and overcome by weeds, past the swamp and the bamboo thickets and stopped in front of Saikia's house. He surveyed the scene for a moment, locked his cycle and marched in. He ignored the muted greetings of the women or the sight of children scurrying away in fear for the safety of their mothers' laps. He strode inside in the officious nature expected of his lot.

The policeman still hadn't spoken a single word, not even a rough insult to move out of his way or a shouted order or abuse.

He moved from room to room, and finding the object of his search absent inside the house, he went out to the back. He found Neal resting under the shade of a coconut tree. Their eyes met for a second, and then somebody offered him a chair, and he settled down with a sigh as if overcome by the inevitability of his task at hand.

He didn't utter a single word that day, not even when spoken to or when a child peered at him with half-closed eyes and asked his mother if "he was the monster everyone is talking about." But he never declined the cups of tea or the fresh fruit and sweets that were sent his way. In the evening, another policeman replaced him. When morning dawned, there were two. The day before the actual shraddha, the number jumped to four. Suddenly, they were everywhere, on the road keeping an eye on visitors, at the back watching out for more visitors, inside the house listening to what was being said and by whom; there was even one near the latrine: he smoked a bidi and spat on the ground every time someone came out. They followed Neal everywhere and never let him out of sight. They waited outside the latrine, fell in behind him when he went to the well to fetch a bucket of water for his bath, watched while he ate, watched while he slept or chatted with visitors or friends. Just to get even, Neal went out to the fields on the third day to defecate. He laughed as the policemen pretended not to notice when he relieved himself on the ground.

They never talked or laughed at his jokes, but he told them anyhow and kept repeating just to irritate them. They never discussed amongst themselves, never passed the odd remark, never told Neal or anyone their intentions, never denied the obvious or refused the food that was still being offered, and the cups of tea that followed one tumbler after another. They stood on guard and did what they were supposed to do.

The soldiers came on the morning of the shraddha in a

cavalcade of three Gypsies. It was about the time the villagers were gathered for the final rites, and the pundit sat cross-legged on the ground and sprayed holy water and recited the mantras by rote. They surrounded the house and hounded out the policemen. They still hadn't spoken and nodded when one of the soldiers ordered them to leave. The house was emptied. Women and children scurried away like frightened cockroaches, while those older were prodded with guns and told to leave. The men had leaned on the side of prudence by staying away since the arrival of the first policeman. The soldiers settled down on chairs to watch as the pundit fumbled his way through the rest of the rituals. When it was time to offer pinda at the site of the cremation by the Dikhow, a ceremony where the soul is offered prayers and food of its liking and sent on its heavenly journey, the soldiers barred their way. They did the best they could by the pond at the back. When the pundit struggled to his feet and declared the ceremony over, two soldiers stepped forward.

One of them pointed at Neal: "You're coming with us."

Neal was certain of such an eventuality the day the policeman arrived to keep watch on his movements. In the days leading up to the shraddha, he prepared himself for his fate, mulling over his life and the time he spent with Ai and his friends. He knew inside him that with the soldiers taking him into custody, his time in this world was over, that he had but a few days to live. His eyes moistened and a sad smile broke on his face.

"What's there to smile about?" said one soldier, poking his ribs with his gun.

Neal gasped in pain. "Let me change, put on my clothes now that I can."

"You won't be needing any." The soldier slapped his cheek.

Another soldier rushed forward. He struck Neal on the head with his gun. Neal dropped on the ground, where he remained, face down and barely breathing.

"Behenchod," said the soldier.

The leader barked an order: "Uthao sale ko. Isko to khabar leni hai." Take him away, he needs to be taken care of.

Two soldiers moved to either side of the fallen man. They grabbed him by his arms and dragged him away.

Ai watched from a window of her house with tears in her eyes. If only the soldiers allowed her outside or listened to her pleas not to punish Neal for the good he had done. Once or twice she tried to force her way out, but they raised their guns and threatened to shoot her. Then she saw him, his body limp and lifeless, two of the soldiers throwing him in the back of the van like some dead animal. She couldn't bear to watch as the soldiers drove away in a cloud of dust, her cries drowned in the roar of their engines.

Ai struggled to her feet and stumbled outside. The scent of freshly-cut bamboo and the acrid smell of burnt wood hung in the air. She wandered about the courtyard not knowing what to do before walking to Saikia's house almost on an afterthought. There was not a soul to be found, not even a mongrel seeking shelter. She went out to the empty pandal at the back and its starkness reminded her of Neal and his agony. Her heart pounded in anguish and she kneeled on the ground and cried. It was the desperate wail of a woman whose tears come from her womb. Then, as suddenly as her tears flowed, they stopped. Like so many occasions before in her life when all seemed lost and the inevitability of the loss pushed her to move forward, she rose to her feet.

Everywhere lay evidence of a rushed ritual and an abrupt end to the ceremony. Ai sorted out the things that lay strewn about. She picked up what she could and swept the rest into a neat pile in a corner. A few chairs lay scattered on the ground. She arranged the lot one atop the other till it was almost as tall as herself. In the makeshift kitchen, the food cooked for the bhoj was still keeping warm over the coals. She checked the contents - rice, lentils, vegetables, fish curry, even a few bottles of pickles. She covered the vats, holding down the lids with stones. Satisfied, she lit a lamp inside the house, shut the windows and closed the door after her.

She went to look for Sarmani. She should be able to help her carry out what she had in mind. Not the gaonbura, not after telling her son and Neal to leave the village. How dare he! Such thoughts rankled her mind as she walked down the road. Everywhere she saw huddled groups of people. They whispered to one another and cast wary glances over their shoulders as if they expected soldiers to rush out from behind the trees at any moment. Ai turned into a narrow path and past a larger throng.

Sarmani saw Ai when she looked up from her pounding of a pile of black pepper seeds.

"Good for you, Ai," she said. "At least you've the courage to be doing something. Look at the rest of us - goats for slaughter. We're not even ashamed."

Ai told Sarmani what she had in mind and what she wanted her to do.

"Are you sure we shouldn't be talking this over with the men?" she said.

"They are useless," said Ai. "They would rather be sheep and live with their heads bowed than be tigers and roar like the lord of their lands."

Sarmani nodded. "Comes from being afraid of pain. But what can they do, what can anyone do in the face of such force?"

"Not bear everything silently, suffer if they have too."

"What if they take offense?"

"They won't. Not when there is the promise of hot, spicy food."

"Would you like me to come with you?" said Sarmani.

"Do as I tell you and it will be help enough," said Ai. And she walked away from the village, past her house and the empty one by its side, a lonely figure in a dark night. She moved forward, a frail body bent with age, but burning with a fierce desire not to let go. Tiny, winking lights from lamps glowed distant and cold in the windows. They vanished behind a bend in the road as if a giant hand had reached out to wipe them away. She was enveloped by the fields spreading out on either side of her, damp and drowsy in brooding meditation. Ai hardly noticed any of it. She was far too lost in her thoughts.

A yellow light poured into the verandah from a bulb in the daruga's room. A policeman came out on hearing Ai's footsteps.

"What do you want?" he glared at Ai.

"I want to see my son," said Ai. "The one you took away at noon today."

The policeman stared at her in the gloom. "You're Manav's mother, aren't you?" When Ai nodded, he appeared pleased at the confirmation. "You're here for the other boy? Well, he isn't here."

"Not here? He should be there..." said Ai, pointing at the house where they had kept Manav.

"We didn't make the arrest," said the policeman with a wave of his hand. "The Army did. He's with them."

Ai pleaded with him. "Please, how can I see him?"

The policeman laughed. "I can't help you there. The Army doesn't listen to us or trust us because they think we were too nice with you." He was silent for a while. "If I were you, I'd be thankful I had another boy."

Ai stared at him feeling utterly helpless. Then, at the thought of Neal suffering at the hands of his captors, she sprang to her feet. No, she had to find him even if it meant going to the end of the world. She paused to sort out the directions to the Army camp in her mind before rushing out.

Ai had been walking for the better part of an hour. She was cold and tired. Everywhere around her were trees full of scary shadows. In the quiet, her breathing sounded like the harsh wind on a stormy night. A beam of light cut through the darkness. A van much like the one that carried Neal away rounded a bend on the road. It caught Ai for a moment in its glare before racing past. The trees and bushes, which rose like monsters in the light of the headlamps shrunk into the shadows. When she turned another bend in the road, another van wheezed past. Ai realized she must be getting closer to the camp. She imagined she heard the voices of people - stern commands, fierce whispers, even a scream or two. Then, gunshots.

She walked a little faster.

They came out of the trees all of a sudden. Ai almost fainted in fright. A couple of lights stung her eyes and she raised her hands. Ai stared at the men - soldiers - she made out three, but she heard more footsteps beyond the light of their torches. The soldiers stood undecided as if from the surprise of stumbling on a secret and puzzling about what it meant. They pointed their guns at her and whispered amongst themselves.

"Run, run while there's still time," a voice inside Ai urged, but she found she couldn't move. She took a deep breath and pulled herself together.

"Who are you?" said one of the men, lowering his gun and taking a step forward.

"I'm a mother...," said Ai, and the men burst into laughter.

"Every woman is or will be - god willing," said one soldier. "But that's not the answer we're looking for. Don't you think it's a little late for an old woman to be up and about in the middle of nowhere at this time of the night?"

"How can I worry about the time when I'm about to lose my son," said Ai. The soldiers gathered around her not certain what she meant. "Some of your people took my son away today from the village. I'm looking for the Army camp to see if I can find him, beg them to release him. He isn't doing very well."

A soldier stepped forward. He had an unshaven face and was built like a giant. "He is not with us. We don't know where he is."

"Where have you taken him?" said Ai. "Please let me see him, let me give him these warm clothes." She held up the packet in her hands. "He hasn't eaten properly for two weeks. I want to see if he's all right."

"Don't worry, woman," said the giant, covering her face with a shower of spittle. "We take good care of people like him. He is safe where he is."

"Have you hurt him?" said Ai. "He is just a boy. If he has done anything wrong, forgive him, let him go."

The soldier ignored her. He turned to his men and spoke in a language she couldn't understand. A van started up somewhere and its lights burst forth from behind a cluster of trees. The engine growled and strained, there was the sound of tires swishing through a patch of mud, and it roared on to the road. A soldier pointed to the van.

"Your lucky night, woman. You're coming for a ride with us."

Ai squeezed in at the back between two men. The cold steel of their guns touched her neck with every movement of the van and sent a chill down her spine. But she didn't cringe or draw away. She wasn't afraid anymore.

In a room inside the military camp, Neal sat on the floor and shivered in the cold. He was clad in the same dhoti he had been wearing since the cremation, and it was struggling to hold itself together. He dozed off every now and then, and when the pain became too much to bear, he'd wake all of a sudden as if from a bad dream and gasp for air. The pain would rise again from deep within him as if somebody had thrust a red-hot knife into his body reminding him of the horrors he'd been through all afternoon - the rope burns on his wrist, the bruises on his back when they dragged him behind the van, the swollen soles of his feet where they hit him with a cane and, when he thought it was over, they wrapped him in a blanket and rained blows on his body. He started to bleed from his nose and passed out, and then they must have let him go, dragged him to this room.

Neal heard footsteps approaching - the rapid steps of boots banging on the hard floor mingling with slow, unsteady steps of someone else walking alongside. He took a deep breath and braced himself for more pain.

The door opened and a light peeked inside.

"See, there's your bastard," a harsh voice said to someone. To Neal: "Hey you, get up. You have a visitor."

Neal obeyed. He tried to rise, but fell. The soles of his feet hurt, and the slightest pressure sent spasms of pain to his head. A face peered inside. It stared at Neal in the bleakness, straining to see the figure curled up on the floor. Neal thought he saw a wet glint in those eyes, but the pain was sheer agony. The soothing comfort of blackness enveloped him in its embrace and the pain slowly diminished. Ai! He could hardly recognize her.

"Enough," said the harsh voice, pulling her away. He snatched the packet from Ai and threw it at Neal's feet. "These are for you. Put them on, have some shame."

The door clamped shut. There was the sound of a struggle, and a sharp rebuke from the harsh voice, followed by the thud of someone falling. A moment later, Neal heard the footsteps move away.

Everything was dark and quiet. And quite painful.

Ai spent a sleepless night on a bench in front of the mess, shivering in the cold and swatting at mosquitoes. The cook found her a blanket and she covered herself the best she could. She sat bolt upright when someone shook her by her shoulders. When she uncovered herself and blinked at the strong morning sun, the soldier with the rough, unshaven face was towering over her. At a word from him, two soldiers stepped forward. They grabbed her arms and marched her towards a waiting Gypsy.

They left her by the thickets and disappeared into the morning haze.

Ai trudged home weary and defeated. Her throat was parched and sleep tugged at her eyes. She made herself a cup of tea and settled down by the window. She soon dozed off. She was awakened by a commotion somewhere outside. Voices drifted to her ears. They grew loud and shrill. She stepped outside and squinted in the direction of the noise. In the distance she saw people gathering at the chowk in front of the namghar. A dhoti-clad man, the gaonbura, ran out of a narrow path overgrown with bamboo, giving the impression of a mouse scurrying out of its hole. The crowd parted to let him through. He clambered up the few steps to the verandah. Ai stared at the people on the verandah - the gaonbura and a young man she hasn't seen before: someone from the Sangathon?

"What is happening?" she said to a young lad beside her.

"See for yourself," he said without turning his head. When she spoke to someone on her right, all she got was a severe "Ssshhhh, listen."

"People," said the gaonbura. "We've made a mistake, we've blundered, committed a sin. We've turned our backs on the very person who risked everything to be a son to a dead man he hardly knew, and who now is facing the greatest danger to his life." His voice was steady though with the odd tremor of apology.

Those in the crowd looked at each other and drew closer.

"People," the gaonbura continued. "Because of our cowardice, because we chose to be silent and suffer, the Army took away Neal. Now I hear they've Manav's mother in their custody because she was brave enough to love him and look out for him while we sat like scared mice in our homes. She, an old woman, she had the courage to take them on, walk to their camp, demand they let him go."

Those in the crowd gazes dourly at the gaonbura and at each other. A group of women who hadn't yet heard about Ai's escapade gasped in disbelief.

The gaonbura watched the faces of those in the crowd close to him. He appeared disappointed by the sullen silence that followed his speech. This must be what the people wanted and, now, when he was telling them what they wanted to hear all along, all he received in reply were a sea of silent faces. He cleared his throat and said: "Don't you think it's time we followed her example, go to their camp, the police station, wherever they are holding Neal, make them release him before it's too late?"

"What does he mean by that?" said one man.

"These Army fellows, they'll torture him to death, that's what he meant," said another.

The gaonbura's voice flew to them:

"Maybe I'll suffer for what I'm telling you, maybe they'll take me away, beat me, torture me, but I'm ready to face anything, all the blows and bullets they send my way because if we don't stand up to them, a day will come when they'll take away anyone they want - our daughters and wives, sisters and mothers. I say it's time we march to their camp and demand they release the mother and the boy."

Those in the crowd debated the gaonbura's proposal. Their voices grew louder. Somebody turned and spotted Ai.

"Look she's here."

162

"She's back."

"They released her."

"Scared of an old woman."

"This is what I think of them!" One man spat on the ground.

Ai stared back at the faces. A clamour of voices surrounded her:

"Tell us what happened?"

"Put her on the verandah."

"We want to hear what she has to say."

Ai was escorted to the verandah. The gaonbura and the young man stepped aside. Ai found herself standing in front of so many people for the first time in her life. Words deserted her. Her mouth was dry and her tongue felt like a piece of meat struck in her throat. The crowd grew impatient.

"Say something," the gaonbura urged.

"I saw Neal in their camp yesterday," said Ai, and the crowd drew closer. "He didn't recognize me at first. He tried to stand up, but he fell like a sack of grain. He tried to speak, but he couldn't utter a word, and then he fainted."

A combative look appeared on everyone's faces. Angry voices raised slogans against the Army and the government. A few hurled her questions:

"Why did they take you?"

"Did they beat you?"

"Have they no shame?"

Ai stood like a statue not knowing what to say to the furious well of questions. Tears brimmed in her eyes. She grasped a chair to steady herself. Someone helped her to it. A glass of water was thrust in her hands. She sipped the water and wiped away her tears.

The gaonbura spoke again. "I say we stop this nonsense. How dare they hit the mother? Have they no respect for age? We are going to march to their camp now. And we're not coming back without Neal."

The crowd responded with chants of approval. A hum of indignant voices rose in the air.

Those young shook their fists. Those older suggested prudence. Not a soul noticed a cloud of dust approach the village. The lone police Jeep that patrolled a hundred square kilometers of its jurisdiction came to a halt.

The havildar stepped on the ground, a grimace on his face. He flourished a cane, which hung from his fingers and trailed the ground. The other policemen positioned themselves around the crowd, which parted to make way for the havildar. He staggered up the steps to the verandah. The gaonbura barred his way, but a push sent him tumbling on the floor. Angry voices rose in protest. The havildar stepped forward. His eyes observed the gathering for any sign of disobedience.

"Who's talking there?"

A policeman at the back grabbed a young man by his hair and slapped him across the cheeks. "Was it you, you son of a bitch?" He shook him by his collar.

The crowd grew silent. No one moved. Ai dropped her head and went back to her tears.

The gaonbura struggled to his feet. "People, we're not going to be cowed down by their threats. We must…"

"Shut up." The havildar struck him over his ears.

The gaonbura swayed and fell holding his face. "They come and take whoever they want, do whatever they like. We can't allow this to go on any longer…"

"Take him away," said the havildar. Two of his men grabbed the gaonbura by his arms and led him down the steps. To everyone in the crowd, he said: "You people, don't you have any work to do? Go home now before I break it up."

A young boy - the gaonbura's son - rushed forward to free his father. A policeman held his hands in one of his and struck him on the face and chest with his fist.

"Stop hitting him," said Ai, unable to take it any longer.

"Why should you hit him?" A voice shouted from the crowd.

"Come here and say it," said the havildar, brandishing his cane. "I'll show you."

"You wouldn't dare." A well-built youth stepped forward.

The havildar moved forward waving the cane.

"Don't let him, people," urged a voice in the crowd. "Beating and killing people has become a drug for them - their hunger is never satiated. They always come back for more. Don't let the policeman hit him."

Ai rose to her feet. They still hurt from her exertions of the previous day. She grabbed the chair for support. "My dear people, if they take the gaonbura away, they'll beat him to death. They're beasts. We mean nothing to them, our lives, our work have no meaning in their eyes. We can't let this go on."

"You dumb woman!" The havildar turned towards Ai.

A sandal flew through the air. It caught the havildar on his cheeks. He stepped back surprised. A ripple of laughter broke through the throng, followed by shouts of encouragement. More things flew out of the crowd: potatoes, pebbles, even a fresh catch of fish. The people pushed forward. The policemen at the back looked around scared. More and more people came running in a state of great excitement. They surged towards the gaonbura and his two captors. The two policemen were pulled aside, punched and kicked.

"See," the gaonbura raised his hands in triumph. "If we're in this together, nobody dare hurt us. If we don't stand up for one another, who will do it for us?"

The people gathered around him. Two of them placed him on their shoulders. They carried him around the village in a procession, stealing glances at the policemen and shouting slogans that rose to a crescendo.

"How dare you take the law into your hands?" said the havildar. "Put him down this instant."

Nobody paid him any heed. More and more people joined the procession. It organized itself, men leading, women behind, children following. Before the astonished eyes of the policemen, it turned eastwards past the swamps and the bamboo thickets, and on the road towards the Army camp.

13

The daruga was sitting down to a cup of tea when he heard voices ringing in his ears. They died out in a faint echo, carried away by the wind. From his vantage he saw the road a long way and not a soul was in sight. He wondered what was taking the havildar so long. He heard the voices again, a faint trickle of men and women shouting and children mimicking the adults. A moment later he saw them, a line of men and women on the road leading out of the village, the men in front, the women behind them, the Jeep following the procession, the children seated on its bonnet. He downed the tea in a gulp and called out to his men. They rushed to the entrance, but the procession was already crawling away from the outpost.

"The military camp!" It dawned on the daruga. The Jeep found a way past the people and came to a halt in front of the police outpost. "I told you to stop them, didn't I?" said the daruga. "Not carry their children."

The havildar answered with downcast eyes: "They were too many. They refused to listen to us. I took the gaonbura into custody, but they freed him, punched the men. They are going to the Army camp to get that boy released."

"I can see that," said the daruga. He has to stop them somehow, stop them before anything terrible happens. He'd skirt the villagers, take the longer road west through the village and wait for them before they reached the camp.

He shouted at the driver: "Turn the Jeep around. Hurry."

Major Billy Banduk, the officer in charge of the camp, stabbed out the remains of his cigarette on Neal's shoulder and strode out of the gate. The villagers saw him and silence descended on the crowd.

"Who are this people? Why are they here?" he said to one of his men.

"They are from the village," said one soldier. "They've come for the man in our custody."

"Get rid of them. I don't want any disturbance here," said the Major.

The gaonbura approached with folded hands. "Please, sahib. Release the boy in your custody, give him to us before you do him any more harm, spare his life."

The Major turned to the soldier by his side. "What is this nonsense? How dare he come here and talk to me like that? Why aren't the police here?"

"They're on their way," said the soldier.

The gaonbura fell at the Major's feet. "Don't harm him, sir. Let him go. If he has done anything wrong, forgive him."

The Major kicked out in anger. His boot caught the gaonbura on the forehead. He fell with a cry of pain. A trickle of blood flowed from a cut above his eyes. Several villagers rushed to the gaonbura's aid. The Major raised a hand and a couple of soldiers stepped forward. The villagers retreated.

"Tie him up," he ordered.

A soldier twisted the gaonbura's hands behind his back and tied them with a wire. When he cried out in pain, the soldier slapped him across the face. The villagers shouted in protest. Their faces grew dark and hostile, and their eyes burned with anger.

The Major addressed the crowd. His command of the language was poor and he spoke in a colourless, halting voice. "Your leader here...we'll hand him over to the police. Apart from him, I don't see why any one of you should waste your time here when you can go home and rest, do your work."

A young man stood up. "Why do you have to tie him up? He is just an old man. What harm can he do? You're the ones doing all the harm..."

A soldier grabbed the man by his throat and shook him like a tree. He gave him a push, sending him sprawling on the road.

"Enough of this nonsense," said the Major to his men. "Clear it up. Quickly." At a signal from him, the soldiers moved forward, pushing the villagers back.

"Stop it, you brutes," said one man, when one soldier grabbed a girl by her hair.

The soldier turned his attention on the man and the girl retreated to the back of the crowd. "You son of a bitch, how dare you threaten us." He swung his gun and struck the man on the face.

Another man leapt in front. "How many do you think you will kill?" When the soldier turned towards him, he shouted: "Don't you dare hit me, you filthy dog."

"Oh, you're a brave one, aren't you?" The soldier swung his gun again. It struck the man on the forehead. He fell on the ground without a sound. Two women rushed forward.

"Is he all right?" One of them asked.

"He is dead." The first woman wailed.

"They killed him." The second woman wailed after her.

The soldier snorted. "He is not dead, just knocked cold. When he wakes up, he'll know how to behave next time."

A murmur of anger rose from those in the back. The men armed themselves with stones, branches from nearby trees, whatever they found lying around. The women cowered behind them. They covered the children with their bodies. The unconscious man remained in a heap on the road, blood oozing from his nose. The gaonbura sat by his side, hands tied, head throbbing with pain from the blow.

A mile from the camp, the Jeep crawled to a halt. The driver struggled for a while, then shrugged his shoulders. The daruga swore under his breath and ordered his men to walk the remaining distance. They broke into a run when they heard the angry voices of the villagers.

The Major noted the arrival of the policemen with a sigh of relief. He marched inside with an expression bordering on disgust. The soldiers retreated. The policemen took up positions around the crowd.

"You've done enough damage," the daruga addressed the villagers. "Go home now and let there be no more trouble."

Ai stood up. "Give us Neal and let the gaonbura go, and we'll leave."

The daruga shook his head. "Neal is in their custody. Unless they hand him over, I can't do anything. The gaonbura is under arrest for assaulting the Major - he has to come with me."

"That Major kicked the gaonbura. How can he be arrested for something he didn't do?" said Ai.

"I'll have to take their word for it," said the daruga. "Even if it's not what they say, I still have to take him in."

"Take Neal too, save him."

"He is their responsibility. My opinion doesn't count. I can't do anything about it."

"But you must," said Ai. "Otherwise they'll kill him."

The daruga shrugged his shoulders. Ai moved to the front of the crowd and squatted on the road with a determined expression on her face. Several villagers joined her.

"I'm warning you. It's against the law to block a public road," said the daruga.

"Do as we say or we won't move," said Ai. "Cane us, shoot us, we don't care."

"Don't you have family of your own? Don't you belong here?"

said one young man.

"Don't forget there's god," said another.

"Aren't you an Assamese? Traitor!"

"I'm ordering you to break it up this very moment," said the daruga.

More villagers moved forward in reply. A stone flew through the air. It missed everyone and landed in the bushes by the road. The daruga was left with no choice. He had to get the demonstration over before it got out of hand. Already news of it must have reached the neighbouring villages. Soon more people would arrive. The crowd would increase. Then, anything was possible. He gave the order.

The policemen raised their canes. The villagers realized there was going to be a baton charge. They shielded their heads with their hands. At a command from the daruga, the policemen waded into the crowd. Several villagers fled at the sight of the charging policemen. Those in front including Ai stayed firm. A policeman swung his cane at Ai. She ducked her head and it struck her on the shoulder sending a spasm of pain shooting up her injured hand. The second blow knocked her to the ground. She saw policemen hitting people left and right and kicking at those fallen. She tried to rise to her feet, but she couldn't move. Her head dropped and the shoulders sagged. When she tried to speak, her voice quavered and broke.

The baton charge stopped.

The people regrouped in the shade of the trees on the other side of the road. Ai sat on the ground quite unmoving, her strength gone, overcome by defeat and pain. Cries of people injured in the charge buzzed around her. Most had bruises of some sort on their bodies. A young woman - Ai couldn't recognize the face - wiped dirt and blood from her face. Another spat out a broken tooth. They used handkerchiefs to clean themselves. Someone brought a pail of water. Ai extended her palms for a drink. More people arrived in a hurry. They were updated by those present. Their voices merged in a hum which expressed little hope.

The policemen cleared the road. The gaonbura was pushed into the back of an Army Gypsy. The injured followed, trussed up like chickens for the market. A couple of policemen jumped in after them, their feet on top of those injured. The soldiers went back to their posts. The road emptied.

Ai saw the daruga coming toward them. His steps resounded over the asphalt. The next moment, he was standing beside her. For a second, his glance filled her with fear. She tried to rise to her feet, but her knees gave away.

"You're all fools doing things you know nothing about," said the daruga in a reproachful voice. "If that stone had struck one soldier, they'd have started firing, and all of you'd have been dead."

"Praise the lord," said one man in a furious voice. "We should be grateful for our broken bones and our bruises. At least we're alive."

"So we should thank you for beating us up," added one woman.

The daruga gave her a sharp glance. He said in a firm voice, "Let me handle this. Go home, now. Everyone."

Neal slept well into the morning, but it was an uneasy sleep. He still bled from his nose, and every few minutes he'd struggle for air and wake with a start. The pain in his body never eased. Every now and then, a spasm rose deep within him and brought tears to his eyes. He was grateful for the warm clothes he had on, but he still shivered from the cold, and his feet were numb and fingers swollen. Then the pain ceased like it was never there.

The door opened and two soldiers entered the room.

"Get up," said one. "Enough of your beauty sleep."

When Neal didn't budge, the soldier kicked him on the side. There was a grunt of pain and he made a sound like air escaping from a balloon.

"Bloody bugger," said the other, prodding him with his boot. "Think he is dead?"

"Who cares? Bring the motherchod outside. We'll put him in the shower."

They dragged Neal down the corridor. In the stink of the toilet, they placed him against the wall, straightened his head and opened the tap. The cold water stung and Neal opened his eyes. A thousand fires burned inside him, the flames rising till the heat became unbearable. The feeling was soon past and the fires went out, doused by the water, which set off a flood of agonizing sensations all over his body. They stopped after a minute, and then he couldn't feel a thing more. His head drooped and Neal crashed to the floor. He laid still, his mouth half in the drain and half out of it, water and air coming out of his mouth with an awful choking sound.

One of the soldiers leaned forward and closed the tap.

"Sick bastard." He spat on him.

"Behenchod, what do they eat? A few blows, a kick here, a kick there and they fall like dry leaves."

"They don't get enough to eat."

"But look at their spirit. They want to fight all the time."

Sometime later, the camp doctor went to report to the Major.

"Is he alive?" said the Major, a grimace on his face.

"He is breathing."

"He is alive."

"He is in a bad way," said the doctor. "He needs to be hospitalized."

"I can't allow it," said the Major.

The doctor looked at him, a confused look on his face. He held his gaze and nodded.

"Do what you can here. I want him alive for a few more days," said the Major.

The doctor gave Neal a few injections - what he could find in his bag - and took a blood sample.

A few hours later, the daruga faced the Major, a tired smile on his face. He told him what he had in mind.

"Not possible," the Major shook his head. "He is too valuable for me to let you've him. The next thing you know, he is out on bail planting bombs for my men to get killed."

The daruga persisted. So did the Major. The daruga argued. The Major argued back. The daruga went away. He came back the next day. Neal still hadn't woken up and the Army doctor had come back with a disturbing report. The daruga repeated his request. There had been a march to the police station, stones had been thrown and tires burnt on the road. A youth lost one eye after a scuffle with the baton-charging policemen. Too many returned home to the village with badly bruised limbs from the beatings. The situation was getting worse. The SP had called and wanted to know what was going on. There was still no report in any newspapers. The people were getting desperate. Members of the Sangathon were using the opportunity to organize a public protest. If they had their way, there would be a coterie of photographers waiting for the situation to get out of hand. There'd be more shot or injured, a house or two set on fire, the police Jeep in flames...

The Major raised his hand in a gesture of impatience. "All right, all right. You can have him. He is of no use to me. The bugger has viral encephalitis."

It was Rajen, the gaonbura's son, who brought Ai news of Neal's release. "Nobody has seen him, but several of our people have set up a vigil in front of the Army camp, and they think they saw the daruga leave with him."

"How is he?" said Ai. "Why hasn't he come home?"

The young boy looked about nervously. "He is in a bad way, Ai. The police have taken him to the big hospital in town. Everyone's saying he is dying."

Ai let out a cry, her mind full of anguished thoughts. They have beaten him, tortured him like he was always afraid they would. If only she could see him somehow, take care of him. There has to be a way. She threw a chador over her shoulders and rushed out of the house with Rajen. Several villagers, who had heard about Neal's release and came to inquire, followed the two. Ai walked rapidly, following the familiar path out of the village. "What if the daruga doesn't tell me where he is?" remained her constant needle of worry. She staggered up the steps to the daruga's room and stopped.

A constable barred her way.

"Do you know where my son is?" said Ai.

"He isn't here," he said in a stern voice.

"They released him today. I heard he is in a bad way. Please let me see him," said Ai.

The policeman opened his mouth to speak and stopped. Somehow the agony he and his fellow policemen inflicted on the villagers in the last few days pricked his conscience. When he spoke again, it was with more consideration than he was usually wont to give. "He is at the Civil Hospital in town. He has encephalitis. Daruga sir is with him."

"Do you how he is?"

The constable shrugged his shoulders. "He must be in a bad way. Otherwise why would the military bother releasing him to us?"

"Can't we see him?"

"When the daruga comes back he'll tell you when you can see him," said the constable. "Maybe he'll take you to see him."

Ai pleaded with him. "Please, can't we go on our own?"

This suggestion produced a chorus of approval from the accompanying villagers. They discussed the pros and cons of going to town on their own. But with the sun setting and the only bus to town leaving in the morning, there was little they could do except wait.

Evening fell. A full moon cast the earth in its light. The news of Neal's release had spread through the village, and more and more people came to visit Ai and inquire about him, only to return home disappointed when they found he was in hospital. It was late at night by the time everyone left. At midnight, Ai went to bed, but sleep eluded her. She tossed and turned in bed and looked expectantly in the direction of the door every time she heard a noise. She waited for someone to knock at the door and take her to Neal, tell her all is well. But no one came. Not a dog barked in the village. The sole fox came and went without a sound.

At dawn, Ai washed, said her prayers longer than usual, and made herself a strong cup of tea. Then she hurried to the police station. "No, the daruga hasn't come yet and he hasn't phoned either," the policemen told her. There was nothing they could do to help.

Ai did not know what to do, but some of the villagers had already discussed about such an eventuality the previous night. They decided to visit Neal on their own. Several hours later, two villagers who had been to town the most, escorted Ai and Rajen to the Civil Hospital at Burton Road, and past a clerk at the reception, who pointed out directions in exchange for ten rupees and a pack of bidis.

The ward for prisoners stood at the end of a dark corridor close to the toilets. A policeman stood guard behind a collapsible gate at the entrance. He bared a set of yellow teeth when Ai asked to be allowed in.

"Go back," he said, waving the baton in his hands. "No visitors allowed."

"Beat me. Put me here," Ai said to the policeman, and he stepped aside.

The ward was a large, well-ventilated room with two rows of beds. The windows were barred with an iron mesh and two policemen sat on a concrete bench outside. Ai moved past the first row of beds. Out of the corner of her eye, she saw Rajen rushing to a corner bed. She filed past the second row. There was still no sign of Neal. She noticed one patient cordoned off by a partition. She parted a curtain and gasped. In her surprise, she knocked over one of the screens. It fell on the floor sending a medicine cabinet and a smattering of enamel trays all over the room. Several of the patients started out of their sleep. A doctor in a white coat and a nurse rushed inside.

"How did she get in here?" said the doctor.

"What are you doing here?" the nurse demanded.

"Lucky the screen didn't fall on the patient."

"Wouldn't have made any difference."

Ai remained oblivious to their presence. She stood like a statue, her eyes on the wasted figure on the bed. With a cry she rushed forward and hugged the emaciated body. Neal was cold to touch, and when she held his hands, the fingers were lifeless and limp. His eyes were closed and sunk in their sockets. His cheeks had fallen in and the skin had a deadly pallor. One of his hands was cuffed to a bedpost.

"Neal, my son. What have they done to you?" said Ai, her eyes brimming with tears.

The doctor and the nurse slid into the narrow space between the beds. They checked their patient.

"How is he?" said Ai.

"Can't you see he is dying?" said the doctor, pointing at Neal's unconscious figure.

"Please, please, can't you save him?" Ai pleaded.

The doctor ignored her. He checked Neal's chest with his stethoscope. The nurse returned with the policeman at the gate. He held Ai by her arm and marched her out of the ward.

Rajen was waiting for her outside. He helped her to a bench in the waiting area and went to get a bottle of water. Ai held her head in her hands and wept. It was a common sight in a public hospital. There were sick and dead people everywhere. Almost everyone was in the grip of a horror in their lives. Nobody noticed her.

A thin figure appeared at the entrance. He glanced around, then slid into the seat beside her.

"Ai," said Hirok. "Neal is in a bad way. There is very little hope."

The day wore by. Then another, and yet another. The wait seemed never-ending, an endless trial of patience and perseverance. Ai had run against a wall that was too high for her to climb, too long to follow and find its end. No, she won't be allowed to visit Neal, see him for a few minutes, steal a glimpse, touch him, see life ebb out slowly, be there when it ends. No amount of argument, not even the most plaintive of pleas moved the policemen on guard. There wasn't a soul inside them, nor the slightest pity. Ai wouldn't give up. She scuttled in every three or four hours praying for a change of heart, but the policemen on guard would hear nothing of her requests and pushed her away every time:

"We told you not to come back."

"Why bother seeing him when he can't see you?"

"Go to a temple. Say some prayers. He's going to need them."

In the afternoon, Hirok and Phukan brought news of the two detained men. Neal's condition has shown no signs of improvement. The gaonbura was to be released from hospital in a day or two and shifted to the district jail. The two villagers suggested they return home now that there was very little they could do; after all, they had families to look after and fields to toil. Ai didn't say anything in reply, but sat staring into the distance. By evening, she was running a slight fever. She vomited, felt better, then worse.

The next morning, Ai walked slowly to the ward. Manav's words rang in her ears and there was a deep churning of conflicting emotions inside her. She wanted to stay for Neal, but knew she had no chance of seeing him, not even a glimmer of hope. Neal was dying and she could do nothing about it, not even be with him when the time came. As she approached the corridor, she noticed a commotion inside the ward: harried voices and hustling feet; doctors and nurses rushing past; even a crowd of hospital staff watching. Ai lowered her head and pushed through the crowd.

A policeman approached her. She hadn't seen him before or he her.

"Someone's in a bad way inside," he said.

"Do you think it's my son?" said Ai. "He is in the corner bed." When the policeman nodded, Ai pushed past him and he let her.

Neal lay on the bed, his nose flared, his body going into convulsions with every breath of air. A doctor sat on a stool by his side. He held Neal's free hand, checking his pulse and shaking his head. After a minute or so, he placed Neal's hand by his side. Ai wanted to interrupt and ask what was happening. The doctor turned to leave, a defeated look on his face. The nurse appeared to be doing everything within her power with the realization that it was not going to be enough. The policeman at the entrance hurried off and returned with two of his colleagues. One of them stopped the doctor on his way out.

The other filled out a form. There was a brief exchange of words by the door.

Ai was torn between her desire to stay by Neal's side and her wish to know what was happening. She ran after the doctor. He stopped when she called out to him.

"He's my son…" she said.

"I know," said the doctor. He paused for a moment. His face bore the expression of a man faced with an unpleasant task. "He's in a bad way. We've done all we could."

Ai nodded. "His arm…do you think he can run away when he can't even breathe?"

The doctor stopped. A brief apologetic nod of his head and he called a policeman over. "That dying man. Why is his hand still cuffed? How could he possibly escape now?"

The nurse came running out of the ward. "Doctor, please come back."

The doctor ran after her with short, quick steps. Those in the crowd gasped at the sight in front of them. Neal's neck was arched in agony. He opened his eyes and glanced around the room. They came to rest on Ai. He opened his mouth as if to say something and reached out with his hand. Ai stroked it, not daring to breathe. With a stiff movement, he threw back his head. There was a tired sigh, the body gave a shudder and the head fell over his shoulders. Ai sank to the floor, moaning in agony at the passing, her hands over her face. The two policemen outside watched with their faces pressed to the window. A couple of policemen bustled in followed by a nurse. There was a brief exchange of words. A new prisoner was on the way and they needed the bed. One of them moved towards the bed to remove the cuff on Neal's wrist. He fiddled with the lock for a few minutes. The other policeman elbowed him out for a try. Soon every policemen in the vicinity arrived to show the others how to unlock a handcuff. When the sweepers came to remove the body, they were sent away. The Inspector arrived an hour later demanding to be told why the dead man was still on the bed. A constable stepped forward to explain.

"The lock's jammed, sir," he said. "We can't free the body."

14

It took an entire day and more to free the dead man from his fetters.

The news of the death and the crisis of the jammed handcuff spread through the town. A crowd gathered outside the hospital gates demanding to be let in. Some carried large placards denouncing the government; others shouted slogans and swore at the policemen on duty. Not much later, a coterie of reporters forced their way in past the police barricades. They took photographs, interviewed the nurses and doctors and had their cameras confiscated at the gate. They left protesting against curbs on the freedom of the press. Several hours later, the hospital superintendent arrived. He glanced into the ward, whispered to the doctor on duty and disappeared.

The day passed. As the sun set and lights came on, the other patients in the ward grew uneasy. They exchanged glances and remembered their prayers. More and more people evaded the police in groups of twos and threes to see for themselves yet another example of police brutality. Those who came expecting the worst left with shocked expressions on their faces. There were whispers of a protest rally. A procession with the dead body. Even a general strike. Several human rights activists arrived. They asked questions, demanded to be shown the relevant papers. This, that. They took photographs and interviewed people - Ai, for instance. She wept through the entire interview, but nodded her head when Rajen recounted the events.

A convoy of siren-blaring cars arrived late in the evening. Heavy footsteps and loud voices rushed into the ward on shiny shoes. Afterwards, there was a hurried meeting in the corridor between several important looking people in stiffly-starched kurta-pajamas or safari-suits, and a policeman with a bodyguard, the Superintendent of Police. They ignored Ai on the floor, still waiting for Neal's body.

"Damn it," said the bureaucrat. "Just when things were getting under control this had to happen. Why can't these Army fellows be a little discreet?"

"We can't allow the body to rot here," said the local MLA. "It'll give these militants a rallying point and the opposition an issue. I can't have my constituency running all over me, not with the elections just months away."

"Fodder for the cows," said the SP, a grimace on his face. "The military - dumping their misdeeds on us."

"I heard the Amnesty people are already here," said the MLA.

"Not Amnesty," said the SP. "I checked. Some other organization - new one - too many nowadays. This is quite fertile ground."

"It's good business - death. People actually make a living out of keeping scores," said the bureaucrat. He wished he could finish this unpleasant business and hurry home. "I heard they're planning to call a bandh or a procession with the dead body."

"I've my men in place," said the SP. "I won't allow it. It will be business as usual tomorrow."

The MLA frowned. "Good, good. I don't want to be held responsible for any trouble when I return to Dispur." He paused. "I can't understand why you've to handcuff sick prisoners when there are guards everywhere. Now there will be questions asked…"

The SP shifted uncomfortably in his shoes. "We've everything under control. The body won't be here in the morning," he said. "I'll see to that."

The bureaucrat lit a cigarette and paced the corridor. Once

or twice, he glanced in Ai's direction. He stopped midstride and turned. When the two other men glanced at him, he smiled: "I found us someone to pin this on. It should make everyone happy - the press gets a scapegoat, the activists someone to vent their ire and the militants a target." He stopped and burst into laughter. "It should also keep the masses happy. It will send a signal that they are still heard." He called the men closer and explained.

A few feet away, Ai listened to the conversation with a heavy heart.

A mile down the road, Hirok and his friends grasped hot cups of tea and made plans for the morning.

In the village, a bus pulled up in front of the namghar. In the darkness of the night, a flurry of footsteps rushed out from inside. Young and old, men and women boarded the bus.

In town, a couple of policemen knocked down the door of a locksmith not far from the hospital. The man was woken up, sobered under a bucketful of water and led away. An hour later, he settled down on the floor beside Neal's body. He lit a packet of incense sticks to keep out the smell and the mosquitoes and stuck them here and there - in gaps on the floor, and a few in the nook between lifeless fingers. He spread his tools on the floor and set to work. After an hour, he gave up trying to pick the lock and readied his hacksaw. The frail looking blade made no impression on the steel cuffs. It snapped like a crisp wafer. A pile of broken blades built up on the floor. Every now and then, a policeman dropped in to check on the progress:

"Hurry up. We haven't got all night!"

"If you can't cut through, we'll make you saw through the hand."

"Have another peg! It'll give you strength."

An hour into the new day, the locksmith threw up his hands. "Find someone else. You can shoot me if you like."

The policemen discussed amongst themselves. There was little they could do except wake the Inspector. The youngest amongst the three was sent to report their predicament. He returned with his ears ringing with the Inspector's words: "You dumbass, cut the bedpost. Do I've to tell you everything?"

The locksmith who had gone out for a smoke was summoned back. Two hours later, the arm was freed from the bed, but the handcuff still dangled from the wrist. The doctor on duty was roused and the hospital superintendent alerted. He informed the SP, who asked for an immediate postmortem. The SP, aware of the possibility of a march with the dead body, and the MLA's concern at protests, barked off a list of instructions to his subordinate. The Inspector arrived to carry out the SP's instructions. The body was wheeled out for the postmortem examination. Two constables were sent to make arrangements for the cremation. Another was asked to hurry the paperwork along.

Dawn was still a couple of hours away.

Ai and her entourage slept pitifully that night, unaware of the developments. Not far away, Hirok and his men moved through the dark streets, avoiding the sleepy policemen manning the various checkpoints. Just out of town, the bus from the village was waved to a halt. The passengers were made to disembark and frisked. They were told to turn back. When they refused, they were caned. Men, women and children scattered like scared pigeons in the darkest hour of the night before dawn. The bus was seized and the driver arrested.

The postmortem was hurriedly completed. The paperwork already was.

In the early hours of the morning, in a deserted cremation ground by the Brahmaputra, a party of policemen and sweepers lit a kerosene-drenched, hurriedly-assembled pyre. When it was all over, the sweepers set to work. They ferried a few buckets of water from the river and doused the flames, then swept the area clean and piled fresh soil on the blackened earth.

The sun rose behind their backs in all its splendour. The party turned to leave. The Inspector stumbled. He looked down at the offending article at his feet. There was a smile on his face as he picked up a dark piece of twisted metal.

"It's come out," he said, holding up the handcuff.

As the sun shone against an azure sky, a crowd gathered at the gates of the hospital, which had been locked on the Superintendent's orders. They were incensed by the refusal of the gatekeeper to let anyone in. A buzz of voices rose in dissent. Those in front made critical remarks about the hospital authorities. Those with breakfasts for friends and relatives inside looked upset. Those waiting for the release of Neal's body talked of the injustice of the law. The gatekeeper shrugged from behind the iron grille and pointed at the policemen by his side, but they looked on nonchalantly and passed comments on the pleasant weather.

"Can't let you through," said the gatekeeper when Hirok moved forward and asked to be let in. "Nobody can unless they've a patient inside."

"You fool," said Hirok. "My brother is dead inside and I'm here to take his body."

Ai watched the exchange from the other side of the road. She saw a vocal group move forward and demand the body be handed over. A side-gate opened and some of the people with food and medicines were allowed inside. Those that weren't pushed against the gate and shouted slogans. A few of the men organized the crowd. Ai craned her neck and tried to see what was going on. She heard shouts and orders. As if on cue, a portion of the crowd raced forward and hurled themselves at the gate with all their strength. There was a screech and one of the hinges gave way. The policemen retreated a couple of steps. More of their colleagues arrived. They whispered amongst themselves and observed the onslaught with worried faces.

The crowd prepared for another push when a sharp voice rang out.

"STOP!"

Everyone turned towards the voice.

A short man squeezed out from behind the policemen. "What's all this? How dare you destroy public property?"

The crowd grew silent, but it was more from the surprise of the loud voice emanating from the puny body.

"Who are you?" said someone, recovering from the initial surprise. "We want to talk to the Superintendent."

The man nodded, full of self importance. "What do you want?"

A chorus of indignant voices rang out.

"Only those with patients inside can go in," said the Superintendent.

More voices shouted back in reply:

"We're here to claim a dead body. The one you chained to the bed even after his death."

"Hand over the body now."

"Yes, we want the body. We've to pay our respects."

The Superintendent raised his hand: "We haven't got a claim as yet."

Ai was carried to the front of the crowd. "I'm the mother," she said, watching the many curious eyes on her.

The Superintendent shook his head. "She is not the mother. Calling each other mother and son doesn't make them so."

"You bastard," someone swore at him.

Men and women rushed forward in anger. They shouted at the Superintendent, who sought shelter behind the police barricade. Ai was conveyed to the back of the crowd. Before her flashed anguished, agitated faces:

"Isn't it the god-given right of a man to have a proper funeral?"

"You killed him, you murdered a fine man. At least give us his body. Let us honour him."

"Look at their guilty faces, look at the criminals. They are the rascals and yet they yield all the power."

"Time they are taught a lesson."

Hirok's voice rose above the bedlam: "We demand the right to cremate our friend and my brother whom you tortured to death. We ask that the guilty be punished for their crime."

Loud voices rang out in support. Those in front shook the gate. Someone threw a brick. The policemen raised their shields above their heads. It sailed over the gate and landed in their midst. The crowd roared in approval. Men, women and children rushed around picking up what they could find. The shopkeepers in the vicinity downed shutters and locked their doors. The rickshaw pullers and the auto drivers fled. So did the roadside hawkers selling tea and clothes, and the barbers and masseurs.

The crowd grew at an astonishing rate as news of the protest spread. More and more people arrived every minute until they filled the street. Ai found herself backing up the steps of a shop. From her elevated position, she saw figures in khaki approaching from the rear. As they drew nearer, she saw them clearly - heads helmeted, one hand holding up a shield, the other clasping a stout cane. Those in the crowd noticed the policemen.

"Careful!"

"There are more of them at the back."

"More like them sneaking up on innocent people."

Ai was lost in a sea of people. She watched the faces in the crowd. There were few that appeared scared while some were thoughtful, but most expressed hatred. She tried to spot her son in the crowd, Rajen and the two villagers.

The policemen were almost upon them. They spread out and positioned themselves across the street. Fingers tightened on batons and shields, stones and rocks. Tense silence. Hostile faces.

A loud voice broke the stillness. The SI leading the posse said: "I order you to disperse. Now!"

Stifled murmurs rose to a crescendo in the crowd. Slogans rang out from somewhere in the middle. They mixed with expletives and obscene gestures from those in front facing the policemen. There was much pushing and shoving. People sought solace in each other's presence in collective bravado.

"I'm warning you," the SI's voice boomed over the people's heads.

Those near him shouted back:

"Give us the body."

"Beasts."

"Can't a dead man have the dignity of a proper funereal?"

At a command from the SI, several policemen kneeled on their knees. They loaded large canisters into big muzzled guns, aimed at the sky and fired. The shells flew through the air in arcs of white gas, landing in clouds of hissing smoke. People ran for cover. Cries rented the air as the tear-gas stung their eyes. Some covered their faces with handkerchiefs. Those in front charged with stones and sticks. The missiles crashed into the policemen's shields. At that moment, the SI gave the order. The policemen charged with their canes. The air was filled with the hurried shuffle of running feet. Dulls thuds of canes hitting flesh and bone. People falling, screaming in pain. Policemen standing over those fallen and letting loose a barrage of blows before advancing forward.

Ai crawled into a gap between two shops and covered her head with her hands. She heard a volley of boots scampering

189

past. Policemen chasing, people fleeing. Rough voices shouting commands, women crying, children wailing. Then, sound of gunshots. One, two. Several. More shouts. Screams. Ai raised her head. A mass of fallen bodies littered the road. A few were struggling to their feet. Some of the faces were bloodied. Most had the expression of being overcome by a force way beyond their imagination. Someone touched Ai on her shoulders. She turned and saw Rajen, disheveled, a cut below his eyes. Beside him was Hirok, his shirt torn and covered with blood.

"Let me go, it's nothing..." he mumbled, holding on to Rajen, his eyes closing.

"They shot him, Ai," said Rajen. He too was bleeding from his mouth. "A cut, nothing much, but they got him in the shoulders." He looked around to check if anybody was watching and whispered: "The people are getting together again. They're going to charge the SP's office. There are many injured. I must go and help them." He set down Hirok besides Ai and thrust a wad of soiled notes into her hands. "Take him away from here, away from the police. I found the money in his pockets. You'll need it. No use waiting here for Neal's body. They've already cremated him. That's why they refused to hand over the body to us. That part is over now."

"They removed every shred of evidence," said Hirok, opening his eyes. He held on to Rajen and rose to his feet. "That's not all. They beat up most of the people from the village last night. They were coming here in a bus to take away Neal's body. So many injured, didn't even spare the children."

Ai listened with a shocked expression on her face. Tears smouldered inside her like a spiteful volcano.

Rajen saw the policemen returning through a corner of his eyes. "They're coming. You must leave."

"They haven't seen us yet," said Hirok. He turned to the young boy. "I've an idea. How fast can you run?"

190

The few remaining people who came back to help the injured were scattering now, disappearing into gaps between houses. Rajen watched the policemen with a frightened expression on his face.

"Think you can do it?" said Hirok, placing a rock in his hands.

"Easily," said the boy.

"Go, now," said Hirok, and Rajen ran as fast he could.

He stopped a few metres in front of the policemen, took careful aim and sent the rock flying towards them. The policemen turned, got a glimpse of a small figure in gray and took off after him.

"Hurry," said Ai, helping Hirok to his feet.

"I'm all right, it doesn't hurt," he said, spitting out more blood. "The policeman hit me on my teeth. But I got him good, punched him on his stomach, beat him with his own cane. I...I don't know how I got shot..."

"Yes...yes, but let's hurry now." Ai was urging him on, leading him away from the policemen. She imagined they were hiding behind trees, and at street corners, waiting for them, leaping out to arrest the two. They stepped through a narrow lane and came out on a large road. Not a soul was in sight, not even a dog. A tire burned a few feet away from a litter of discarded sandals and shoes, rocks and debris. There was an emptiness in the air, a hurtful silence, broken only by the cries of birds on roofs.

Hirok's shirt was soaked in blood. With great difficulty, he staggered forward. "I'm all right, I can walk," he kept reassuring Ai, refusing every offer of her support.

Ai shook her head. "We'll rest," she said. She helped him to a seat in front of a deserted shop, its wares still on display. "Here, let me get you some water. You'll feel a lot better." She propped him against the wall and checked his wounds. He was still bleeding, but it was more of a gentle ooze. He suddenly slumped forward and was silent. Alarmed, Ai looked around for help. She ran down the road. Nowhere was a soul in sight. Not a sound broke the stillness except for the hiss of the bamboo barricades burning. Every shutter was closed, every door locked. Not even a pharmacy was open. Her heart pounded. She was scared now, scared for her son. There was the sound of wheels behind her. She turned in surprise.

"Don't you know there is a curfew in town?" said a familiar voice.

A faint smile creased Ai's face. "What are you doing here?" she said in a surprised voice.

"Looking for the two of you," said Phukan, jumping down from the rickshaw.

"Hurry," said Ai. "He's in a bad way. We've to get him to a doctor."

Ai hovered between sleep and waking. The events of the last few days flashed before her like a portent of things to come. Random images filled her mind: Neal's hollow face as he gasped for air with his last breath; the stricken villagers coming to take Neal home; the policemen beating up those protesting Neal's death. She saw everything clearly now. The day's events appeared perfectly rational to her. Every blow, every shot was a pitfall on the rough path to a glorious outcome. In spite of everything, she was at peace, and a gentle light flooded her soul, making her feel wanted and useful. She was no longer the woman so full of fears and alarms for her son. That woman no longer existed. She had gone somewhere far away, consumed by the fire of her emotions, which had purged her spirit, charging it with new strength.

Ai heard urgent voices and opened her eyes. For a moment

she wondered where she was. The room was dark and she lay on a couch not far from a large window. Photographs adorned the walls - tattered, framed occasions that once meant something, but now, didn't matter. Above her, Gandhi gazed out from behind a thick layer of cobwebs surrounded by portraits of gods and goddesses, their palms raised in muted blessings. Then it all came back to her. The rickshaw had come to a halt in front of a door at the end of an alley. An old wizened head held a door open as Phukan carried Manav inside. No words were spoken, but there was an exchange of nods. "The doctor," Phukan had whispered to her. They followed him through a labyrinth of corridors, past this very room, and into a larger one. On an elongated metal table, under a light that hung from the ceiling, they placed her unconscious son. The doctor went to work, cutting away his shirt to reveal his injuries. There was a big bruise on his back and a cut on the side made with a blunt object; a tear in the shoulders where the bullet had gone in. Everything covered in a layer of caked blood...

The doctor and Phukan were talking.

"The bullet is out, but he has lost a lot of blood," said the doctor. "We need to get him to a hospital."

"No, we can't," said Phukan. "Not when he has a gunshot injury."

"I know people who can manage it for us. It'll need money."

"Money is no problem, but you've to take care of him here. He is a marked man and they'll be watching out for him. Give him a few days. He is a tough village lad, he'll be all right."

The doctor furrowed his forehead, but nodded. "It's a terrible risk."

Ai turned and saw Rajen. He came over when he saw she was awake.

"Things are really bad outside, Ai," he said in an awestruck voice. "I saw this group of people - goondas, and they are using this opportunity to settle scores with the police. There were two policemen waiting in their Jeep. The goondas came from behind and thrashed them, set fire to the Jeep. When the other policemen returned and saw what happened, they went on a rampage. They came upon this group of peaceful protestors - they were sitting on the road, blocking the traffic - the policemen didn't even give them a warning. They beat the group to pulp. When the people started running, they fired. I saw two of them fall, shot in their backs."

"That is no way to treat people," said Ai, overcome with pity. "So much suffering, livelihoods ruined, people beaten and tortured, killed like animals…"

Rajen watched her with an expression of anguish. "Ai, when will it all end, when will we've what is ours? When will they release father…" He stopped. "I shouldn't be so selfish when so many people are getting killed every day. We are all one and shouldn't draw apart, not at this time."

Ai realized the boy had grown into a man in the few days he had been away from home. There was a newly discovered maturity that shone through him.

The door burst open and Phukan, who had gone out, came back with the news that the police were making arrests. "But they can't possibly find us here," he said.

The doctor poked a head into the room and smiled. "Your son, he has come to. You can see him now."

When Ai looked out of the window the next morning, the sun was a demure sentinel in a bland sky. From what few inches she saw of the road outside, it was empty and forsaken. Wearied by the events of the previous day, most people slept late or stayed inside the safety of their homes.

Rajen ventured out after breakfast and returned with disturbing news. "I heard the government has been dismissed.

The Army is in charge. They are everywhere."

"Everywhere?" said the doctor.

"Well," Rajen hesitated. "I saw a couple of them."

Phukan, who had been sleeping, let off a yawn. "Who told you all that? Our information is that it isn't due for another month."

"Everyone's talking about it, even the police," said Rajen. "A Jeep-load of them came looking for someone a mile down the road - didn't find him, of course. So they arrested someone else in his place."

"The poor man," said Ai, shaking her head. She sighed, but without grief, and this amazed her. She realized she was becoming like the others, immune to pain and suffering and everyday loss.

"He belonged to the gang that killed a policeman yesterday at Graham Bazaar," said Rajen.

"A goonda," said Phukan. "They give our cause a bad name - opportunists, the worst kind. He will be dead by the time they are through with him. The police only want someone to vent their anger. It doesn't matter who."

"The real culprits always get away," said the doctor without looking up from his newspaper. "No mention here of President's rule."

Ai's face fell. "But he's innocent."

"Who cares," said Phukan. "Like I said, the police are happy to have someone in their net. The goonda - he's one because he doesn't give a damn who else suffers for him as long as he's free."

Ai nodded. She found Phukan strangely fidgety today. He was simpler and happier in the face of much adversity. There was much strength and purpose in his thought and work. The sudden development appeared to have pushed him to the edge and there was a grim expression on his face.

"Do you think they'll come here?" said Rajen.

"Let them try and arrest me," said Phukan. "They'll find themselves in the land of their forefathers." He produced a gun from behind his back.

Ai gasped. Rajen watched fascinated. The doctor kept reading the newspaper and appeared not to hear their talk. Now and then, he would put the newspaper aside and leave the room to check on Hirok. Time passed. Everyone in that house in the midst of so many houses rested.

A few miles away, a few hours later, a driver started the engine of his bus. It was cramped with people from the surrounding villages: vegetable vendors, traders, office-goers, those who had come to visit friends or relatives in hospital, all caught in the events of the day before, now eager to leave town. There was excited chatter about what happened, how many were injured and killed, and how many injured and killed the authorities were admitting. They soon settled down. A few of them chatted with their neighbours. Others adopted a meditative look closing their eyes to the din. The journey started with much relief and happiness. Tired faces glowed with the anticipation of going home. They watched a ghost town from the windows, glad to be leaving its confines, but wary still of the shimmering tension in the villages now that the protests had spread throughout the state. There were policemen everywhere, even a few soldiers. Just out of town, the bus was stopped at an Army checkpoint. The soldiers boarded the bus. They made everyone get down and kneel on the ground - men, women and children in a chastised line of bowed bodies by the road. They tore open the bags and poked through the contents with their guns - clothing for children and medicines for the old, toys and condiments, this, that - before sending them on their way.

The bus continued its journey. More checkpoints, more prodding gun barrels. It stopped every now and then in front of a familiar road leading to a village to let down a few relieved passengers. They all felt like coming to a place that was no longer theirs. The fields were deserted. The crop stood lonely and forlorn. No one seemed to be working. The children were confined to their homes by worried parents. Fewer people were about, and the shanty shops in the chowks were closed and shuttered.

Everywhere it was the same. People were silent and suffering.

The sun set. Evening fell. The electricity was cut. Lamps flickered and glowed through gaps in the windows. In Dikhowpar, electricity remained a figment of the imagination, a mass of dangling wires from tall concrete poles that brought little cheer to the people. The phone rang at the police outpost. Its shrill ring echoed through the pensive surroundings. A constable picked up the phone. He listened to the terse voice, put down the receiver and went to call the daruga.

The daruga was sitting down to an early dinner. A minute later, the daruga was running to take the call, spitting food from his mouth and wiping lentils from the ends of his moustache. The SP rarely called, and if he did, it had to be something important. He picked up the phone with trembling hands and held it for a moment in silent prayer before placing it over his ears. Like the constable before him, he listened stiffly, only longer. His expression underwent a remarkable transformation. Not a single word escaped the daruga's lips except for a whispered 'Yes, sir' at the end. He returned the phone to its cradle and remained lost in thought for some time. Then coming to a decision, he hurried to his quarters. He had a brief conversation with his wife. He left her in tears to talk to Nina.

"Something came up," he said, struggling to explain what was causing him considerable confusion. "I'm under investigation for Neal's death. I've been suspended with immediate effect. You've to leave."

15

In town, in that house in the midst of a maze of alleys, time stood still. Ai paced its confines or stopped at the window to check out the deserted road. Sometimes she rested on the couch drifting through a myriad of thoughts and worrying about her son, who passed the agony of his pain in the solace of slumber, interrupted by short periods of agonizing wakefulness. Rajen idled around with the restless energy of a boy his age. He followed Phukan everywhere. Every now and then, he watched him check his gun and take potshots at imaginary policemen.

It was during such a moment, three days later, that they heard a knock on the door. Ai sat up in the couch. The doctor poked his head out from the examination room. Rajen glanced up from the book he was reading. Everyone had a worried look on their faces. Everyone looked at Phukan.

"Open it," said Phukan to Rajen, quite unperturbed. "If it's the police, all of you pretend you were threatened by me to take care of Hirok."

Ai rose from her seat. Such visits no longer distressed her - she had no premonition of danger. She opened the door. Their visitor was a little boy. He looked around the room and came over to Phukan.

"The police," he said. "They're coming here. You must leave now."

The suddenness of the announcement froze everyone. For sometime nobody moved. They looked fearfully at the boy, who glanced around with scared eyes.

Phukan broke the silence. "Who told you?"

The boy fished out a letter from his pockets. "He said to burn it," he said, his eyes on Phukan, not convinced he would. Turning on his heels, he ran out of the door.

Ai bolted the door after him. "What are we to do now?" she said.

Phukan read the slip, tore it into pieces and put them in his mouth. He turned to the doctor. "Hirok - can we move him?" When the doctor shook his head, he said, "But we have to. If they get hold of him, he is done for."

Someone pressed against the door rattling the latch. Muffled voices. A boy crying.

"They're already here," said Phukan.

"Don't open the door. Quick," Ai said to Phukan, "place the table against the door. If it's the police it will hold them for a while."

"It's too late," he said, a defeated expression on his face. He sat down on the sofa.

The others turned towards him in astonishment. There was a loud rap on the door. A voice shouted "Open up, now," followed by more pounding on the door.

The doctor withdrew into the examination room. There was the sound of a latch sliding into place. The banging on the door grew louder, the voices harsher. It shook as if in the grip of a beast. Phukan shrank further into the sofa. A splinter of wood flew into the room. Ai grabbed Rajen and pulled him behind her.

The door burst open. Six or seven policemen entered the room in a surge of khaki. A timid Phukan was overpowered and disarmed. His hands were cuffed behind his back. Ai and Rajen were marched to a corner of the room and told not to move. The policemen searched the house. They broke open the almirah and rummaged through the papers, throwing most of it on the floor. One of them noticed the door leading to the examination room. They tried to open it. Finding it locked from inside, they showered a volley of blows with their guns and feet.

Ai watched with an anguished expression on her face. Rajen gripped her hand. Phukan presented an impassive face when the officer questioned him.

"Who is inside?" he said to Phukan. When he didn't reply, he struck Phukan on the face.

Ai found the sight of an armed man beating someone with his hands bound behind his back revolting. But it was not as frightening now as it was before. With time, her hatred for these uniformed men had grown, and the hatred consumed her fears. The door shattered under the onslaught. One final kick and it hung by its hinges like a lifeless body at the end of a rope. The policemen rushed inside in a torrent of cries. Ai held her breath. Phukan watched with muted glimmer in his eyes. The officer had a triumphant expression on his face as his men emerged a minute later with the doctor.

"There is no one else," a policeman stepped forward to report.

It started to rain and the raindrops pattered against the window. Inside the cell, it grew dark and cold. Ai sat in a corner, mulling over the events of the day. Where was Manav? How had he escaped? How did they know they were there? And Phukan - why was he acting so strangely? A smile broke over her face when she recalled the bewildered expressions on the policemen's faces. "How could he escape when we've the house surrounded and the road blocked?" she heard them whispering amongst themselves. They were herded them out of the house and led to a police van. Everywhere she saw traces of their violence: broken doors and smashed window panes; shoeprints on doors; scared faces watching without a word. The street was lined by a wall of faceless people in a shroud of khaki. They were hustled into the back of the van and brought to this brick-red building and separated. She was pushed into the cell and the door locked.

It soon grew dark. A bulb came to life in a corner. It cast a long shadow of Ai on the floor. Once or twice she heard footsteps moving down the corridor. Her eyes closed and she dozed off. Gray figures with thick arms and masked faces were doing the rounds of the building waiting for their turn to torture her. She heard cries from the cells around her - animal cries full of pain and suffering. She tried to run away, hiding from her captors in the shadows of tall buildings in a town bereft of people. It was night, and she was on the road again, looking for her son in a house without a front door. She stumbled and fell. Two people rushed out to help - Rajen and the good doctor. But Phukan? What had they done to him? What are they going to do to her? They'd be coming for her soon as soon as they were done with the others...

The door opened with a screech. A tall policeman entered followed by a constable. He looked down at Ai from his enormous height and gestured at the startled mother.

"On the floor," he said, pointing with his fingers.

Ai obeyed, recoiling when bare skin touched the cold concrete. She took a deep breath to calm herself before looking up.

The policeman sat down on the stool and crossed his legs, the tip of his boots pointing at Ai. He took a file from the constable and shifted through the pages. "I'm told your husband was a Gandhian," he said, "that you've a portrait of the father of the nation in your home."

Ai nodded. "Until the soldiers burned it with my house."

The policeman shook his head. "Sad, sad, but you can't blame them after what went on in that house right under the man's nose."

"I saw a portrait of Gandhi at the entrance of this building," said Ai. "I'm told there are portraits of Gandhi everywhere, most government offices. Do you think they do very pious work? At least in my house, I cleaned the portrait every day."

"Oh, we owe him this country and that makes it our duty to honour him even if we sometimes forget to dust his picture. That doesn't make us worse than you and your son," said the policeman. "Pity your son doesn't realize what a great man his father was, how much he sacrificed for his county."

"My son has enough sense. It is the government which abuses its power."

"Aha, so sedition is sensible. What of all the killings, the threats, the kidnappings? Your people have ruined this land, turned its green valleys red."

"You should tell the soldiers that, the beasts they are. The police are no different. They don't even spare children."

"Pity you are old and a woman at that."

"Oh, don't pity me! I've seen how much sympathy your canes have for people of my age."

"Enough! So where is Hirok, where have you hidden him, where has that coward run?"

"I've no son by that name."

"Well, whatever you call him. Manav, freedom-fighter, revolutionary, motherchod."

"I haven't seen my son for a long time. Please let me know when you find him."

The policeman flung the file at Ai. "We know he was in that house, we know you've been with him every inch of his wicked ways, and yet you pretend you haven't seen your good-for-nothing son? Do you think he'll get far with that bullet injury? I heard he lost a lot of blood. Now with the police looking for him, he can't be doing too well. What if the soldiers get him first?"

"God is with him."

"God was with that other fellow as well. But he still ended

up dead and such a pitiable death too."

Ai kept her eyes on the tip of his shoes. For some reason, its dull shine fascinated her.

"The good doctor has been very cooperative," continued the policeman. "And the boy, he can talk, I can tell you that - can't stop once he gets started. Only that young man, he won't open his mouth. He is a bit stubborn, but once we are through with him, he'll be singing like a bird."

Ai's shoulders dropped and a sigh escaped her lips. Her mouth opened as if to say something, then stopped.

"Yes, yes, go on," said the policeman "Don't be afraid."

"Nothing," said Ai. "Only...aren't you afraid that one day you might have to answer for your actions, that the very god you are laughing at now sees everything?"

The policeman burst into laughter. "An old witch's curse from an accursed bitch like you - it won't affect us in the least." With a laugh he lumbered out. The door was locked and the light switched off.

Ai shrank to the floor. She sat with her head between her hands, her heart pounding with grief and the painful consciousness of her helplessness. She was haunted by the thought of Rajen carried off by a group of armed men and Phukan screaming in agony at the pain inflicted by his captors. Within her heart gathered a cloud of bitterness for the people who had meted out so much pain and injustice. An utter weariness gripped her soul. Throwing back her head, she gave a long, low cry into which she poured all the pain of her heart.

In a comfortably furnished room a few meters away from Ai, the Superintendent of Police sat observing the young man in front of him. Above his head, a fan dangled from a hook in the ceiling and its slow movements ruffled the few hairs on his head. Behind him, Gandhi observed from his perch on the wall, masked by the glare of a fluorescent tube. An orderly sat by the door while a couple of policemen stood guard outside with bored expressions on their faces.

"They won't talk," said the SP, scratching his bald pate. "That boy, he has quite a spirit, but he is wasting his energy for a lost cause. You know that better than me."

The young man nodded, a wry smile on his face. "He has seen a lot in the last few days and it has hardened him, made a man out of a boy. But he'll break and so will that old bastard, sir. They will spill out all you want to know."

The SP laughed. "We wish we could break a few bones, cut them up a bit, but we made a very public arrest, so we must keep them in good shape. The human rights activists are already asking about them. They are more worried about you though." He paused. "If you had done your work, I wouldn't have to worry about such things."

The man lowered his gaze. The smile on his face vanished. "I don't know how he did it, sir. He was too weak to move. I checked in the morning. He barely recognized me."

The SP drummed his fingers on the desk. "I had such high hopes. This would have shown the Army people that we're most capable of doing our job. I feel let down again. First the bomb blast, now this. How many more blunders do I've to bear?"

The man shifted in his seat. "You know how the Sangathon operates. Most times the right hand doesn't know what the left is doing. I didn't have any inkling about the second bomb. Barman doesn't tell me anything."

"Of course, he doesn't," said the SP, "which means he is doing a good job of manipulating whoever he likes. I'm surprised that after spending so much time with him you'd have learned something useful."

"They're clever, sir," said the man. "They'll go to any lengths to keep their secrecy." He paused. "This won't happen again, sir."

The SP nodded. "Better not. I cannot lose more face with the military waiting for every opportunity to tell us how to do our job." He rang the bell. "Time you leave. We'll arrange for your release in a week or two. In the meantime, enjoy your rest."

The tall policeman returned in the morning. Again with the same questions put in his admonishing manner and stories of the doctor's fading health and Rajen's blistered back. Ai kept her eyes on the floor and ignored him. She was half-afraid he would strike her, but he clenched his fist and left muttering to himself.

The rest of the day passed in a fog of vague remembrances, interrupted by the entry of an orderly with a plate of stale food. Ai wandered about the cell, and when her feet ached, she sat down by the skylight and watched the colours of the changing sky: blue and starkly fresh in the morning, a tired azure after noon and a gloomy gray with the approaching evening. She was exhausted from her confinement and longed for the open spaces of her village. Her lips were cracked and her mouth was dry. Hunger gnawed at her stomach. Her hands trembled and chills ran up her body. Once or twice, she drank water from a pitcher, which tasted bitter and quenched neither thirst nor quelled her hunger. She tried to gather her thoughts, but all she felt was a dreary, depthless void, which grabbed at her and tried to pull her in.

Evening brought with it a visitor.

A woman entered the cell followed by a policeman. Ai heard the gentle shuffle of her sari and looked up in surprise. The woman introduced herself. She sat down on the floor by Ai's side, took out a sheaf of papers from a bag and explained. She told Ai about her 'rights' being violated, how nobody could keep her confined without a 'trial.' Bits and pieces about 'charges' that she couldn't make any sense off, and newspaper reports about their 'illegal' confinement creating a hullabaloo outside.

Ai was pleased with what she heard. "Well, I've never heard anything like this before. I never knew we've any of these 'rights.'" But she was more concerned about the others. "How is Rajen? And the doctor? Phukan? The policeman was telling me the doctor is sick and the boy hurt."

"The boy is fine. I met him before coming here," said the woman, her eyes seeking out Ai's to reassure her. "No bruises anywhere on his body or he'd have told me. The doctor is sick, something to do with his heart - an old condition. We're getting someone to take a look at him. Phukan has been sent to jail. Good for him, it will spare him a lot of pain. He is a wanted man and it will be difficult to get him out."

Ai was silent for a while. She wondered if this kind woman would know anything about Manav.

"I've been to the house, if you can still call it a house," she said, darting a glance at the policeman. "There is no one there except for a guard. It has been ransacked and turned upside down. Maybe they expect your son to come back."

Ai stared at the woman. She held her hands and kissed them. If only she could talk properly with this nice woman who knew so much. She understood her being so discreet with a policeman inside the cell in a police station teeming with men looking for a hint to her son.

The policeman tapped the floor with his cane and pointed at his watch.

The woman glared at him, but nodded all the same. "They think they can do what they like, but it's time they are taught a lesson or two," she said, rising to leave.

Just before dawn, the bulb in the cell flickered to life. The door opened and two policemen rushed inside. They shook Ai awake by her shoulders.

"Get up," they shouted, startling her out of her sleep.

For a moment, Ai couldn't bring her mind to focus and wondered what was happening. The light from the bulb stung her eyes. She peered at the policemen through half-closed eyes. They grabbed her arms and marched her outside through a dimly lit corridor. Outside, it was still dark. The road was deserted save for the huddled shapes of people sleeping on the pavement. An engine was running somewhere. Ai was marshaled towards the sound, her feet moving in tandem to match the two policemen's rapid strides. Somebody held a door open and she was pushed inside. Her gaze fell on Rajen.

"What's happening?" she said.

The young boy gave her a scared look. "They're taking us somewhere. Do you think they are going to shoot us?"

She held his hands. "Don't worry. They wouldn't dare. Besides, we are not important enough to be tortured or shot."

"Are we going to jail then?" said Rajen, after a moment's pause.

"Without seeing a judge? I doubt it," said Ai. She patted his hands. "We'll soon find out."

The door in front opened and a man slid into the driver's seat. He nodded at the two and started the van. A minute later they were on the way.

Rajen turned to Ai: "Why isn't there a guard?"

She shook her head. "I don't think they are going to shoot us, that's why. Maybe they're going to take us somewhere else."

"Without a guard?"

"I'm an old woman," said Ai, smiling at Rajen. "And you are just a boy."

They drove for a long time, a constant whir of wheels over bumpy roads. Ahead of them, the sky changed from a deep shade of gray to a light crimson, then a bright orange. More and more people appeared on the road, walking or cycling to work: farmers with plows balanced on their shoulders, vendors with vegetables, milkmen with vats of milk dangling from their cycles, fishermen with jakois hanging from their hips.

People were rising to another day.

They sped across the road at a fast pace.

Ai began to recognize the sights: the bridge on the Dikhow, the Deopani namghar, the road leading to the maidams; then, the shops beneath the cluster of trees at the crossroad; behind them, the vigorous green of lush fields. A familiar face or two.

The van came to a halt in a cloud of dust. The driver jumped down. He came to the back and opened the door.

"You're home," he said. "You're free to go."

16

Magh approached. In the village, it was quiet for a change. The days passed in a whir of foggy mornings and murky evenings. The fields took on a golden hue, and a brisk wind chilled the air. Elsewhere in the state trouble brewed like a crooked crone's broth. Bombs burst with frightening regularity and people were killed like rats in traps. In a time of plenty, the odd ripple of laughter echoed through a village as it reaped the fruits of a season of hard work. There was the odd bit of news about Hirok, and occasional whispers and hurriedly flung words of well-being. Then one morning, Nina appeared at the front door like an apparition, a smile on her face, but Hirok never came nor sent a message.

At night, Ai lay in bed worn out by the bustle of the day, a dull ache in her heart as the darkness clawed at her. During the day, she stood by the window, her arms crossed, gazing out without seeing. She watched the path leading out of the village for hours on end and could barely breathe from the anguish in her heart. On and on she stood until her feet ached or someone called.

Not far away, the grocer squatted in the undergrowth by the swamp and pondered his fate. His business had taken a beating after the villagers got together and started their own store close to the namghar. In a village coming to terms with a season of devastation, he prowled looking for an opportunity to avenge himself. A few nights before uruka, the day of the feast to celebrate the harvest, as the pithas baked in iron pans and their sweet smell wafted through the air, he got the first whiff.

It was a cold night and a mist hung about the village like a sinister cloak through which trees and houses sprouted like evil designs. Half drunk with a bottle of laopani inside him, he sat on his haunches outside Ai's hut scratching an itchy leg. His stupor was broken by voices drifting to his ears. He stood up with a start. He moved forward, jumping from the shadow of one tree to another till, like before, he was in a familiar part outside the verandah. Ai and Nina sat on the bed, their backs to the window. A lamp flickered in the breeze by their side and pushed slivers of light at the night through gaps in the wall.

"The government has given safe passage to everyone in the Sangathon to come home for Bihu," Nina was saying. "Now Hirok can safely visit us."

Ai shook her head in the way of those who had little faith in hope. "I don't trust the government - they're always quick to make promises. It's just a ruse to get everyone home and then arrest them. It makes their job easier instead of looking for them all over."

Nina chuckled. "No, they can't do something like that, not after making a public announcement. I wouldn't have come otherwise."

Ai wanted to ask her where she had been all this time, but decided not to. She was glad she was there and she was happy for it, but she missed her son, missed the mere assurance of having him around. Could Nina know and not tell her?

"How'll we find out if they break their word?" she said.

"They wouldn't dare. Don't you understand, Ai?" said Nina. "The public is the judge and executioner here. On one side is us and on the other side is the government. It's like a balance - if they break their word, the people come over to our side. If they don't, the people will believe the government is sincere. Everyone stands to gain."

Ai nodded. It was as if she was starting to gain perspective on a problem she'd looked at purely from a personal angle. "So it's a matter of faith."

"No," Nina laughed. "It's more like the politics of faith. With elections not far off, the government has to show to the public it's doing everything possible for peace. Isn't that what everybody is fighting for?"

"So peace is like the football," said Ai. "It gets kicked around by everyone, but only one team can score a goal."

Nina smiled. "Now you understand. Think of it as a game. It's a game everyone plays - the police, the soldiers, the government, us. Everyone knows about the players in the other team, their weakness, their strengths. Everyone knows what the other is doing. Everyone is playing catch up."

"But it's a game that takes lives, causes so much pain, such loss," said Ai.

"It's a game played without mercy," said Nina. "Nobody gives a finger's width. Everybody plays to win." She was silent for a while. "And lives - death is life's shadow. Where would we be without either?"

The grocer listened with interest as Ai and Nina exchanged news - a death here and a wedding there, just like the fox behind him perked its ears to his shallow breathing. There was the odd snippet about Ai's plans to attend a wedding in a nearby village the next day, and her bitter plaints about a son who had lost his way home. When Nina leaned sideways and blew out the lamp, the grocer left. He took the path out of the village, a ghostly figure swimming through a sea of white smoke.

A few minutes past the midnight hour, the grocer burst into the police station. The constable on duty sat with a glazed look in his eyes, a bottle of liquor by his side. He frowned at the interruption of his late night drink. Somehow his loneliness found favour with the grocer's isolation and culminated in both of them finishing off the entire bottle. Dawn found them in the presence of the new daruga, his loud voice booming through the outpost as he towered over the two and demanded an explanation.

The grocer flinched at a pounding headache and stammered his story. The daruga shook his head, a look of disbelief on his face.

"You're still drunk," he said.

"No, I'm not," said the grocer. "I saw her with my own two eyes."

"I've heard about the power of your eyes. I've seen the damage they had done."

"You must take my word."

"Your word has no meaning now," said the daruga. "I can't risk trusting you, not after all the trouble you caused. One more dead or missing, any more arrests and I'll have a riot in my hands."

"But...," the grocer started to protest.

The daruga shrugged his shoulders. "Doesn't matter anyhow, we can't do a thing now."

The grocer let out a sigh of exasperation. "Why?"

"You've heard about the safe passage to militants to visit their families for Bihu, no? We can't do anything as long as the offer stands. Not to forget the elections, which are not far off."

The grocer glared at him. "So that's it. You let a criminal and an extremist run wild planting bombs while you sit and allow it because of a few measly votes."

The daruga glared at him. He lit a cigarette and turned the information over in his mind. He came to a decision. The Army was in charge of counter insurgency operations in the area. They don't have to follow rules set by the babus at Dispur. He'd pass on the information, leave it to them to decide. If they arrest the girl, he'd have all the credit; if they choose to sit on it, they can take all the blame.

Several hours later, Ai was passing on final instructions to Nina about the fresh batch of baking she must do for the guests she expected for Bihu. "Don't forget the coconut scrapings," she said, folding a cardigan into a jute bag. "They must be fried just right or they'll burn."

Nina patted her hands. "I'll take care of everything. You just have a good time."

Ai was soon on her way to the neighbouring village, the setting sun in front of her. It was a three mile walk, but she had company for the journey, and expected to be back by nine.

Not far away, the grocer struggled past a meal of rice and lentils. He'd trundled home weary with the lack of sleep and burning with his humiliation at the hands of the Major. His words rang in his ears. "I don't have time to be judge or jury," the Major had barked at the daruga. "There has been enough nonsense, too much time wasted for nothing. Peace is not my call nor is elections." He pointed to an imaginary scrap of paper in his hands. "You see the names here. Well, that's all that matters. The day I cross out each and every name in this list, I can leave this god-forsaken land for ever and not have to deal with double-crossing swine like him ever again." This with a severe look in the grocer's direction.

The grocer pushed away his food.

His wife hurried to his side, a worried look on her face. "Is something wrong with the food? Is there too much salt?"

The grocer ignored her. He stood in front of the mirror, a small broken piece of the full-length one he once had. He rubbed the thick stubble on his face and stared at the deep set eyes riding the sneer on his face. He turned away in disgust, seething with anger. So this had come of his devotion to the country, his service for its unity. After all the risks he took, the beatings he endured, he'd become a joke, and a useless vagabond of the struggle, despised by his community and deserted by the very people he served. He looked at his watch. He wasn't very sure about the time, but there wasn't a moment to lose. Ai's house was only three furlongs away and if he took the shortcut through the forest he could be there in ten minutes. He slipped on his sandals - the only good ones he had left - and hurried out.

Ahead of him, ten minutes away, a group of men crept forward, hiding behind the bushes that lined the path, their faces painted, eyes scanning the forest in front of them. They stopped when they heard footsteps. Their leader signaled to one of the men. Swiftly, on silent feet, he approached the thin, unsteady figure. The grocer never heard a sound as strong hands grabbed him from behind. He'd even less time to feel any pain as the man slit his throat with the knife in his hand.

As the moon slid behind the clouds the men moved into position. They watched the fire burn in the hearth in the kitchen. Hunched in front of it, surrounded by a smattering of pots and pans, squatted Nina. Her hands moved rapidly as nimble fingers laid out a wafer-thin layer of ground wheat on a hot pan. When it warmed up in a sticky sheet, she placed a filling of sweetened coconut shavings, folding it with a wooden batter and tapping it a couple of times before putting it away.

The wind picked up the aroma of the freshly-baked pithas carrying it to the men hiding behind the trees. The neighbour's dog, attracted by the smell, slipped through a gap in the fence. It stopped at the sight of the men creeping forward. There was the sound of a bird calling out, which rippled through the surroundings. The men broke cover and ran towards the house. The front door was kicked open and the soldiers rushed inside, pointing guns and scrambling feet hurrying from one room to another. Nina was overpowered. A gag was forced into her mouth, and her hands tied behind her back. The soldiers searched the house and ransacked the furniture, kicking out at the dog, which followed them, barking all the while. A soldier grabbed it by its tail, pinned it to the ground, and ran a knife through its throat.

Nina was dragged by her hair and brought before the Major, who lit a cigarette and sat on what remained of the chair. He took a long look at her before barking off a number of questions in broken Assamese.

The terrified girl, scared out of her mind at the sight of the armed men, trembled with fear. Deep down she realized her end was near. The soldiers had come without any policemen. They were not there to make an arrest. Somebody had been spying on her, and she'd been found out.

The Major waited impatiently for an answer. "What is your name?" he repeated for the umpteenth time.

Nina kept her gaze on the floor. A soldier stepped forward and struck her across the face. The blow sent her sprawling across the room. When she struggled to her feet, he hit her again, and again. She closed her eyes and prayed for a painless death.

The Major observed her moving lips and closed eyes with increasing irritation. Her silence was taken as defiance, another example of the obdurate locals waging their stupid struggle for freedom. He didn't waste any time pondering over her. He nodded to his men waiting for his signal. They grabbed her by her arms and marched her out. They left the house in disarray and the front door open. Then a gust of wind came in and blew out the lamp, leaving the house in darkness.

They took Nina to the Dikhow. In the grassy slopes of its banks, the soldiers tore into her like beasts. They raped and ravished her and, when they were done, one of the men put a bullet in her head. Two of the men carried the dead girl to the water's edge and pushed the body into the river. It was around the time Ai returned home.

She and her two companions had enjoyed themselves all evening, meeting up with friends and relatives they thought they'd never see again, and who appeared before them like wonderful coincidences of fate. The food wasn't bad, the conversation engrossing, and by the time they managed to pull away, the wedding was long over, and the foxes were out in the fields.

As they approached the house, one of the women in the group nudged Ai and pointed to the house. "Why isn't there a light?"

Ai, attuned to the alarms of the times, shrugged her shoulders. The first feeling of unease touched her when she found the front door hanging by its hinges. She frowned in the darkness, the bad feeling inside her turning to one of extreme foreboding. She pushed past the women and ran inside. Like the soldiers before her, she hurried from one room to the other, searching for Nina, calling her name. All she heard in reply was the whisper of a breeze blowing through the house, and the leaves stirring in response in the trees outside. One of the women sat in a corner and cried.

Ai searched for a match. When she found one, she lit the lamp. Only then the full scale of what must have happened became apparent. It was as if a storm had passed through the house. The furniture was overturned or broken, and the neighbour's dog lay in a pool of blood near the back door. She ran to her neighbour's house just round the corner, as fast as an old woman could run, desperately hoping some unexplained circumstances had forced Nina there. But the woman shook her head and ran after Ai to see for herself.

A couple of hours later, a group of villagers collected in the cold outside the police outpost. They were greeted by the constable on duty, who appeared after much pounding at the door. He frowned at the disturbance. No, the daruga had gone to town on an important errand. He was in charge now and he was busy, but he'd spare them a minute or two.

Soumen, who led the delegation, settled down on a chair and pointed the constable to one. He explained the purpose and circumstances of his visit. He finished with a query: "So do you've her?"

The smile vanished from the constable's face. In an instant he was certain of what must have happened. The grocer's plaints rang in his ears. He shook his head. "Do you think she has eloped?"

"It is possible," said Soumen, "but why anyone would kill a dog and ruin the furniture while running away?" He pointed at the wireless. "We don't have time to waste and a life is at risk. Perhaps you could find out. You're in charge."

The constable shrugged his shoulders. "The army doesn't listen to us. They are their own masters. What can I possibly do?"

The villagers discussed amongst themselves. If the soldiers have her, she was good as dead. Time was of essence. Words of anger rang out. Questions were hurled at the constable:

"Were you aware of this?"

"The police normally accompany the soldiers. You must have known."

"Tell us where she is and we'll go and find her even if we've to fight."

One of the villagers suggested torching the outpost. "It's of no use to us anyway. The police never help us and we are better off without the lot."

Another suggested making an example of the constable. "He knows. He's not telling us."

"Then we'll make him tell us." A villager pushed forward.

"Yes, let's teach him a lesson." The others chorused.

Soumen raised a hand to calm the men. He knew it would take only a flicker of insanity to turn the spark into a fire. The villagers realized no help was forthcoming from the police; as always they must fend for themselves. They huddled together in a hum of worried voices. In the quietness before dawn, they organized themselves into groups of twos and threes and started their search for Nina. The news about the disappearance spread to the neighbouring villages and more and more people joined the search parties or formed one of their own.

They looked everywhere - by the river bank, on the grassy, bush-thronged embankment, amongst the reeds in the swamp, in the bamboo thickets, even in the areca plantations. There was talk of a march to the military camp, but not a soul had seen a soldier in the vicinity of the village or heard anything amiss. After much debate, the plan was abandoned.

They couldn't find a trace of her anywhere.

Three days later, Nina's body, now mottled with fish bites and breeding maggots, washed up a few miles downstream on the Dikhow. Her face bore a shocked expression and her eyes had a dull, vacant look. On her forehead, a mark much like a bindi where the bullet had gone in. A rotting gag still filled her mouth. A crowd collected on the spot. Tempers frayed at the slur on the village. Revenge was on the villagers' minds. All they needed was someone to vent their anger if not the actual culprit.

The news of the discovery of the body reached the daruga while he was returning from his rounds. For a stunned moment he wondered if it was the same girl the Army had taken into custody. He dismissed the thought as quickly as it entered his mind. The Major had told him the girl was in the camp and would be handed over in a day or two. With a hurried word to the constable, he pedaled as fast as possible to the site of the incident.

Like most policeman of his ilk, the daruga possessed a keen

nose for trouble. It had stood him in good stead during the long years of service and, on many occasions, rescued him from tight situations. He heard the shouting first. When he saw the crowd from his vantage on the embankment, he hesitated, wondering if it was safe for him to venture into a sea of pent-up feelings. The situation was bad enough, but if he did nothing, it could take a turn for the worse.

Someone in the crowd spotted him. Their voices reached his ears:

"Look, the police have come. Always too late to do anything."

"Pompous fool."

"Why is he here?"

Wiping sweat from his brow, the daruga plunged into the sea of people. He pushed through the crowd, swearing and swinging his cane to reach the water's edge. As soon as he saw Nina's face, he knew he made a mistake: the cold eyes, the ghastly colour of bloated flesh, worms wriggling out of her belly. The bilious taste of the morning meal came to his mouth. In a split second it occurred to him what must have happened. He looked at the faces surrounding him and noted the fire in their eyes, and the anger in their mouths. Everyone screamed vengeance. For the moment the law had lost its relevance. The smell of decaying flesh stung his senses. Faces blurred. The shouting ceased. He fainted. "It is these extremists," he mumbled before losing consciousness.

After the daruga pedaled away, the constable in the outpost fretted at the prospect of someone in khaki facing an irate crowd, recalling the ugly situation from a few nights back. He sent a wireless message to the police reserve twenty kilometers away with an update on the situation and a request for advice. A few minutes later, the SDPO read the dispatch, a frown spreading across his face. He knew how bad the situation was elsewhere in the state and was proud of the fact that at least in his sub-division, it was normal as it could get. Fewer people were getting killed and, with the Army in charge, he was happy to abdicate responsibility for counter insurgency operations. But he was not going to take any chances, not when his promotion was due. He made up his mind. He'd send an armed party to the site to make certain the situation was all right. He gave the order.

The first sight the police party got from their perch on the Gypsy on the embankment road was a policeman lying on the ground surrounded by villagers. In the din the villagers remained oblivious of their arrival. One of them sprinkled water on the daruga's face; another held a lemon peel to his nose. A few made jokes about the daruga. The others gathered around full of advice. The policemen in the Gypsy thought otherwise. One of their colleagues had been lynched by an angry mob. Their uniform had been insulted. The law broken.

The Gypsy came to a halt in a cloud of dust. The policemen jumped out, guns drawn and aimed at the villagers, who stared back in utter bewilderment. Two of them came forward to explain. The policemen stood undecided. One of them snapped out an order. In the hullabaloo, no one heard what was shouted. Guns boomed. The two advancing villagers fell in a heap where they stood. The others panicked and scattered. A few scrambled up the embankment. Some hid in the ditches created by bites of the Dikhow. Several jumped into the water and swam away as fast as they could. The firing lasted less than two minutes. Of the thirty odd villagers who gathered out of curiosity, only a handful escaped unscathed. Most of them lay on the ground, writhing with pain and crying for help.

It started to drizzle. The cool patter of rainfall on his face woke the daruga. For a moment, he couldn't make out where he was: cries of terror, bodies strewn around him, some screaming in agony, others lying still, blood everywhere. He blinked at the sight, and then a policeman appeared out of nowhere.

The policeman stared at the daruga with an incredulous expression on his face before saying: "You...you're all right?"

The daruga nodded. "I fainted. The heat and the smell got to me, I guess. I'd to pedal all the way here."

The other policemen in the party rushed towards the daruga. They looked at him with an expression of shock on their faces. One of them felt his neck, another checked his chest. The first one there took it upon himself to explain to the others. "He fainted. The villagers were trying to revive him." He pointed at the lemon peel in the daruga's hands.

They looked at one another, their expressions ranging from the impassive to the aghast. There had been a mistake, an error of judgment. But they'd been there before and so knew what to do. One of them was already on the radio.

"Sir, there has been an attack..."

A couple of miles away, his clothes dripping wet from the sudden shower, Hirok heard the gunshots like distant pops of crackers going off. He stopped on the narrow forest path and listened. The wind picked up and brought with it the smell of putrid flesh. As he moved deeper into the forest, the smell grew stronger and more persistent. Ahead of him, he heard the animated drone of flies.

Hirok stopped and parted the leaves of a bush. Behind it lay the grocer in a languid repose of death. One lifeless eye stared at him. His mouth hung half open as if in surprise. The thin, spindly hair was gone along with a part of the scalp, eaten by an animal by the look of it. His swarthy features were dwarfed, shrunken by death. Just beneath his chin was a dark slit on the throat. It was concise and perfect.

Hirok wiped his hands on the grass. He loathed him when alive, but in death, he pitied him.

17

As the fireflies burst forth in the night, a band of people rode the back of a lorry on the road to Dikhowpar. Shortly afterwards, it veered off the road and followed a cattle track for a few miles before climbing the kutcha road on the embankment bordering the Dikhow. It came to a halt not far from where they'd been shot, and what remained of it - faint trickles of blood on the sand baked brown by the sun on which vultures and eagles swooped down during the day and scratched their beaks and, now, ants made a beeline.

They knew nothing of the machinations behind this hush-hush visit. Shortly after the dead and injured reached the hospital in town, senior police officers gathered for an urgent meeting at the SP's office. They reached agreement on a number of decisions. One of them was not to punish the policemen responsible for the firing. "It'd only show us as the guilty party," said the SP. "Besides how could they know what was happening. They did what they thought best." The second decision was on their version for the press. "We'll tell them the policemen were attacked by a mob of villagers armed with bows and arrows," said the SP. "I already have two men in hospital to show for the attack." The final decision was to dispose of the dead without delay. There would be an armed escort to ensure the cremations were done before the night is over. To make matters secure, it was decided to clamp curfew on the village and its surrounding areas for a few days. "I want shoot-at-sight orders and I want law and I want order. That village is like a pot of poison," said the SP, a flustered expression on his face. The local MLA, who had hurried to the meeting on hearing the news, was told to stay away from the village. "We don't want your people trampling all over with offers of sympathy and promises of punishment. It'll only make the situation worse," the SP told him, knowing how easy it was to convince him. "I'm sure you'd agree with elections not far away."

A couple of policemen rushed to the back of the lorry and opened the tailgate. They ordered the men to lower the shrouded bodies. Under their watchful eye the villagers piled on stacks of logs one atop the other to make the pyres. When they found they didn't have enough wood, they chopped bamboo from the thickets by the river bank. At a signal from the policemen, a priest stepped forward. He sprinkled holy water on the unveiled corpses and chanted the final prayers. A middle-aged man in a dhoti shivered in the cold and stepped forward to light the first pyre; the others did similarly with the other pyres. As the flames rose in the sky, the villagers drew closer and warmed themselves. In the moonless night, the pyres shimmered in the dark waters as six people were sent on their final journey.

It was a weary village that greeted dawn. A pall of gloom enveloped it in a shroud of grief. From all around came the sound of suffering: women weeping for their husbands, children crying for lost fathers, a brother shedding tears for a dead sibling, mothers beating their chests lamenting lost sons - tormented souls shaken by the turn of events that had swept the village. For the villagers struggling to comprehend the murder of Nina, it was even more difficult to accept the death of so many from amongst them in the matter of a day. Living, laughing people that were there the previous day no longer existed; it was as if a pestilence had sneaked up on them to snatch them away forever.

Nobody spoke that day. Words, even those of sympathy, had lost their meaning. People moved in a daze. As the day advanced, they squatted on the grass under the shade of trees or sheds or sat on their haunches and mourned in the awkward silence between them. The fields were deserted, and the road was a serpent skin laid out between yellowing fields, speckled by lazily moving dots of soldiers keeping an uneasy vigil. There was no sign of the playful prance of children: they sat in silent huddles at the feet of their parents. Those old were too stunned to speak and sat like statues staring into the horizon with their feeble eyesight. The namghar was deserted save for a mongrel resting on its steps. Its lamps won't be lit until after the funerals. In the village chowk, the lone shop was closed and shuttered. Further away, a widow wept alone. Then Ai got all the women together and made peace.

The grocer, finally, was one of them.

From the window of their house, Hirok watched the soldiers patrolling the road out of the village. "Bastards," he said, closing his eyes in an effort to get some sleep.

Ai came in, hard of breath and pressing her hand to her chest. She sat down on the bed by his side. "Who could've done such a terrible thing?" she said about the grocer's death. They avoided discussing about Nina knowing how much it hurt, how painful it was to learn the manner of her death.

"Too many people had too many reasons for killing him," said Hirok. "Why do you bother? He only got what was coming to him."

"That is all in the past. He's one of us now," said Ai. When Hirok gave her a blank look, she explained: "Everyone's agreed his name should be included with the others for the public funeral."

"Doesn't lessen his sins one bit," said Hirok. "How can everyone forget what he'd done? Jogen kai, Molu ka, Neal - they all suffered because of him." A pause. "Nina."

Ai shook her head. "What else could we do? Everyone in

the village is in pain. We all agreed we've to stay together to move forward."

"The police and the military aren't so forgiving," said Hirok. "There'll be new searches trying to find out who did it. Gives them an excuse to create more trouble, kill a few more."

"Let them do their job and we'll do ours," said Ai.

Hirok scratched his head. "Well, who could've killed him? Must have been someone who knows their way around here, someone who knows he kept his ears and eyes open."

Ai started and through her mind flashed the names of possible suspects. "I can't think of any. Everyone disliked him for sure, but nobody hated him enough to take his life."

"That's what I meant," said Hirok. "Nobody would want to dirty their hands by killing him. He had outlived his usefulness to the police once the villagers started avoiding him. His information was becoming useless."

"You mean they…"

Hirok shrugged his shoulders, his eyes still on the soldiers. He noticed that as the day advanced their colours changed, becoming gray blotches by late afternoon, then turning into dark dots, which disappeared with dusk. By late evening, he heard the thud of their boots on the gravel, and the squeaky flinch of the bamboo fence outside when they stopped to rest and lean.

Late at night, sharp knocking on the door. A familiar voice whispered through a gap in the door. Ai opened the door.

"Is something wrong? Has anyone been arrested yet?" she said, letting Rajen inside.

Rajen shook his head. "I don't know, but the soldiers are everywhere. Can't avoid running into them."

"You shouldn't be out so late," said Hirok from the other room.

The young boy was silent for a while. "What could I do?

It's not easy to remain in the house when so much is happening. Besides, if they see anyone during the day they'll beat or arrest you."

Hirok poked his head out through the door. "Haven't they started searching yet? They'll need to show something for their efforts."

"What can they hope to find?" said Rajen. "Bora deserved what he got."

"No," said Ai, pointing a stern finger. "You shouldn't talk of the dead like that."

"They couldn't just sit and let it be known that the law no longer exists here," said Hirok. "If the police pick up somebody, it'll demonstrate to their own sick hearts they still have a society where they can do as they like."

The young boy fastened his eyes on him, then at Ai. "People are saying Bora spied on Nina, brought the soldiers here."

"How can anyone know?" said Ai.

"I still think he deserved his death," said Rajen. "He'll suffer. God will punish him for what he did."

"Let god decide that," said Ai. "But everyone has the right to die with dignity."

The young boy jumped up with great agitation. "Then what dignity of death was there for Nina? She had the worse and now the murderers are running free and putting on a dumb charade of being keepers of the law."

Hirok stepped forward and placed a hand on his trembling shoulders. "You go home now," he said in a firm voice. The touch of his hands and the strict tone sent the boy scurrying.

Rajen took off through the back, past the cluster of trees and the bamboo thickets, following an overgrown path. It was dark in the forest and he moved by instinct, flirting from one gap in the bushes to another, his body brushing the shrubs, making a slight shuffling sound. Ahead of him, a group of people crouched in the undergrowth, fingers on triggers and eyes peering into the darkness. They listened to the wind, but all they caught was the sound of foxes howling and crickets chirping all around them. They'd been waiting for close to an hour and glanced impatiently at each other in the dark. Still ahead of them, a thickset, bald man stepped into the familiar path from the embankment. A tall figure emerged from behind the shadow of a tree and greeted him.

"I thought you wouldn't make it," said Phukan.

Barman nodded. "I almost didn't. The soldiers - they are everywhere."

They talked in urgent whispers as they walked along the faint trace of the forest path.

"That stupid man," said Barman. "What is he doing here? I told him to stay away. The situation is bad here and it's getting worse."

Phukan let off a low laugh. "Love makes a man do crazy things. How could he stay away when his girl is raped and killed?"

Barman was silent for a while. "Any idea who is responsible?"

"Your guess is as good as mine," said Phukan.

"Who else? It is these Army bastards."

"Don't you think we should do something about it?"

"We must. Somebody must have told them about her. Bora?"

"He's dead. They found his body in the forest."

"Now that complicates matters."

Phukan coughed. "Any instructions?"

"You'll know when it comes…" said Barman.

His sentence was cut off midway as strong hands seized him in the dark and pinned him to the ground. The light from a torch shone like a beacon in the dark and Rajen stopped in his tracks. He crept closer. Four masked men tied Barman's hands behind his back. A tall man stood facing him.

"I suppose with you and Hirok dead, it'll be the end of your struggle in this part of the world," said the tall man, laughing.

Rajen heard a feeble riposte from the tied man.

"You, Phukan, you are a traitor and a disgrace to your mother."

Phukan kicked out at Barman. The thud of boots hitting bone sent a chill down Rajen's spine. It sent the captive man sprawling on his back. Phukan stepped forward, finger pointing at the fallen man. "You, you are the traitor. You sold out this country. You are the one who plant bombs and hold people to ransom. You and your kind, you have ruined this land."

One of the masked men grabbed Barman by his hair and pulled him to his feet. He glanced around as if querying something. The others around him nodded and watched in expectation. A knife appeared in his hand. He ran it across the throat. There was a burst of red around the neck and a choking, gurgling sound. He let go and Barman slowly toppled forward.

Rajen started to scream. Then someone grabbed him from behind and clamped a hand over his mouth.

"Be quiet," whispered Hirok, slowly releasing his hold.

They crouched behind a tree, and Hirok placed his hands on the frightened boy to calm him. They watched two of the men drag the body into the bushes. The light was lowered, probably placed on the ground, and it spread outwards casting an eerie shadow of bloated tree trunks and shrubs. They heard the sound of digging, and a spade hitting rock. The light appeared once more, pointing here and there, then at the ground. The body was dragged out from the bushes. Two of the men struggled to right it before pushing it into the shallow grave. More hurried shoveling, sound of boots patting the ground, hands being wiped. One of the men cut off a few branches and dragged shrubbery over the grave. Soon it was no longer noticeable. The light was switched off and the men moved away into the night. Once more silence descended in the forest.

A fox waited not far away. It had tasted human flesh not many days back; now, it was getting used to its tender taste. When Hirok and Rajen moved after the group, it scraped away the soil from the grave. Ten minutes later, the two ducked behind the jackfruit tree by the pond. Hirok realized they were looking for him, but he was more worried about Ai, worried they would harm her when they found he was not at home. There was no sign of the masked men, but the wind brought the faint noise of their panting. One of the men to their right let out a low cough. There was a hissed order and the sounds ceased. Hirok's mind churned with a thousand thoughts. Why Phukan? How could he have been compromised? The Sangathon always checked the antecedents of its recruits. No, he told himself, it was not possible. He was one of the most trusted men in the organization, entrusted with the most secret of missions. Why would he do something like this?

They waited and watched in the darkness for some time, and then Phukan stepped into the light of the verandah and knocked on the door. Another man followed Phukan. Bent low, he hurried past the verandah before ducking into the shadows of the house beneath the window. The light of the lamp fell on his hands through a gap in the wall and Hirok caught the gleam of metal on his hands. A gun!

Hirok motioned to Rajen to wait, pushing him into the bushes by the pond. He listened for the other men. There was one to his right, a few feet inside the gate; two more to his left somewhere between the pond and the kitchen. He circled the house, past the dark silhouette of a man near the midden, and moved towards the grain store attached to the house. He stepped inside, holding his breath when the door squeaked. From his place between two sacks, Hirok saw Phukan talking to Ai.

"...I was in the area and decided to drop by. Besides, I haven't seen you in such a long time, not since Dibrugarh," he was saying with his usual nonchalant air.

Ai appeared pleased. "We thought you were still in jail. When did you get out?"

Phukan pointed to the wall. "What happened to Gandhi's picture? Don't tell me - it burnt when the soldiers set fire to the house." He paused for a moment. "I was lucky. The police didn't have anything to put on me. There were no witnesses and Hirok was gone. They dawdled for a while, then let me out."

"The gaonbura is not so lucky," said Ai. "The poor man, rotting in jail and everybody has forgotten what he is in for. Can't you do something to help him?"

"We're outlaws in the eyes of the law. Our word has no standing," said Phukan. He changed the subject. "I was hoping to meet Hirok. Where did you say he went?"

"I didn't say," said Ai in her usual calm voice, and Hirok grinned, pleased with the answer. "He left all of a sudden. He didn't tell me anything about your visit tonight."

Phukan shifted in his seat. His eyes caught a cockroach scurrying past and put a foot forward to crush it. "He isn't supposed to."

Ai found this a little strange. "It's cold outside. It'll do you good to have a hot cup of tea inside you. If you are hungry, I can cook you a meal."

"No time for that, I must leave."

"Spend the night here. If he comes back you can meet him."

"No, I must go," said Phukan. "You know how it is, the lives we lead." He was suddenly fidgety for some reason. He glanced around the room and looked at Ai suspiciously. He paced the room lost in thought. He stopped near the window and paused for a moment. "Give Hirok my regards when he comes

230

back," he said. "No...no, don't do that. Don't tell him I was here. Let me surprise him another day." Without another word he left the house.

Hirok gave him a couple of minutes, five, before stepping outside. Like before, he crawled away, his eyes alert for any sign of Phukan and his men. He stopped every few feet to listen for any sound, but all he heard was the bland emptiness of a silent night. He moved past the garden patch and the beds of spinach, past the areca trees, and the coriander bed, darting into the bushes by the pond.

"Rajen," he called out.

There was no reply.

"This is no time to fall asleep," Hirok whispered, moving forward.

But there was no one there. The men were gone, the courtyard was empty, and Rajen had vanished.

At dawn, when the darkness gave way to the incandescence of morning, Hirok turned homewards. He spent the rest of the night searching for Rajen, but he was nowhere to be found. He looked everywhere he could think off - near the bamboo thickets, by the swamp inside the boat, the narrow gullies leading off the road, all the nooks and corners only they knew. When he exhausted all his options, he returned to the forests behind the house. But they were dark and empty, and quite forlorn. All he found was a looming threat behind every tree and bush, which teased at the helplessness inside him. He stumbled on a mound of soil and his eyes fell on a smudged pate showing through the dirt. Barman was a good leader, but he was gone, and his passing was already a distant event in the face of Rajen's disappearance. He covered the head with fistfuls of soil and went his way.

Hirok sat down by the pond. A mist crept up on him in a cloak of white. As the sunlight streaked through the trees, he wondered what had happened after he left Rajen. There wasn't a sign of a struggle anywhere near the bushes, a snapped twig or broken branches. Above him, the leaves on the jackfruit tree stirred in the breeze as if trying to tell him something. When he watched his reflection, a stranger with deep set eyes glared at him. He frowned in anger and tossed a pebble into the water. It sent a ripple across the pond and the fish feeding on the surface scattered here and there.

Hirok spent a restless morning in the house. When Ai brought him tea and news of Phukan's late night visit, he kept his gaze fixed outside the window. Ai frowned at the silence and went away mumbling to herself. Not far away, the olive-green blotches with stubs on their backs moved like lazy dots on the road. Their humdrum movements soothed Hirok's eyes and he dozed off.

He was awakened by loud knocking on the door. Ai rushed to the room, pausing before opening the latch.

"Who's there?" she said in an anxious voice.

"Me," said an unfamiliar boyish voice.

"Rajen?" said Ai, sending a questioning look in Hirok's direction.

"Please hurry up and open it," said the voice.

Ai lifted the latch and pushed the door open. A young boy limped in. He was crying. His shirt was torn and spattered with blood, and his fists were clenched. His face was smudged with dirt while scared eyes watched from a shrunken face.

"What happened?" said Ai, rushing forward, recognizing the boy.

"I fell down and hurt myself," he said between tears. He pointed to a cut on his cheeks and another on his knee.

"Let me have a look," said Hirok.

"I'll get the tincture," said Ai, rushing off.

"I'm all right," said the boy, wiping away tears with the

back of his hand. He pointed to the blood on his shirt. "I was playing with my kite in the forest when I heard shouts, somebody crying. I went closer to have a look. There were many people there. One of them saw me. He called out to me. I was afraid. I ran away, but there were so many of them. I fell down and one of them grabbed my shirt and dragged me away. Now Ma is going to spank me."

Hirok held the boy in his arms. "No, she won't," he said, trying to soothe the frightened child.

"You don't know her," said the boy.

"Is that why you came here instead of going home?" said Hirok, taking the bottle of tincture from Ai, who hurried off again. He dabbed the tincture in the cut. The boy closed his eyes and gritted his teeth.

"No," he cried as the medicine stung. Then as if pushed by the pain, he said: "They slapped me for running away. Thash! Thash! Thash! One of them asked about you...he gave this." The boy opened his fist and a piece of paper fell on the floor.

Hirok picked it up, smoothed the edges and held it in front of his eyes.

"What is it?" Ai returned with a glass of milk.

Hirok thrust the paper into a pocket. "Nothing, just a message." He beckoned to the young boy. "I'll take you home. Your mother must be worried."

"What about the milk? Let him have it first...," said Ai, but Hirok had already left with the boy.

A short distance away from the house, Hirok faced the boy. "You said you heard someone crying - did you see who it was?"

"Does it have anything to do with the note?" said the boy.

"None of your business," said Hirok, deep in thought. "What were you doing so far out anyway?"

The boy looked at him with frightened eyes. "There was someone. I didn't see his face, but he was crying. The men were

233

pretty vicious. They struck him on the face. He tried to get away from them, but they surrounded him and kicked him till he was all bloody." He clamped his mouth shut and refused to answer any more questions.

They walked the rest of the way in silence. The boy lived not very far away and Hirok led the way, avoiding two soldiers on patrol and a brood of startled ducks, past the bamboo thickets and through hedges of thorny shrubbery and flowering bushes. The boy pointed to a narrow path and they stopped in front of his house.

"The boy that was crying, I know him," he said all of a sudden, looking up at Hirok with large frank eyes.

A woman, his mother, crept up behind him. She grabbed him by his arms and boxed his ears. "You monkey, where have you been all morning? What have you done to your clothes?"

"He fell on the road," said Hirok, "but he is a brave boy."

"Doesn't matter how brave he is when he should be at the study table," said the woman, glaring at Hirok. She held her son by his arms and pulled him into the house.

"Well, stay home now," Hirok called after them, half-wondering if he should ask the mother to let him have a chat. He thought better of it.

Ten minutes later, Hirok was scrambling the few feet down to the water's edge in the swamp, the words in the note banging away in his mind. He uncovered a rope and pulled in what appeared to be a bed of water hyacinth. As soon as it was within touching distance, he dragged a small boat aground. From his pocket he removed a knife with which he cut away the tarpaulin to uncover a trunk. He unlocked the trunk and sorted the contents. When he was satisfied he had everything he needed, he settled down to work.

A few miles north of the village, a group of men squatted on the ground and watched their leader wipe his hands on a handkerchief. He spat on a figure lying on the ground and settled down by their side, a look of utter disdain on his face.

"The things we've to do to earn a living," he said to no one in particular, and the others laughed.

"Doesn't appear to know much, does he?" said one of the men, striking a match.

The leader leaned forward and lit the cigarette dangling from his mouth. "He isn't one of them, but he's at a dangerous age. You never know - what if he picks up a gun? Better be safe than regret later."

The other men chatted amongst themselves:

"Do you think he'll come?"

"He is a bloody idealistic moron. He'll come."

"He'll have a plan of some sort and the blessings of Mao and Lenin. Nothing will come of it."

"Right now he must be looking for Barman."

"Maybe he'll send the old hag."

"They've got everyone involved, haven't they?"

"The next thing you know they'll be producing baby insurgents."

"Maksudas."

The leader puffed away in silence, his eyes gazing into the distance, his mind turning over all manner of possibilities, drowning the hum of conversation around him. He glanced at the body, then upwards at the gloomy sky. Then coming to a decision, he drew one last puff of the cigarette and jumped to his feet.

"Okay, enough of it," he said. "It's going to rain and we've work to do." He turned to one of the men, pointing at the boy on the ground. "Throw him in the pit and make a good job of it."

18

A light rain was falling by the time Hirok finished work on his contrivance, which he taped to his body. He repacked the trunk, covered the boat with the tarpaulin and pushed it out to the water.

Ai was waiting for him when he returned home.

"Why haven't you eaten?" he said, noticing the two overturned plates.

"How can I eat without you?" she said, watching him go out again. There was the sound of the hand pump winch and water splashing. Hirok reappeared, shaking his feet dry at the door and wiping his face on a gamocha. He sat down by her side and Ai served their meagre meal. They ate their food in silence. A sparrow pranced in through the open door. It stopped when it saw the two bent over their meal. When Hirok extended his hand forward for a tumbler of water, it flew away with a shriek.

"They've Rajen," he said all of a sudden. "Phukan and his men have him," he added, when Ai looked up from her food and stared at him.

"I thought you said you showed him home last night," said Ai.

Hirok pushed away his food. "It's all my fault."

"And what was that about Phukan?"

"He is one of them. Too bad we found out too late," said Hirok. "He's been working for the government all along. Last night we saw him kill Barman, the man he was supposed to guard with his life. There were four other men with him. They planned to do away with me too, that's why they came here. We followed him here. I left Rajen by the pond and hid in the granary. I was worried he'd harm you when he found I wasn't at home."

"Dear me," said Ai. "How could he? How could he turn his back on the very people who cared for him? But…why did he save you in Dibrugarh?"

Hirok shook his head. "I don't know. Perhaps he wanted me well enough to kill. Perhaps he was waiting for orders, more information, glory." He paused for a moment. "I think he invited the police over to have me arrested."

Ai calmed herself with great difficulty. She thought she had seen everything, but the world never ceased to surprise her. She glanced at her son. At that moment she saw something different: a terrified look in his eyes, which contrasted with a fiercely determined look on his face.

"Your life is in danger now," she said.

"Rajen is worse off," said Hirok.

"Can't we do something? March with the entire village to wherever they are holding the boy?"

"It won't do."

"What if we try?"

Hirok was silent for a while before he answered. "They've the entire village surrounded by the Army, every road patrolled, every house watched. Do you think we could get far?"

Ai grew thoughtful. She sensed Hirok had already decided what was to be done and nothing she or anybody said would make him change his mind.

"I saw that boy give you a note," she said, almost in a whisper. "What did it say? Is it from them?" She waited for an answer. "Well?"

"They want me to come and get Rajen, Ai," said Hirok. There was a pause. "If I don't, they will kill him."

Ai closed her eyes, afraid even to breathe. "My poor boy," she thought. "Now, they would kill him for sure." A tear trickled down her cheeks. She wiped it away. "I wish you wouldn't," she said. "What if they've already killed him?"

"Perhaps," said Hirok, "but what if they haven't?"

"They'll kill you," said Ai.

"They are beasts and they kill without qualms."

"Who doesn't?"

"I know it'll be hard on you, Ai."

"It's always been hard."

"It's too late for anything, Ai," said Hirok, looking away.

A vague emptiness tugged at her heart. It told her of more pain and a coming loss. She wanted to say many things, but her heart was heavy with pity and the words wouldn't leave her lips. "We're all going to die," she thought. "This is all going to end."

In the forest north of the village, near where the oil pipeline passes close to the railway track by the Dikhow, three men sat in the rain in the shelter of a machan waiting for news from a scouting party. Their eyes scanned the forest below them, their bodies taut, fingers feeling their guns. They sat with the patient anticipation of hunters waiting for prey. Not far away, Hirok made rapid strides in the slush, his eyes alert for any sign of soldiers on patrol or Phukan's men. Every few minutes, he stopped to catch his breath and check the explosives taped to his body or feel the plunger in his pocket. Unlike the men waiting for him, his mind was blank except for his worries about Rajen's safety. Phukan had mentioned a location for the rendezvous, a place familiar to both from their days of secret meetings and hiding from the military. If only he could sneak up to them, find the boy and escape. He moved from one tree to another, crouching in the dense undergrowth, then moving forward again.

They found Hirok a mile from the camp. There was the cracking of twigs and the shuffle of feet behind him. When Hirok turned to look, another man had materialized in front. The one behind Hirok pointed his gun, while the one in front frisked him for a gun or knife.

"He's clean - such a shame," he said. He let off a low laugh. "Makshuda. Didn't expect to be jumped like this, did he?"

"Takes courage to come unarmed, my friend," said the other man.

"To think it's all wasted on a lost cause."

"He doesn't know it's all over."

Despite their jibes, they appeared a little afraid, staying out of Hirok's reach. The one behind kept his gun on Hirok's back.

"Walk," he said, and the one in front led the way.

They moved into the forest through a maze of trees and elephant grass. The rain fell with unbridled ferocity and the ground became softer and soggier. Large clouds swirled in the sky covering the sun and sending a pall of darkness over the land. An hour of walking brought them to a clearing in the jungle ringed by a row of huts built on stilts.

Hirok noticed four of these thatched bamboo dwellings and a couple of machans on the trees occupied by armed lookouts. He heard voices, brief snatches of conversation that vanished with the wind. Then, a familiar face. Phukan appeared from behind a patch of tall kohua. He read his thoughts.

"You like it, eh," he said in a taunting voice. "Just temporary arrangements to get rid of pests like you." He paused for a moment. "I'm surprised you came."

"Where is Rajen?" said Hirok.

"He's dead and buried and in another world," said Phukan, running a finger across his throat.

"You shouldn't have. He was just a boy."

"Boys grow up to be someone like you. I don't want to fight

him when he's all grown up. I don't want to be at this job all my life weeding this land." He studied Hirok for a while, a smile on his face. "You know, with you gone, it'll be the end of your rutty little revolution in this part of the world."

"There will always be someone around to take my place," said Hirok.

"Oh, there will always be a few fools around," said Phukan. "Otherwise what would happen to people like us? We'd be out of work."

"You're the bigger fool."

Phukan laughed. "No greater than you. What if I tell you your leaders sold you for their share of the gold?"

Hirok spat on him. "They'd never do that. You...you are the traitor. You'd sell your own mother if you could."

Phukan laughed. "If it comes to that, sure. But I must tell you, I feel like I've done a good deed every time I put one of you down."

"Why did you save my life at Dibrugarh?" said Hirok.

"I had my reasons," said Phukan. "I was looking for a bigger catch, and I was hoping you could help me tie up a few loose ends. I had such high hopes."

"You called the police?"

"I'm the police. But you didn't do badly either escaping."

"I was there the whole time. The police are blind."

"Not any more. With a few more like you dead, we can claim success. The military will soon be gone."

"I saw you kill Barman. You murdered a fine man."

"A seditionist. I should've killed him earlier."

Hirok looked at the men around him and at Phukan. He realized his fate had already been decided. There was no getting out now. The rain was letting up. The sky was lit with the last colours of the day.

"What are you going to do with me? Arrest me?" he said.

The men chuckled.

"You refuse to recognize authority and yet want to be arrested?" said Phukan.

"His heart approves of the government, but his mind hates it," said one of the men. "It doesn't matter now, does it?" The man raised his gun.

Another man sneaked up behind Hirok.

Hirok took a deep breath. If he'd to make a move, it had to be now. "Tell that man behind me to stop now," he screamed, his thumb on the plunger inside his pocket. "Or I'll blow all of us apart!"

The man stopped undecided.

"What?" said Phukan, a look of utter astonishment on his face.

"I'll blow us apart if anybody moves," said Hirok.

"My men searched you back there…"

"They were looking for guns and knives."

"I don't believe you."

"You've no choice."

"I know," said Phukan, and lunged forward.

Hirok ducked. His thumb pressed the plunger.

Ai couldn't sleep all night. As soon as it was light she jumped out of bed. She washed, cleaned, prayed and rushed through her everyday ritual of routine. A vague premonition grew inside her, but as the morning progressed she found her fears receding into a corner of her heart. When her work was done and the waiting began, she sat down by the window, a glass of tea by her side, her eyes on the road winding away.

She waited and watched, and she forgot about her tea.

Ai was suddenly filled with fear. Her thoughts churned like an evil machine spouting all sorts of scary portents for far worse times. "Where was Manav? Why hasn't he come back? And Rajen?

241

Is he safe? Why aren't they back? How much more of this agony did she have to endure? When would this all end?" Her eyes closed in the moist warmth of falling rain. From outside came the hum of voices on the road. Shouts and screams. She heard the gate slapping shut. Someone's bare feet pattered across the courtyard and the door flung open.

"Haven't you heard?" Sarmani burst into the room, breathless with excitement.

Ai sat up on the bed. Her heart pounded and her face tightened.

"They've found another body in the forest," said Sarmani. "They haven't identified the man. It seems part of the face has been eaten away by some beast. Some are saying it is someone from the Sangathon."

Ai sighed with the awkwardness of the knowing. Sarmani waited with her hands on her hips.

"Aren't you coming to see?" she said, taken aback by Ai's lack of interest.

"What's there to see?" said Ai, slipping on her sandals.

"Everyone thinks the police or the Army did it. Does it matter? They're all the same," said Sarmani in an anguished voice. "How many of us will be alive if things are allowed to go on like this?" She stopped and looked at Ai. "But it gets worse. There is word they have picked up Rajen for the murder of the grocer. That kid and murder - it grows outrageous by the day. Do you think he can reach up to that man's height and slit his throat?"

There was the sound of running feet and two women rushed inside.

"Come quickly," they said. "There is going to be trouble. The police have come. Some are saying soldiers are going to raid the village."

They hurried outside and plunged into the bedlam on the

road. Groups of people milled around watching the approaching blur of khaki. The people looked at her with a mixture of respect and indifference. She caught snatches of remarks passed in worried voices:

"Do you think they'll shoot us?"

"Too many to shoot. They will lathicharge us, burst a few tear-gas shells and let us disperse."

"What if they shoot?"

"It's only the police. Who's afraid of them?"

Soumen's voice leapt out from the din.

"Quiet, everyone," he said. Two youths, new faces, probably from the Sangathon, hoisted him on their shoulders. A silence fell over the crowd. The little groups merged into one. Eyes turned in his direction. "Have you heard, people? Do you know another body has been found in the forest? Do you know the gaonbura's son has been taken away by agents of the government? Do you know they now deny any knowledge of him? Have you seen what has happened to our village? How these men in uniform turned our lovely land into killing fields, how this fertile soil sprouts dead bodies?"

Someone in the crowd said: "What can we do? We can't fight them?"

Loud retorts and murmurs of discontent passed through the crowd.

Soumen raised his hands to calm the people. He searched in the crowd and pointed to Ai. "She may not know it yet, but I've just been informed by these two young men that her son is no more because his life was the price they wanted for the gaonbura's son. In trying to save Rajen, Manav was killed." He stopped for a moment, adding in a choked voice, "So was Rajen, tortured and cut to pieces."

The words hit Ai like bullets out of a gun. Her head reeled at the news of Manav's death. She stared at the wall of faces that turned to her. They drew closer. Sympathetic hands lent her support and lowered her to the ground. A murmur of angst rose from within them. Furious voices burst forth like spiteful crackers:

"How many more of us will have to die till their hunger is satiated?"

"Murderers."

"Rascals."

"Down with the police."

The crowd swelled. More voices were added. The distant line of khaki became a marching band of armed policemen. Heads turned. Angry feet moved forward. Bare heels and torn sandals in a flurry of hurt feelings. Voices rose to a crescendo of slogans.

Ai stood still. The world grew quiet around her. The faces receded into the background. Her eyes were stung by hot tears. A stab of anger shot through her. She watched the people move forward to face the police party. All reason deserted her. She quickened her steps and caught up with the rear of the crowd. She waded into the mob. Someone recognized her. The crowd parted to let her through. She was in front with Soumen and Sarmani, and the two young men, with the children prancing along. They moved past the waters of the swamp and the bamboo thickets, and towards the open fields. The figures in khaki took on the shape of men with guns.

The daruga's powerful voice rang out.

"Stop!"

The crowd slowed. There was much pushing and jostling. Hearts thumped in anticipation of trouble. A few climbed down to the fields for a better view. Those at the back raised their heads and looked into the distance in confusion, not sure what was going on. Those in the middle felt safe and waited. The air was charged with excitement. Most seemed not to know what to do. A few assumed a show of bravado. There was only a moment's hesitation. The crowd picked up pace again. Loud voices ranted the air:

"How many do you think you can kill?"

"You think you're brave, but throw away your guns and face us if you can."

"It's time you are taught a lesson."

The daruga's voice boomed over the crowd, a tinge of desperation to it.

"Stop, I'm warning you!"

A shudder passed through the crowd.

"If we stop now they'll destroy us, take our souls," said Soumen.

"The time for stopping is past," said the two youths at the front.

A roar of approval echoed through the crowd. Voices blended into a rumble of hostility. Feet moved forward again. The policemen spread across the width of the road. Their guns gleamed in the sunlight.

"Disperse now," ordered the daruga.

The crowd hesitated, stopped, then moved forward. Ai's eyes met Soumen's for the flicker of a moment. She noticed the two youths were no longer there. Those behind pushed at her as if wanting her to face the police. They slackened their pace and kept a safe distance behind those in front.

At a command from the daruga, the policemen raised their guns.

"If you don't stop I'll have to fire," the daruga cautioned in a terrified voice.

The crowd thinned behind those in the front. People running, agitated voices. Screams. Shouts.

"Run!"

"Get back."

"God, please help."

Those in front moved forward with a resolute doggedness. Those behind fell back, then gathering strength from those ahead of them, pushed forward again.

"Into position," the daruga's sharp voice rang out.

The policemen kneeled on one knee and took aim.

The daruga took a deep breath and raised his pistol.

"Fire!" he cried.

*Finest Literature and
Best Literary Criticism*

ROMAN *Books*
www.roman-books.co.uk

MINI NAIR

THE FOURTH PASSENGER

'An inspirational story . . . a terrific read' *Publisher's Weekly*

'A lovely novel . . . affecting and inspiring' Shashi Tharoor

'A feel-good read' *The Bookseller*

Set in Mumbai during the Hindu-Muslim conflict of the early 1990s, *The Fourth Passenger* is the story of four women raised with traditional Indian values, whose partnership give them the temerity to stand up against the religious extremism. Having reached their thirties and disillusioned with their lives and husbands, their decision to open an urban food stand is mingled with their memories of a distant past when two of them loved the same man. But, in order to establish their fledgling business, they must contend with individual temperament, extortionists, ruthless competitors, and most importantly, the prevailing religious intolerance.

Mini Nair has had two of her books published in India. A post graduate in chemistry, Mini Nair lives with her family and twin daughters in Mumbai where she was also born and brought up. *The Fourth Passenger* is her first novel.

Hardcover | £14.99 | $24.95
ISBN 978-93-80905-06-8
Available at your nearest bookstore

www.roman-books.co.uk

SUDHA BALAGOPAL

THERE ARE SEVEN NOTES

Can music really communicate emotions better than words? Is a person born with music embedded in his DNA? Could two souls bound by music ever find a connection outside of it? Like a superbly arranged musical composition, *There are Seven Notes* endeavours to sing a song to reveal the unseen bonds between life and music. Eight year old Hamsa suffers through her vocal lessons to satisfy the cultural aspirations of her family—a skilled singer steps away from his professional performance to re-assess his life—and a celebrity father's musical hopes for his son are dashed. The seven stories in *There are Seven Notes* reveal the pervasiveness of classical music in Indian culture: an attempt once again to fathom the distance between life and art.

Sudha Balagopal was born and raised in India. Her stories have appeared in a number of magazines of international repute. An avid listener and admirer of Indian classical music, Sudha has lived in the United States for the past quarter century. *There are Seven Notes* is her first book.

Hardcover | £12.99 | $19.95
ISBN 978-93-80905-04-4
Available at your nearest bookstore

PIERRE FRÉHA

FRENCH SAHIB

What happens when a Frenchman falls in love with a young Indian guy? Set in India with a French protagonist, and written by a Frenchman, French Sahib is a French-Indian love story revealing the taboos of Indian society and the hypocrisies of French milieu. On his arrival in India Philippe is confronted with the traditional Indian values which are very unlikely from the country he hails from. When young Dipu wants to marry Philippe it is the stereotyped social values that become the stumbling block in their romance. How can they confront the unbridgeable gulf between the traditional East and the modern West? In *French Sahib* Pierre Fréha tells that amusing tale of identity, individuality, love and universal human need for connection and belonging.

Pierre Fréha was born in Algeria at the time when the country was a French colony. He has worked for many years as an independent, freelance writer. He visited and stayed in many countries including India. He has seven novels to his credit. When not travelling, he lives in Paris.

Hardcover | £15.99 | $24.95
ISBN 978-93-80905-09-9
Available at your nearest bookstore

FIONA McCLEAN

FROM UNDER THE BED

'Compelling . . . fulfilling read' *The Bookseller*
'More than a journey . . . an experience' Mary Wood

Alice loves to paint pictures of fish. Her only problem is her addiction to cakes and pastries. To feed this obsession, she steals . . . and to rid herself of her spoils, she makes herself sick. Stick thin, Alice puts her fragile mind into the care of a psychiatrist, Professor Lucas, and tries to learn the rules people should live by. But her recovery soon brings a new and dangerous addiction—Brendan. As Alice struggles to cope with Brendan's violent outbursts, her dying father and poverty, she takes solace in her job at a massage parlour where she finds comfort with motherly Helen. But these are just temporary respites as her life with Brendan spirals downwards becoming a nightmarish maze.

Fiona McClean was born in Dusseldorf, Germany as the daughter of an army family. After studying Fine Arts at the University of Wales, Newport, she now lives the life of an accomplished painter in South France. Fiona loves to spend her time writing and painting, walking and horse riding. *From Under the Bed* is her debut novel.

Hardcover | £14.99 | $24.95
ISBN 978-93-80905-05-1
Available at your nearest bookstore